BearPaw Resort
Book One

W0006698

CAMBRIA
HEBERT

PROLOGUE

Bellamy

SQUINTING DOWN AT THE ADDRESS SCRAWLED ACROSS THE crumpled piece of paper clutched in my hand, I reached to lower my sunglasses from the top of my head, only to realize I'd left them at home.

Figures.

Of all the days to forget them, it was a day I would find them useful, not just for the sun, but to conceal the expressions in my eyes. It was too late to turn back now, considering I was about a block from the place I needed to be.

At least, I thought I was.

I wasn't familiar with this part of town. It wasn't a place most people recommended visiting, unless of course you had to. Like me, right now. Putting the paper right in front of my peepers, I made sure for like the fiftieth time that I actually was reading this right.

Yep. 666 Ghetto Street, up ahead and on the left.

Right past the burning trashcans and through the doorway to hell.

Snorting to myself, I shoved the paper into my pocket and walked ahead. This neighborhood wasn't *that* bad. I mean, nothing was on fire. And the address definitely wasn't 666. I would tell you this, though: if it wasn't broad daylight, I wouldn't have come here.

Father or not, it would have been a hard pass.

It wasn't dark out, though. In fact, it was still early in the day, not quite lunchtime. Also, I hadn't seen or heard from my father in three years. When he called me out of the blue just yesterday, I wondered how the hell he got my number because I was so surprised he'd called at all.

He wanted to see me, he said. He had something important to tell me, he said. Please come, he said.

What could I say? I was a sucker. Well, that and I had some daddy issues because he wasn't ever around. When he was, it was few and far between, which even then was more than my mother wanted. I made sure not to tell her about this little visit. She would have thrown a fit, and it wouldn't have been pretty.

I'd just tell her about it after.

Maybe most grown women wouldn't have been so quick to jump when someone who disappointed them time and again called. If I was smart (and did what dear old Mom instructed), I would have given him the finger and hung up the phone.

I wasn't smart. As proof of this, I would later look back on today and realize how right my mother was.

In fact, my father's indifference had the reverse effect. It made me want to jump faster and higher when he called. As if *this time* I could finally prove I was worthy of his attention. *This time* he would see what he'd been missing all these years.

With a heavy sigh, I stopped in front of the rundown brick building that appeared dingy and ready to crumble. Notes of warning shivered along my spine and tickled the back of my neck. Gazing up at the rusty fire escape, cracked windows on almost every level, and then finally to the sky, which was heavy with dark, ominous clouds, I decided to shove aside the nerves tightening my stomach and move forward.

Cautiously, I pushed open the door leading into the bottom floor and poked my head inside. It smelled like sweat and pee, trash and leaves littered the hallway, and part of the carpet was missing, revealing cracked concrete floors.

Eyeing the dark stain I sincerely hoped was not blood, I rushed around the corner and bolted up the stairs, moving as quietly as my sneakers would allow.

By the time I arrived at the third floor, my heart was pounding and I was quietly gasping for breath. I knew I was being ridiculous. The place was rundown, but it wasn't like someone was chasing me. Still, adrenaline surged through my veins and made it hard to not feel I was in imminent danger.

Trying to shake off the feeling, I stepped into the hallway and felt a little better when I didn't see any bloodstains. He was the third door on the left. As I approached, my fist lifted to knock, but before my knuckles could rap on the dirty wood, it swung open.

A set of bony fingers curled around the edge of the wood as wide eyes peered out, making me feel I was in some kind of horror film.

"Dad?"

My father reached around, snatched my wrist, and pulled me swiftly into the apartment, shutting the door.

Rubbing my arm where he'd grabbed, I walked into

the tiny space, gazing around. The place was a dump. And I wasn't being rude. Or snobby. It was actually a kind description.

The only furniture in the entire place was a stained mattress without any sheets or blankets lying on the floor and a chair that looked like it belonged at one of those old metal card tables.

Oh, there was a lamp. It was brass, had no shade, and the lightbulb was busted.

It smelled in here, too. Mostly of sweat. And fear.

I didn't realize fear had a scent, but taking a breath of it now, I found it was distinctive.

"Bellamy," he said, moving into the room behind me after he did up the chain lock. "Thank you for coming."

He moved to hug me. I stiffened, but he didn't stop. His arms went around me and squeezed. After a moment, I forgot this was weird. I forgot I didn't want to be here. I felt like a little girl again, back on that day when he pulled me into his arms and explained he had to go away and I probably wouldn't see him for a while.

A while turned out to be five years.

I hugged him back, sniffled, and stepped away.

"What are you doing here?" I glanced around. "And in a place like this?"

"Thank you for coming," he said, wringing his hands and glancing to make sure the lock was indeed locked.

I noticed he seemed to have aged exponentially since the last time I saw him. Yes, it had been about three years, but he was only in his forties... yet he looked closer to mid-fifties.

His brown hair seemed thinner, his body leaner. There were worry lines in his forehead and around his mouth and eyes. His clothes were rumpled, and he had this overall vibe about him. He was nervous. Almost skittish.

Joseph Cutler was a lot of things in life, but nervous and skittish were not it.

"It's so good to see you. I've missed you."

"Dad," I said, sweeping a glance over him again. Concern was taking over any other emotion I might feel upon seeing him again. "What's going on here? What's wrong?"

"Listen, sweetheart. We don't have long. You can't stay. I just wanted to see you, even if for a moment."

My stomach sank. "Why don't we go have lunch? My treat. There's this diner a few blocks away. I'm sure they have pie," I said, smiling a little. My dad liked pie.

Without waiting, I started toward the door.

"No!" he said swiftly, moving in front of me and holding up his hands. My steps halted. "We can't go. *I* can't."

"Why?"

His shoulders slumped. "It's nothing you need to worry about."

"Then why did you call? Why are you in town?"

"I came to see you. I—" His throat worked. "I came to say good-bye."

"Good-bye?" I didn't really need to ask. I knew.

As in good-bye forever. Not, *I'll see you in five years.*

He came forward and grasped my arms. "I got into some trouble, made a bad business deal." He began, glancing at the door once more. When his eyes returned to mine, they softened. "Do you remember that time we went on vacation?"

I nodded. "To B—"

Quickly, he put his hand over my mouth and shook his head. His eyes widened, silently telling me not to say anything. When he pulled back, he put a finger to his lips, telling me to be quiet.

"That was the best time of my life." He confided. "I should have been a better father. We should have had more times like that."

"We still can," I told him. My heart squeezed uncomfortably. This whole conversation was not what I expected when I stepped into this ratchet building today. Maybe the address and unexpected call from him should have been the first clues.

He smiled a wistfully. Leaving my side, he went toward the bare mattress and lifted a navy duffle bag from the opposite side, placing it on the bed. The sound of the zipper was quiet but distinct. My father reached inside and pulled out a white envelope with the flap tucked into the opening in the back. It was thick as if it were stuffed full, and one of the corners was bent.

Without a word, he lifted the flap of the leather messenger bag draped over my body and tucked the envelope inside. "Take this," he said, his voice catching just a little.

"You need it," I answered, glancing around pointedly.

"I need you to have the last piece of me that's clean."

I felt my brow wrinkle, puzzling over his words. I didn't understand what he was saying.

Before I could ask, his head tilted to the side, listening.

I listened, too, at first hearing nothing, but then a few faint sounds seemed to filter up from the lower levels.

"They're coming," he said, part gasp, part whisper.

"Who?"

He slammed his entire clammy palm over my mouth. The pupils of his eyes were dilated, making them look black and wild. I felt the tremble of his fingers against my face, and I was instantly shaking, too.

"Move," my father ordered so low I wouldn't have heard if he didn't shove me backward with the demand.

I stumbled, but he kept pushing. Even though I was in front, I felt as if he were dragging me toward the narrow doorway crudely placed in the wall. My sneakers hit the peeling linoleum, sticking instantly. My father shoved, and I faltered backward.

Motioning for me to be silent, he quickly pulled open the single cabinet door on the tiny vanity in the bathroom. I watched in disbelief as he quietly pulled out the panel on the inside, the piece that was supposed to be attached to the wall.

The sound of pounding footsteps rumbled out in the hall, making me jolt.

My father grabbed me, forcing me toward the tiny cabinet. My body was rigid, but he pushed anyway. I wasn't going to fit. This cabinet was so small. I wasn't going to fit.

He kept shoving, I felt the edges of the door scrape me. Stinging pain radiated down my arm. Stifling a cry, I noticed the hole in the wall, beneath the panel he'd removed. It looked almost as if someone had chewed the drywall.

Panic assailed me as my body forced its way into the tiny space between the wall of the bathroom and the main room. I struggled, genuine fear clawing my throat, making it feel as though my trachea were collapsing.

Before I could scramble out, my father leaned into the cabinet and motioned again for me to be quiet. Out in the main room, someone banged on the door. I heard the rattle of the chain my father so carefully put into place.

His hand shot into the wall, caressing my cheek. "I'm not a good man, but I do love you."

Another bang on the door, and my father pushed the paneling back toward the hole, making the space even more claustrophobic than it already was.

I pushed at it, stopping it from sealing me in. "Daddy?"

"Don't make a sound."

Then the paneling was slid over the hole, and the sound of the cabinet closing filled my ears.

It was dark in here. Pitch black. The space was so small my shoulders ached from being pressed between the two walls. The electric box inside the wall jammed into my hip, but there was nowhere to move, so I sat there just feeling the pain. The same scent of fear lingered in here as if this wasn't the first time someone had squeezed themselves in here. As if hiding was a regular thing.

I struggled to breathe. Terror unlike anything I'd ever felt before strangled me. The sound of a door bursting open came through the walls. The sound of that damn chain swinging, clacking against the wooden door frame, penetrated my skull like a jackhammer.

Muffled voices reached my ears, low mumbling, and then a louder yell.

The familiar sound of my father's voice carried through the drywall. His pleading bounced around my head.

What was happening? Who was out there with him?

A man with a deep voice barked an order for silence. Quiet fell for a stretch of time, but then my father spoke again.

A loud boom exploded. Despite the tiny quarters, I fell back, my body twisting sideways as something ripped right through the drywall above me, right where I'd just been.

I would have screamed, but the sound caught in my throat. My mouth opened wide, but nothing came out. A thin sheath of light seemed to blind me in the darkness.

I blinked, trying to understand what had happened.

Shaking almost beyond comprehension, another scream rose up my throat. I felt it build and push against the other one still lodged there.

I forced my fist against my lips, pushing my knuckles into my mouth so there was no chance any sound could escape.

My chest burned. With no place to go, they pummeled my chest and throat until I was pretty sure I might faint.

Staring at the stream of light suddenly stretching across the space, looking sort of like a laser beam, I realized something.

There was a hole in the wall. A ragged, ripped hole.

From a bullet.

The loud boom I'd heard was a gun being fired. The force of the bullet ripped right through the wall and would have killed me if I hadn't fallen back.

A hard slap and the sound of a grunt made me forget about my almost demise. Carefully, I lifted my head, angling my face in front of the bullet hole, and squinted out into the room.

There were two men. Big guys, like wrestlers on TV. Their suits strained against their bodies, the fabric looking tortured and about to rip.

One man had blond hair, the other none at all. The one without hair had a big tattoo of a spider on the back of his neck.

I shivered. Forcing my fist back into my mouth, I

watched as the one man grabbed my father and held him so the other could plow his fist into his stomach.

The air in him whooshed out. His body folded over the arm holding him. As if he were a ragdoll, he was yanked back up again, only to have a meaty fist slammed into his face.

Tears, fat and quick, spilled over, slipping down my cheeks and dripping off my chin and jaw.

"You didn't think you could hide forever, did you?" the man with hair said, punching my father again.

The bald man let him go. His body crumpled to the floor in a sad heap. I couldn't just sit here! I couldn't just hide in this tiny hole and watch him.

Slap! Kick! Groan.

"Hiding is useless. Crone always gets his man."

"Please," my father said, spitting out blood. "I'll do anything."

I started to move, to try and wedge myself out from between the walls. As if sensing what I was about to do, my father surged to his knees, blood dripping down his face, and stared toward the hole as if he knew I was watching.

A very slight shake of his head made me go still.

The man with no hair pulled out a gun, making a show of screwing on a long-barreled silencer. Obviously, it was just a way to prolong what he planned to do. Obviously, these men weren't worried about being heard. They'd already shot through the wall.

"Any last words?" the man with hair intoned.

My father stared at the wall. A single tear slid down his cheek, mixing with his blood. "Tell my daughter I love her."

Both men stepped back. My father glanced up.

A bullet from each gun fired.

The sound of the metal slapping into my father's body was something I would never forget. Blood splattered on the wall behind him. His body fell over motionless.

Squeezing my eyes shut, I bit down on my fist until the unmistakable tang of blood filled my mouth. I kept biting, kept staring through that tiny hole at my father's body as life pooled out.

I shook so hard I pretty much vibrated. My mouth was so dry it was an effort to peel my tongue up to swallow. I felt my own blood coat the back of my throat, but in that moment, it didn't feel like my blood I was swallowing.

It felt like his.

I sat there while the men dumped the contents of his duffle bag all over the mattress. I sat there while they made a joke about the way he soiled his pants in death. My eye stayed glued to the hole as the man with hair hit a button on his cell and spoke.

"Tell Crone it's done," he ordered, gruff.

When he was done, the bald man walked into the bathroom and took a piss. The sound of him relieving himself was almost too much. Black spots swam before my eyes, and the room around me spun.

"Let's get some lunch," one said.

I sat in the tiny space long after they'd gone. My body shook and trembled for so long I honestly thought it was a permanent state.

My father's eyes were open, still staring at the wall. Still watching, making sure I was hidden.

When I finally crawled out of the wall, I stood over his body, staring down as his blood seeped into my shoes and clung to the soles.

Glancing over to the heap of his upturned bag, my

eyes landed on a photo. The edges were worn, and one side was ripped.

Bending down, I picked it up. The image blurred, dimmed, and then came back into focus. I didn't notice the blood on my hands where I'd bitten myself or the crescent marks on the opposite palm from my fingernails.

It was a picture of a memory. Of a younger man standing in the snow, his daughter smiling beside him.

That was the best time of my life.

Clutching the photo to my chest, I stared back down at my father, and finally, I started to scream.

1

Bellamy

ONE YEAR LATER...

~~I STAYED LATE AT WORK BECAUSE I LOVE MY JOB.~~ I STAYED late at work because I had nothing better to do. I mean, really, trying to tell myself that lie was laughable. So laughable in fact that it made me snort even as I tried to convince myself it was even half true.

There was no point. If I couldn't be honest inside my own head, then I probably should have climbed out of that wall that day and died right then with my father.

Harsh.

Sometimes the truth was harsh. But wasn't the truth better than lie after lie? I would know. I lived one every single day.

Correction: it wasn't a lie. It was a new me.

Or so I was trained over and over to believe. For the most part, it worked. Except on nights like tonight when

13

I stayed late correlating files because thoughts of going home and staring at the empty walls of my apartment was excruciating. I wondered, not for the first time, if it would ever get any easier.

To cheer myself up, I stopped at a local grocery place on the corner near my apartment building. I didn't stop here much, though the place was amazing. It was expensive, but beyond that, it made me homesick. Because of that, it probably should have been the first place to avoid tonight as all these thoughts whirled around inside me. It stood to reason, though, that maybe if this place could make me homesick, perhaps it could also make me feel closer to what I missed.

At the very least, I could get a nice bottle of wine.

Wandering up and down the aisles of the little grocery, I breathed in the various scents mingling in the air. Fresh herbs, produce, and the heady aroma of baking baguettes.

I took in a deep breath and exhaled. Some of the tension and restlessness inside me eased.

Tucking the basket into the crook of my arm, I continued on, pausing to glance at the jarred sauces and selection of oils. A tingle of excitement and inspiration swirled inside, leaving my chest a little fluttery. The need to create something that burst across the tongue was almost irresistible.

After indulging in my thoughts for a few moments, I choose a few fresh herbs, some tomatoes that smelled delish, some garlic, and a few other light ingredients. Once those were in my basket, I selected a fresh baguette, still warm.

Fresh bruschetta would go very nicely with the wine I planned on drinking tonight.

Perusing the wine selection, a tingle of something

brushed over the back of my neck. Almost as if someone opened a window or the door and some of the wintry air floated in. I was nowhere near the door, though. And there was no window over here.

Glancing around, nothing appeared amiss, so I continued. As I was pulling out the bottle I chose, I noticed something out of the corner of my eye. I turned, staring down the aisle, as a man disappeared around the corner.

My stomach tightened and prickles of warning—the same kind I'd only ever had once before—assaulted me. Adrenaline flooded my system so fast that everything in the basket began to rattle with the shaking of my body.

Forcing a deep breath, I walked toward the cashier, forcing my steps to be unhurried and casual. All I really wanted to do was run.

Run and scream.

That familiar clawing sensation in the back of my esophagus started, and I cleared my throat, trying to push it away.

After paying for my items and giving the cashier a tight-lipped smile, I used the cold air as an excuse to hunch down into my coat and hurry to my car.

I white-knuckled the steering wheel until I pulled into the parking garage past the security gate. It wasn't much, really, but having that little drop-down arm that required a pass to park inside was better than nothing.

I might have pressed on the *close doors* button inside the elevator a few thousand times as I anxiously stared out into the garage. And I might have nearly tripped rushing down the hall to my door and sagged against it once I was safely inside.

The relief didn't last very long, though.

Instead, my head shot up and I stared down the small

hallway that lead into the rest of the apartment. Suspicion and anxiety with adrenaline was a dangerous combination. Shoving away from the door, I went into my place, flicking on every light along the way. After depositing my groceries and purse on the counter, I checked the rest of the apartment, something that wasn't really unfamiliar to me.

Once that was done, I double-checked the closet, then finally took off my coat and sighed.

I was being silly.

I was.

There was no way anyone had found me. I'd done everything right. Taken every precaution. I was safe.

Then why don't I feel like it?

I poured myself a big glass of wine and unpacked the groceries I'd bought. After about half the glass, I began to feel a little looser. I decided what I needed to do was take a hot shower, put on something comfy, and then make the bruschetta. I could have another overly full glass of wine and watch a sappy romance movie on TV.

Once I was showered, blond hair pulled up on top of my head, and a pair of loose, comfy sweats covered my legs, I carried the empty glass of wine to the kitchen and began cooking.

I'd barely begun when that feeling slinked back over me again.

Dropping the knife, I gripped the edges of the counter and squeezed, watching the way my fingers turned white from the pressure. Beneath my ribs, my heart galloped and an intense urge to flee knocked me back.

Thinking it would make me feel better, I went to the closet nearest the front door and looked inside at the duffle bag sitting on the top shelf, packed.

I wasn't sure what it said about me that it was there, but whatever it was didn't stop me from having it.

After forcing a few deep breaths, I started to push the door closed.

Bang! Bang! Bang!

I let out a low squeal and jumped back, pressing a hand to my chest.

Someone was at the door, knocking. No one ever came to the door.

Creeping forward, I looked through the peephole.

A man in a dark-brown uniform with the yellow logo of a delivery company stood on the other side. His head was tilted down, so I couldn't see his face, only the hat. In his arms was a brown box.

I wasn't expecting any delivery. In fact, I never shopped online. I never did anything online. It was too risky.

"Yes?" I called through the door.

"Delivery!"

"I'm not expecting anything." I watched through the peephole as the man tugged the box out and glanced down at it.

"Bella Lane?" he called out. "Apartment twelve?"

I nodded, then realized he couldn't see me. "Yes, that's me."

"Then this one's for you."

I hesitated, not saying anything. That feeling was back. And this time, I didn't want to try and fight it. "Just leave it by the door," I called out. I'd get it after he'd gone.

"I need you to sign for it."

Don't open that door!

The scent of sautéing tomatoes that were close to burning wafted down the small hallway.

"I'm not able to answer. If you can't leave it, just take it to the store and I'll pick it up tomorrow."

His head remained down, but his shoulders stiffened. "It will only take a second."

I backed away from the door, creeping as though if I made even the slightest sound, he would know.

He knocked again. I tossed my hand out to steady myself on the wall.

Something was wrong. *If you feel like something is wrong, it probably is.*

Backtracking into the room, I fetched my cell out of my purse and dialed 9-1-1 on the screen. Heart pounding, I stood between the kitchen and the hallway, clutching the phone, staring at the door.

Please go away. Please.

Suddenly, I was back there squished between the walls of my father's shitty apartment. The smell of fear and sweat clung to the inside of my nose, and the sounds of flesh hitting flesh made me shake.

"All right, then," the delivery man yelled. "I'm leaving!"

I let out a breath, but I still trembled all over.

I was still too afraid to move, so I stood there for a long time, just staring at the door and listening for something. Anything.

I thought to go check the window, to see if perhaps the mail truck had driven away, but I couldn't get my feet to work.

A faint sound hit me like the boom of a gun. I jerked, and my eyes flew back to the door.

I watched in horror as the deadbolt, which locked, turned slowly… until it stopped.

Unlocked.

The front door creaked like a bad horror film when

the man, who was clearly not a delivery man, shoved it open. He filled the doorway in his brown uniform. His head lifted just as slowly as the door had swung in.

"I have your package," he intoned. The box was dropped, and beneath it in his hand was a gun.

A gun with a silencer on the end.

I screamed and lunged to the side falling into the kitchen. The sound of a shot going off and the bullet burying in the wall was something I was unfortunately familiar with.

In my haste to leap away, my cell slipped out of my hand and slid nearly under the stove. With a cry, I lunged forward, my knees slapping against the floor. My fingers closed around it, but as I pulled it close, the man appeared, shoving me back into the corner of the cabinets.

He pointed the gun. His eyes were empty and void.

Adrenaline surged in me again, and before I knew what I was doing, I reached up over my head and grabbed the pan I'd been using on the stove. I flung it at the man, and he screamed.

Hot oil, vegetables, and the pan itself smacked him in the face. He screamed as though he was burned, batted the pan away, then began trying to brush off the burning food.

I scrambled away, ran down the hallway, and opened the closet door. My hand closed around the duffle as he came at me. I swung, using the back like a battering ram, and hit him in the face. He fell to the side into the wall with a curse. I yanked open the apartment door behind me and ran. Instead of the elevator, I rushed down the stairs. I heard him not far behind, his footsteps pounding closer. Thinking fast, I ducked into the maintenance room just before the door leading out to the parking garage.

Trembling behind the oversized equipment, I heard him rush by.

"She headed toward you!" he said and burst out into the garage.

The second my heart stopped thundering, I knew I couldn't just sit here. I couldn't wait for him to come back. Sneaking out of the room, I went in the opposite direction, looping through the hall until I came to a door that led out on a different street.

Pulling my hood up over my head, I ducked onto the sidewalk and carried the duffle like an oversized shoulder bag.

A cab pulled to the curb up ahead. A laughing couple stepped out.

I ran for it, sliding into the backseat before the door was even closed. The cabby glanced up, surprise written over his face.

"Where to?" he asked.

"Just drive."

He pulled out into traffic, went down the street, and turned the corner. "I'm gonna need an address, lady."

My first thought was the police station. They would know what to do. They had the resources to keep me safe. I opened my mouth to give the address of the precinct. I knew it by heart.

Something stopped me.

A cold feeling wormed around inside me.

Going to the police was what I was supposed to do. It's what I did last time.

And now I was here.

They'd promised me protection. They'd sworn I was safe. My new identity, my new life… it was all perfectly calculated so the men who killed my father couldn't find me.

They lied.

The fake delivery man with a gun back there was proof.

I had been found.

Everything I'd done was for nothing.

Witness protection couldn't protect me. I'd given them a chance. They failed.

Now it was up to me.

2

Liam

THE SOUND OF THE WHISTLE CUT THROUGH THE FROSTY air. The shiny metal fell from my lips and skidded over my coat to land midway down my chest, stopped by the blue chord it was attached to.

Everyone glanced up, and I clapped. "Wrap it up!" I bellowed, a puff of white air bursting out with my words. "Good class today. I'll see you all on the slopes."

A couple of people skied off toward the lifts, and a few began taking off some of their gear.

It only took a second for me to unlatch the board from my feet, bend down, and pick it up. I was so used to doing it I could do it in my sleep.

Walking toward the rack and for my clipboard, I paused when someone called my name from behind.

"Liam?"

I glanced around as a snow bunny in pink came forward, wobbling on the bulky boots and half dragging the snowboard along with her.

"What can I do you for you, Ms.—"

"Heather," she said, cutting me off. It was a good thing, too, because I didn't know her name. God only knew what would have come out of my mouth.

"Heather," I said and smiled.

She tripped, and the board fell onto the snow and skidded away as she pitched forward.

"Whoa," I said and caught her, easily juggling my board and her body. I noticed the way she pressed close a second. Hell, I even let her do it before I steadied her on her own two feet. "Careful there. You almost got a face full of powder."

She giggled and adjusted the goggles on her head. "Thanks."

After a minute of her saying nothing at all and me just standing there waiting around like a dumbass, I cleared my throat. "Was there something you needed?"

"Oh!" she said, her cheeks turning pinker than they already were. "I was wondering if you had any last-minute tips for me? How did I do in the lesson?"

My eyes dragged over her, starting at her boots and landing at her face. She had long, blond hair that hung out of her cap and over her shoulders. It was slightly damp and slightly wavy from the snow. It reminded me of someone.

Of the past.

Keeping my eyes trained on her face, I replied, "You did good today, for a beginner." Then I smiled.

She giggled.

"Just remember to keep your eyes up and not down at the board. Your body will follow your eyes, okay?"

She nodded.

"Cool." I started to turn, and I felt her follow.

I wanted to groan. Usually, I was all good with the attention from the ladies. But not right now. Not from her.

Besides, I had somewhere I needed to be.

As if on cue, a body on a pair of skis slid expertly to where I was heading. The perfection of his stop was amplified by the powder that sprayed toward me.

"Niiice," I said, grinning.

Alex tucked the poles under his arms, his chuckle loud and clear. The reflective green cast on his goggles flashed blue when he lifted them onto the navy hat on his head. "You see that?" He boasted. "One hundred percent perfection."

I grunted and propped my board up on the rack.

Alex's eyes slid toward my groupie and then back to me. With my back turned, I rolled my eyes at him. A nanosecond of surprise flashed in his, but it was gone practically before it appeared.

"Hey there, bunny," he called, hitching his chin at her. "What's your name?"

"Heather," she said, taking that as her cue to come closer.

"You just have a lesson with my man Liam?"

She nodded. "He's the best,"

Alex grinned, a puff of air floating out around his mouth from his silent laughter. His eyes flickered behind where we stood and then back. "Say, ah, how long you around for?"

I wanted to groan. *She must have a friend.* One who wasn't quite as brazen.

"All week," Heather said.

"That your friend?"

Heather glanced over her shoulder and nodded.

I gave Alex a warning look, silently telling him to shut the fuck up. He didn't even acknowledge me.

A slow smile spread over the lower half of his face. "We're planning on hitting up the tavern off the lodge tonight for some drinks. Maybe we'll see you ladies then."

I almost took the ski pole out of his grasp and stabbed him with it.

After the girl giggled and practically promised to be there, she went to retrieve her board and talk excitedly with her friend.

Once they were out of earshot, I glanced at my best friend and groaned. "Dude. Why did you do that?"

"It's my duty to get you booty," he quipped.

I punched him in the shoulder. He slid backward on the skis, but the bastard steadied himself just as fast. "You know I don't need help with that."

He chuckled. "Maybe not, but she was fine and so was her friend."

"So bang her friend," I grumped. "Fuck, have a threesome with them both, for all the fucks I give."

"Whoa." He made a face. "Who threw a snowball in your shorts?"

"No one." I picked up the clipboard and made a few notes before I forgot. "Sometimes it gets old is all."

"Yeah, being followed around and hit on by hot snow bunnies on the daily is just a tragedy."

I gave him the finger.

He hit the underside of the clipboard. "What's up, bro?"

I glanced up. His ice-blue eyes were concerned. "Nothing," I muttered. "She just reminded me of someone."

"Anyone I'd know?"

I gazed off in the direction she'd gone, then out over the tall pine trees heavy with white snow. "Forget it," I said. "It's ancient history."

Alex made a sound, but before he could press, I said, "Thanks for taking my next class. I better head in before the old man sends someone to fetch me."

"No prob." He checked the watch buried under his jacket. "I got some time. I'm going to head in and grab a drink. I'll walk with you."

Alex had his skis off, leaning them on the rack where my board had been before I tucked it under my arm. I didn't leave my board lying around. And it didn't go in the rental space where all the other equipment was stored either. This board was mine and no one else's.

"So, hey, how 'bout those beers tonight?" Alex asked as we went.

I chuckled. "Do you always think with your dick?"

"Don't you?" he asked, glib.

"Touché." But even as I said it, I knew it wasn't true. At least not lately. Lately, I'd been thinking with my head a lot more than my dick.

I wasn't too fond of it, but damn if I knew how to fix it.

"C'mon, Liam. You're probably gonna need a beer after the meeting with Mr. Mattison himself."

"Fine." I agreed. "I'll meet you in the bar later."

He slapped me on the back.

I slid him a glance from the corner of my eye. "But no women. Not tonight."

"How you going to do me like that?" Alex complained.

I laughed. "Fine. No women for me. But you can take your pick."

"Now that's what I'm talking about!" he exclaimed.

I laughed and returned his fist-bump before heading into the employee entrance, then up to my father's office.

3

Bellamy

THE SECOND THE BUS RUMBLED TO A STOP, NERVES assailed me.

What if I was doing the wrong thing?

This thing that I was doing seemed right until I got here and actually had to follow through with my plan.

If you could even call it that.

I was the last one off the bus. In fact, I sat there so long, staring out into the twilight sky and darkening street, that the bus driver appeared.

"This is the last stop," he said, his voice gruff.

I jumped, having not even heard him approach. Pressing my hand to my chest, I blinked up, wide-eyed.

"I didn't mean to scare you, miss."

I forced a low laugh. "Oh, no. You didn't." It was a stupid thing to say because obviously he had scared me. I went on autopilot, though, just muttering the first polite thing I could think of.

"Sorry for holding you up," I said and stood, clutching the bag into my chest. I bit into my lower lip and waited for him to step aside.

"Not a problem," he said and moved.

He called a good night after me as I stepped onto the snowy street.

The bus doors slammed behind me, and he pulled forward before I was even up on the curb. Once there, I stood still, hugging the bag close. Lifting my chin, I stared into the sky that was a deep shade of blue, but not quite dark. Fat, white snowflakes floated from the sky. They reminded me of feathers the way they sort of glided back and forth on their way to the ground.

One hit me in the nose, its icy structure shocking me just a little as it began to melt against my skin. I smiled, the first smile I think I'd known in a long time.

It almost felt wrong, but even so, I couldn't chastise myself for it. Not tonight. Not after everything.

I might be in trouble, but I'd gotten this far. That was something to be proud of.

Along with the smile, a faint feeling of peace took hold in my chest. It was small and fragile, just like the snowflakes that fell around me, but it was there. And just like those white flakes, it was beautiful.

I was scared, doubting every move I'd made in the last day.

But I was alive.

It was a good place to start.

Someone on the sidewalk skirted around me, narrowly avoiding a collision. Pulling my cheeks from the sky, I glanced around at my surroundings.

The place looked the same.

Same but different.

Was there such a thing?

Maybe it was just me who was different. After everything that happened since I was last here, it was pretty obvious I wouldn't be looking around with the same eyes.

The town of Caribou, Colorado, was a beautiful place. It seemed rooted in history with its small-town feel and narrow main street filled with shops and lights. Snow fell here more often than it didn't, and the mountain rose around the town like an intimidating force. The scent of a nearby bakery carried through the wintry air, and my stomach rumbled.

I hadn't eaten for nearly two days, except for some stale coffee and a pack of crackers. I hadn't wanted to take the chance of being seen while getting any food anywhere.

The bus ride had been long, and even when it made some stops, I refused to get off. My life literally depended upon it.

Was I safe here?

I wasn't entirely sure, but it was the only place I could think to run.

I snorted a little thinking like that.

The first and only time I'd been here, I'd run, too. *Run away.*

I vowed to never return, even to get back the chunk of my heart that had unfortunately stayed behind. Even after all these years, I knew it was still here.

I felt it.

Turning, I glanced past the bundled-up people, the cute little shops and lights. I peered through the falling snow up toward the mountain.

Not far in the distance, a large building stood. Close by were long, white lanes that striped down the mountain, and with those were the chair lifts, lit up, carriages going to and from.

My stomach flipped as I stared up at BearPaw Resort. The place where I first fell in love.

The place where my heart was first broken.

4

Liam

My father tsked when I stepped into his large corner office filled with walnut furniture and sweeping views of the slopes.

It was probably one of the nicest views at the resort.

I was surprised he hadn't made this some swanky room and charged triple for it. People would have paid, and his bottom line would have bled black.

However, as astute of a business man my father was, he could appreciate a damn good view.

Besides, say what you would about Renshaw Mattison; he was a hard worker. And if anyone deserved this prime spot at BearPaw, it was him.

"You couldn't have changed for the meeting?" he asked, glowering over his glasses.

"I'm pretty sure this conversation would still be the same if I was dressed in a three-piece suit."

"Appearances mean a lot in the business world."

I availed myself upon the seat in front of his desk,

leaned back, and propped one foot up over my knee. "I'm not you, Dad."

"Of that I am acutely aware."

I grunted. "Well, it's not too late to change your mind."

He chuckled. "I still believe you are the right man for the job, no matter your dress habits."

"That's good, because if I do end up taking over this place someday, I'm still dressing like this."

"Headstrong. Just like your mother."

It wasn't an insult. In fact, I took it the opposite. My father loved my mother more than anything, so for him to say I was like her spoke volumes.

He cleared his throat. "So have you thought about our last conversation?"

"That you want me to take over BearPaw Resort?" I sat up. "I've thought about it."

"And?"

I sighed. "I'm still thinking."

He frowned.

"I'm not the business type, Dad." I gestured to my clothes as proof. "I'm an athlete. I spend most of my time outside. Up until last year, I didn't spend too much time in one place."

"Things are different now."

How could I forget? I glanced down at my knee, then shifted.

"There are plenty of high-level execs here that would kill for this job." I pointed out.

"Yes. Well, they aren't my son."

"Nepotism at its finest," I drawled.

My father gave me a distasteful look and stood. With his hands clasped behind his back, he stared out over the slopes. The lights had come on a few minutes ago. Soon, it would be completely dark. I loved to night board. Night ski. Cruise around on the snowmobile after hours.

"This started as a family business, and that's the way I would like it to remain. I realize you had other plans for your life, but now you're back. You were raised here. I know you know this place like the back of your hand. I could teach you anything else you needed to know."

"I could do the job," I said, confident.

He glanced around. "Is that a yes?"

I smiled, swift. "No. It means I don't doubt my skills at running this place."

"If you still want to teach," he began, "I'm sure it could be worked out."

I laughed. The idea had some merit to it. Imagine the head honcho of this place out there on the mountain, giving ski lessons. People would never expect that.

I liked doing the unexpected.

Some people might even argue that's what I was known for.

"I was hoping to start training you in the spring." My father spoke, glancing back outside.

My eyebrows rose. That was sooner than I realized. "You ready to retire, Dad?" I asked, a hint of teasing in my voice.

He didn't laugh. Instead, he answered, "I just want to make sure you're ready when the time comes."

My brow wrinkled. "Time comes for what?"

He turned from the window and smiled. "For when your mother decides she doesn't want to be a snowbird and books us a winter cruise."

I barked a laugh. So Mom was talking about retiring.

My father watched me, waiting.

I sighed. "It's only February," I replied.

"So?"

"So spring is a few months away. I still have time to think."

Sitting down behind his desk, he nodded. "Yes. You have some time."

"Meeting adjourned?" I pushed to my feet.

"I'll see you at Sunday dinner."

"I'll be there with bells on." I went to the door, already thinking of a hot shower.

"I know this isn't what you expected," he said abruptly.

My chest tightened, and I turned. "No. It's not."

"And I'm sorry about that, son." He came around the desk, tucking his hands into the pockets of his trousers. "But I'm not sorry you're home."

I nodded.

"Maybe it's just fate's way of letting you know BearPaw is where you belong."

"I'll think about it, Dad," I told him, gripping his shoulder. My throat was tight as I let myself out of the office.

It wasn't that I was sorry I was back here with my family and where I grew up and my best friend lived.

It was just hard to let go of the past. Of things that could have been.

5

Bellamy

THE CAB PULLED UP TO THE FRONT OF THE RESORT, AND all those qualms about coming here became storms. I really wasn't sure about this. About being here.

I didn't know where else to go.

I had no one. Unless you counted the cops who put me into witness protection.

snort

Those dudes definitely didn't count.

When I'd been huddled in the back of that cab with my getaway bag clutched in my lap and the cabbie kept staring at me, asking me where to go, the only place that came to mind was here.

Of all places.

I swore I'd never come back, yet here I was.

Honest fact was with the bad I had experienced here, there had also been so much good.

Only once in my entire life had I spent a vacation with my father. Only once had I had his undivided attention for two whole weeks. This was the place we'd spent what he told me was the best time of his life.

The photo I'd picked up from beside his murdered body was of him and me standing on the slopes.

Maybe that was why. Why when I shut my eyes and tried to imagine somewhere my father's killers couldn't get to me, it was the very place I'd been happy with him.

No one knew I'd spent two weeks here eight years ago. Caribou was a small mountain town, only on the map because of BearPaw Resort. The men from Chicago wouldn't think to look here.

I'd be safe.

That's all I really wanted.

As the cab drove away and I craned my neck to stare up at the giant wooden building lit up from within, my stomach dipped and my heart squeezed. There was something else I wanted.

To *not* see him.

Lucky for me, in this the odds were in my favor.

He'd left this place a long time ago. Before I did, actually. I knew he wasn't here. I was glad. Seeing him would only bring up pain and drag up things I'd long since buried.

Hadn't I?

I had enough to deal with anyway. Like hiding from the men trying to kill me.

That little reminder had me walking under the giant wooden awning where cars could pull in for the valet service and people could unload their bags.

Ducking inside the wide wooden doors, I walked through a small entryway with a thick rug on the floor and heat blasting through vents in the ceiling. I hadn't even realized how cold I was until that heat caressed my skin.

Shivering, I approached the set of glass doors that opened into the reception area of the main building. The idea of the little entry I walked through was pretty clever really. Most likely thought of by a woman who was tired of cleaning.

The thick carpet and the extra space... It was for people to track in all the mud and snow they would, and it would all be gone by the time they reached the lobby.

The place looked the same, even eight years later. Pushing into the giant space with soaring ceilings, wooden beams, and a stone fireplace I could literally stand up in, I remembered just how much I'd loved it here.

It was a shame that one event had tainted it.

Shaking off that thought, I wandered inside, taking in the comfortable seating that was grouped together to create various intimate gathering places. Near the large front desk, there was a table filled with cookies, hot cocoa, and coffee. People milled about, laughing and smiling. Some carried bags; others carried ski equipment. There was a couple close to the fire, drinking wine, wearing sweaters they probably got off QVC.

I was so apprehensive I avoided the front desk at first. Instead, I went to the fireplace. Admiring the large-cut stone in shades of grey and tan, I held my frozen hands out toward the open mouth. Heat wrapped around them, and I shivered again.

A giant chandelier hung in the center of the space. It was rustic and, despite its size, felt cozy, not grandiose. The fireplace was double-sided, and past it, the room stretched on toward a huge wall of windows that gazed out over a terrain of snow, white-blanketed trees, and a landscape that frankly belonged on a postcard.

Noise from the bar that was located off the lodge

filtered in. Music and laughter warred with the quieter tones out here.

I thought longingly of a glass of wine and of the bottle I never got to enjoy. Perhaps after I got a room, I could have some sent up. I had to watch my spending, only having what I'd stowed away in my bag, but I deserved some wine.

Hell, I *needed* it.

Sinking my teeth into my lower lip, I glanced over at the registration desk. A man in a dress shirt and tie stood behind the counter. He glanced up and smiled. I looked away.

I didn't even know how much the rooms cost. They could be crazy expensive. I hadn't paid the last time I was here. Oh, to be sixteen again. To not have to worry about bills or responsibility.

You know even at sixteen nothing is perfect. Far from it.

I'd come all this way. I could at least spend the night. If the prices were too high, I could come up with a plan in the morning. I was tired. Hungry. Afraid.

Rubbing my palms down the front of my sweats (yes, Lord help me, I was still wearing these oversized lounge clothes), I padded over to the desk, cautious.

"Hi. Welcome to BearPaw Lodge. Do you have a reservation?" the man said, a friendly smile on his face.

"Hi." I began as my hands started to shake. "I'm afraid I don't have a reservation. Do you have anything available?"

"Hmm." He turned thoughtful. "Let me check, and I'll be right with you."

He turned his attention to the computer in front of him, the sound of his fingers flying over the keys sort of relaxing.

"I do have a room. It has a double bed. Would that be okay?"

"I'll take it," I said, nearly crumpling to the floor in relief.

"Okay, for that room plus the breakfast buffet and a voucher for one free drink at the bar every night after five p.m., the total is…" He paused, his fingers doing something else. "Two twenty per night."

My breath caught. Two hundred and twenty dollars a night! I couldn't afford that.

My shoulders sagged.

The man frowned, seemingly reading the defeated expression on my face. He cleared his throat, hitting a few more keys. "I can take off the buffet, the drink voucher, and move you to a room without a view. Then the total will be one fifty-nine per night."

Worrying my lower lip, I nodded. "Could I reserve that please?"

"Of course." He beamed. "How many nights?"

"Um, I'm not sure," I mumbled. "Just one."

"Name?"

"Bella Lane," I replied on autopilot.

Tomorrow, I could go back into town and look for a motel of some kind. Something much less expensive.

After a few more moments, he smiled. "All right, Ms. Lane, I just need to see a valid ID and a credit card for the reservation."

I blanched.

I didn't have either of those things. I'd run out of my house without my purse. No ID, no cell phone, no wallet… all I had was an envelope of cash and some clothes.

I mean, for heaven's sake, the shoes on my feet were stolen!

"Of course," I said and smiled. Plopping the bag down near my feet, I bent and pretended to rifle through it. "I have those things right—"

I popped up. "Oh no!"

The man's eyes widened.

"Is something wrong?"

"I left my wallet in the cab!"

He made a sound. "Do you know which cab company you used? I will be happy to call them and have it brought back."

"It was a yellow one," I said, knowing just how idiotic I sounded.

This time he blanched. "They're all yellow here, miss."

Tears rushed to my eyes. I didn't even have to pretend. They were genuine and real. There was no way I was going to get a room at this place with no ID and no credit.

Almost eighteen hours on a bus, and now I couldn't even stay.

"Oh now," the man fretted. Clearly, tears made him uncomfortable.

I sniffled, trying to hold back a full-on melt down.

"It's just been a horrible day," I told him, a whimper in my voice. "I've come such a long way."

He fished under the counter and plopped a tissue box down in front of me.

"I'm so sorry to have wasted your time. I'll go."

"Wait!" he said when I turned away.

I swiped at my cheeks and glanced back.

"Where will you go?"

"I'm not sure," I replied. "Would it be okay if I sat down for a few minutes to think?" I gestured to one of the cozy chairs near the fire.

"Of course," he said. "You just want the room for one night?"

I nodded. "I have cash. I could pay."

"Let me just run it by my manager. Have a seat. I'll be right back."

A speck of hope ignited inside me. Not enough to make me feel better, but enough to make the tears stop.

I knew I wouldn't get the room here tonight, but at least I could sit down and figure out my next move. Maybe if I was lucky, he would forget about me, and I could spend the night in the chair by the fire.

I stole a glance over at the tray of cookies and hot coca. My stomach rumbled. It felt dishonest to partake of the treats. Instead, I went back to the fire and warmed my hands some more.

After a few minutes, I was toasty warm and so tired my eyes were watering from the amount of yawning I was doing. The nearby chair looked comfortable and welcoming. I sank into it, tucking my bag of possessions in with me.

A quick glance to the desk told me the man was still off doing whatever he was doing.

I hope he's not calling the police.

The thought was random, almost sarcastic. But oh, it struck me wide awake. Jolting up, my back and shoulders went taut. I looked around as if the police were already here and coming straight for me.

I hadn't technically done anything wrong, but if they were called about a woman with no ID, dressed like a bum, trying to get a room at some fancy resort, they would surely run my name.

They'd send me back.

Back where I'd be a sitting duck.

Back to be murdered.

Visions of my father being shot to death in front of me assaulted my thoughts. I leapt out of the chair and saw the man still wasn't back.

If I ran now, I could still get away.

Scooping up my bag, I rushed around the back of the chair, away from the front desk. I'd take this way around, maybe keep to the wall so if he came back, he wouldn't see me.

In my haste, I didn't watch where I was going. I collided with a large, solid form and bounced back.

Right before I crumpled to the floor, strong hands grabbed me around the arms and hauled me upright.

"Whoa," he said.

Every hair on my body stood up. My heart caved in.

Even after eight years, I'd know that voice anywhere.

I gasped at the same time I looked up.

Gray eyes collided with mine.

The hands around my arms tightened, and shock filled his expression. *"Bellamy?"*

Oh my God. *He wasn't supposed to be here.*

Oh my God.

It was him.

6

Liam

THE TAVERN RIGHT OFF BEARPAW LODGE WAS BASICALLY just like every other gathering place here at the resort. With the same soaring ceiling, wooden beams, and views of the picturesque slopes, no one could say this bar felt too much like a bar.

Even though that's what it was.

The bar itself sat in the center of the room, basically forming a giant U. It was made of pine, and the countertop was a giant map of the resort and surrounding town under a layer of thick, clear resin or something that didn't let all the alcohol spill through.

Off to one side, there was a stage for karaoke or nights when we had live entertainment. There was, of course, a fireplace, and the rest of the space was filled with tables and chairs.

Alex was already at the bar when I walked in. He signaled, and I headed right for him. The bartender called out a hello and held up a glass. I nodded as I took the stool beside my friend.

"Started without me," I said, tapping the side of his beer.

"Honestly, wasn't too sure you'd show."

I made a face. "When's the last time I told you I'd be somewhere I wasn't?"

"Never." He allowed.

The bartender set a full draft in front of me, and I wrapped my hand around it, sliding it closer.

"Thanks, Todd."

"No problem, Liam," he said and moved off to another customer.

"I wasn't sure what kind of mood you'd be in after the meeting with the big man."

I chuckled a little. It was funny to me how everyone saw my father as this big head honcho, and I guess he was. I mean, he basically built this entire place from the ground up, and with it came a lot of business and opportunity for the entire town of Caribou.

Some people referred to him as the founder of Caribou.

Some viewed my entire family as the royals of Colorado.

I just thought of him as my dad.

"I don't know why you call him that, man," I said, sipping the draft. "He used to change your diapers, too."

Alex cackled. "That's why! The big man himself changing our diapers."

I rolled my eyes and snickered into the beer.

"So how'd it go?" he asked.

I stared at him a minute, taking in his long-sleeved T-shirt and black fleece vest. The collar was flipped up so it shadowed his jaw, which was already shaded with dark stubble.

His hair was out of control, as always. But really, it was part of his charm. The ladies seemed to love the way it was cropped super close on the sides in a fade then sort of full and curly on the top.

Alex always said being born to a white woman and an African-American man gave him the best of both worlds: piercing light eyes and tight curls that were still manageable.

His skin was the color of coffee with cream, and it never burned, even when the sun was nearly blinding as it mirrored off fresh snow. He never got a raging case of hat hair, even when he wore one all day, and his light eyes combined with the rich color of his skin always made the bunnies (as he liked to call them) look twice.

"You checking me out, L?" His teeth flashed as he lifted the beer to his lips.

"Fuck no," I argued. "Just wondering how much gel you had to put in your hair to make it stay like that all day."

Alex chuckled. "All natural, my friend. All natural."

"Dad wants to start training me in the spring," I said, quiet.

Alex made a sound. His beer thumped onto the bar top. "As in *this* spring?"

"Shocked the shit outta me."

"You boys want a pizza?" Sharon said as she walked behind us. She'd been working at this resort for as long as I could remember, and to her, we'd be nothing but boys 'til the day she retired.

I glanced around and gave her a smile. "Extra pepperoni."

"Like you need it," she muttered fondly.

"I'm a growing boy."

She laughed beneath her breath. "Keep eating pizza and you'll be growing all right."

"Thank you, Sharon," Alex called out as she walked away.

"Yeah, yeah," she called back.

One good thing about not training constantly was all the pizza and beer I could eat.

"So why so soon?" Alex asked when she was gone.

I shrugged. "He gave some excuse about Mom wanting to take a winter cruise."

Alex gave me a WTF look.

I nodded. It was complete bullshit.

"Maybe he's ready for a break and just doesn't want to admit it." Alex proposed.

"Maybe." I allowed. "He sure does work a hell of a lot."

"You ready for that?"

I made a sound. "I love this place and I want to do my dad proud, but I can't say I'm too eager to work my ass into the ground."

"So what are you gonna do?"

"I told him to offer you the job instead."

Beer spewed out of Alex's mouth and splattered the bar top.

"Clean that mess up!" Sharon yelled from somewhere in the bar.

I swear she had eyes in the back of her head.

Alex wiped at his mouth with his hand. "What the fuck?"

I laughed. Then I laughed again. "Your face."

"Fuck you, Mattison. Fuck you."

I was still laughing when I helped him clean up the mess then tossed the rag into the bucket behind the bar.

A few minutes later, Sharon slid a large pizza dripping with extra pepperoni, sausage, and green peppers in front of us. "I brought plates," she informed us, giving us one each. "Use them."

"Yes, ma'am," I said dutifully.

She patted me on the cheek. "I'm so glad to have you back here." Then her pat turned into more of a gentle slap. "Now eat nice and don't embarrass me. This place is filling up."

I glanced around with a chuckle. It was getting full.

Just to irritate her, I grabbed a slice and shoved half of it in my mouth. Groaning around the cheesy goodness, I grinned, showing the food in my mouth.

"Absolutely disgusting." She shook her head and walked away.

The conversation never did turn back to the meeting, which was just fine with me. I wasn't sure what to think of the entire discussion. I knew my dad always hoped I'd come back here someday and run the place.

Hell, I never ruled it out either. I just never thought it would be this soon.

It was hard to reconcile what was with what could have been.

That thought brought along an image from long ago that had absolutely nothing to do with business.

I tossed the pizza down and picked up the beer for a guzzle.

Fuck. What is wrong with me today?

"Ladies," Alex drawled, rotating on the barstool so he was facing into the rest of the room.

A light giggle answered, and my back teeth came together. I wasn't in the mood earlier, and I was in even less of a mood now.

Alex hit me in the shoulder. "How lucky are we? The

ladies from this afternoon have graced us with their presence."

I took my time setting down the now-empty glass and rotating. My burly attitude was pushed down, and I offered up a smile. "Ladies," I said. "Looking good tonight."

It was true. They both looked hot. I knew I could score with one of them. The blonde was looking at me the same way she had out in the snow earlier. Her friend divided her attention between both me and Alex, as if she were trying to decide.

Man candy. That's all we were.

What a tough job.

If it had been any other night, I'd be up for it. Hell, I'd lead the brigade.

I just didn't feel like it tonight.

"Shall we grab a table?" Alex hopped off the stool and gestured for the women to follow him toward one of the last tables open in the back.

The blonde hesitated, glancing back at me. I gestured to Todd for a round of drinks, then stood. Out of habit, or maybe because I wasn't the uncouth boy Sharon so loved to call me, I placed my hand on the small of the girl's back and led her to where Alex and her friend were already sitting.

She watched me from beneath dark lashes, and I smiled.

I might not be in the mood, but I wasn't an asshole.

Besides, maybe after another beer, I'd feel differently.

At least now this chick didn't leave me feeling this funny sensation in my gut when I looked at her. She was more made up now. Full makeup, tight top that left little to the imagination, and her hair was dry and curled so it didn't wave over her shoulders anymore.

It wasn't the right color blond now. It was too light.

I should have been relieved.

I wasn't.

The second Todd brought us our beers, I took a healthy drink. Alex gave me a look, asking me what the fuck was up my ass. I ignored him.

I let him do most of the talking. Charm was his specialty. It could be argued it was a specialty of mine, too. But tonight, I was content to sit back in my chair and watch the room.

The girl—I think she reminded me her name was Heather—was making it pretty easy. The way she crossed her legs toward me and leaned over the table, giving me a straight view into her bra. She laughed and giggled, putting her hand on my arm.

After the second beer was empty, I realized something. It didn't matter how many beers I drank tonight. I wasn't going to feel different. I didn't get drunk just to get laid anyway. That was something only assholes did.

Abruptly, I stood, fished around in the pocket of my jeans, and dropped some bills onto the table. "It's on me tonight," I said.

"You're leaving!" the blonde exclaimed, eyes widening.

"'Fraid so. I got an early morning tomorrow."

Alex was staring at me as if I'd grown an extra dick. He knew damn well I didn't have an early morning. I didn't do early.

"I can't convince you to stay? Just one more drink?" Heather asked, jumping from her seat and hanging on my arm.

Casually, I pulled back, smiling down at her. "If anyone could convince me, darlin', it'd be you. But not tonight."

Her eyes flickered with shock. She just couldn't believe she'd thrown herself at me and I was turning her down.

I almost laughed.

"Catch you tomorrow, bro." I held out a fist to Alex. He smashed his against it, and I started away from the table.

I only got a few feet when he called my name and appeared behind me. I turned, glancing over his shoulder to see both women watching us from the table.

"You're for real leaving?" he asked.

My eyes met his. "I'm done tonight."

He frowned. "Yeah. Okay. Want me to come back to your place with you? We can just chill." He was a good friend, willing to give up the ass I knew he was going to get tonight.

"Nah, stay. I want details in the morning."

He made a sound. "I don't kiss and tell."

I snorted.

After the shit-eating grin on his face died down, he asked, "Seriously, you cool?"

I nodded. "I am. I'll see you in the morning."

Alex slapped me on the shoulder and then went back to the table. As I left, I heard them laugh at something he said, and I grinned.

Dude was such a player.

The second I stepped out into the lodge into the quieter tones, I felt some of the tension leave my shoulder blades.

Maybe I just wanted to be alone tonight.

To think.

Coming around the back side of the fireplace, a blur suddenly appeared, and it banged right into me.

"Whoa," I exclaimed, automatically reaching out to steady what just bounced off.

A little gasp stopped my heart.

I glanced down into blue eyes I honestly thought I'd never see again.

I blinked, thinking my mind was playing tricks on me. I was only seeing her because she'd been on my mind today.

As if testing to see if she was real, my fingers flexed where I held her. She didn't disappear.

"Bellamy?" Her name ripped out of me like a blast from the past.

Oh my God.

It was her.

7

Bellamy

BREATHING WAS SOMETHING MY BODY FORGOT HOW TO DO.
An automatic action that suddenly became something so
very complicated.

"*Liam,*" I said, the word low and strained. It used up
the very last bit of my oxygen.

His hands flexed again, still holding on to my arms.

That was the problem. The reason my lungs were
burning and my sight was blurred. He was touching me.

I wrenched away, nearly tripping. He reached to
steady me again, but I made a strangled sound, and he
stopped.

The second there was some precious space between
us, I sucked in a ragged breath. Then another.

"You're here," he rasped.

"You weren't supposed to be."

He smiled. Oh, why did he have to do that? The
dimple in his chin appeared, and my knees started to
shake.

Eight years. Even after eight years, he still reduced me to putty.

"Thought about me, did you?"

Every. Single. Day.

"Of course not." I drew myself up, wrapping my arms around my body. Oh God, I looked a mess. I was dressed like a homeless person…

Oh God, I *was* a homeless person.

And I'd come here.

This was a very, *very* bad choice.

He stepped forward, and I took a step back. Liam frowned, and my eyes raked over his face, taking in his features, noting the way he'd changed over the years.

He was bigger now. So much bigger. His hair wasn't as long as it used to be. Eight years ago, it was so long he could pull it into a short ponytail at the base of his neck. He said he liked it that way because it drove his father crazy. Now it was shorter on the sides but still long enough to run your fingers through.

His jaw was more chiseled. Light-colored hair filled it out, defined it even more. And his eyes.

Oh, his eyes.

Still the same stormy gray, the same depths I could get lost in for hours. They were wiser now. Almost more hawk-like, as if he could penetrate even my deepest of secrets with that stare.

The trembling in my knees moved to my hands. I stood there staring at him, unable to speak, looking like a homeless woman and trembling like a mouse caught out in the cold.

"Is your father with you?" he asked.

The words were like a knife right to my chest. I actually winced when he said them.

After my throat worked, I managed to reply. "Um, no. I'm alone."

He frowned. He was starting to see something wasn't right. He would know if I stood in front of him any longer.

There was something about Liam Mattison that managed to strip me bare.

I thought it had been because I was sixteen. But here I was at the age of twenty-four, and I knew it hadn't been my age.

It was him.

"Ms. Lane," the concierge spoke from somewhere behind. "I spoke to the manager, and I'm sorry, but there isn't anything we can—"

I spun. "It's okay!" I cut him off instantly, wishing I could have done it sooner.

"Manager?" Liam wondered from behind.

Of course he'd heard.

The man glanced behind me, his eyes widening a fraction.

"What's this about a manager, Kenny?"

His eyes flickered to me, and I shook my head, begging him to shut up.

"Who runs this place?" Liam snapped.

I gasped. "You run BearPaw now?"

"Yes," Liam replied with all the confidence in the world.

"What about your father?" Kenny wondered behind us.

"Why did you need a manager?" Liam asked, ignoring what he said.

"I… ah…" I began, then went for my bag I'd dropped on the floor. "I should be going."

"Like hell," Liam growled, grabbing my arm again. His hold was firm, but it didn't hurt.

And damn if I stopped breathing again.

"Please don't touch me." I gasped.

Liam frowned but let go. "Stay," he ordered.

Annoyance made me forget the effect he had on me. "Don't you talk to me like that!"

The corners of his mouth lifted, but he stared at Kenny. "I asked you a question."

"Ms. Lane…"

"Lane?" Liam echoed, confused. Then this dark look came over his eyes, and he stiffened. His stare snapped away from me back to Kenny.

"Yes. She was, uh, trying to get a room, but without ID and a credit card…"

Liam's brows rose. He looked back at me. "No ID and no credit card?"

"She lost her wallet," Kenny put in.

My, wasn't Kenny a helpful fellow?

"I see," Liam murmured.

Actually, he didn't see at all. He couldn't possibly.

"Thank you for your time, Kenny," I told the man. I started to rush away.

Behind me, Liam cursed, and I knew he was following.

I'd made it a few steps when suddenly the room began to swim. My feet stuttered, and I felt my entire body wobble.

Someone called my name, but they were so far away.

Suddenly, everything went dark.

8

Liam

ONE MINUTE I WAS WALKING OUT OF THE TAVERN, wanting to be alone, and now I was standing here with a woman, scared as hell she would walk out.

I chased after her, not understanding anything except I couldn't let her get away.

Not this time.

From just a few steps away, I saw the way her body faltered, how the set of her shoulders sort of slumped. The second she began to sway, I started to run.

I caught her before she could hit the floor, cradling her body against my chest. My breath was heaving, my heart frantic.

What is she doing here?

Something's wrong.

"Fuck," I muttered as I stared down. She'd collapsed right in my arms. Her blond lashes swept against cheeks I realized were far too pale.

Carrying her over, I laid her on one of the large

chairs. Kenny hovered nearby. I wanted to tell him to get the hell away, but I held back. If she needed something, he was going to have to get it. I wasn't leaving her side.

Pushing some of the dark-blond hair out of her face, I cupped her cheek. "Bellamy," I said softly. "Bellamy, wake up."

It took a moment, a moment too long, for her to come around. A small sound echoed in her throat, and I leaned closer. "Hey, Bells," I murmured, stroking her cheek. "Come on. Open your eyes."

Her eyes fluttered open. The blue was hazy and a little unfocused, but she smiled.

My heart turned over.

"You called me Bells."

"Yeah," I whispered, stroking her hair again.

"I like it."

It was like someone punched through my chest, grabbed my heart, and squeezed as hard as they could. It almost made me double over, but I stayed where I was. I couldn't look away.

Awareness crashed over her like a bucket of ice. She sucked in a breath, her eyes cleared, and she bolted up. The sudden movement caused her to sway again, and she groaned.

"Easy." I cautioned her. "Just sit back."

"I have to go," she protested.

I bit back the urge to yell at her. Once I was sure I wouldn't, I asked, "How long has it been since you've eaten?"

"A few days," she murmured.

I jerked up and stared around at Kenny. "Get me a hot chocolate and a couple cookies."

He nodded, but didn't move.

"Now!"

He jumped and ran for the table.

A few moments later, he returned with a paper cup and a napkin with three cookies. Even though I wanted to chew it for her and pour the shit in her mouth, I knew I couldn't.

Telling myself to calm the fuck down, I crouched in front of the chair she was sitting in.

Damn, her feet didn't even touch the floor.

"Here," I said, keeping my voice soft. "Eat something."

Bellamy took a cookie off the napkin in my palm and put it between her lips. The way she nibbled it made me anxious. I wanted her to shove it in there and swallow. What the fuck was she thinking starving herself for days?

Jesus.

When the cookie was just about gone, I pushed the hot chocolate under her nose. "Drink."

"You're bossy," she said, stuffing the rest of the cookie into her mouth.

"All the more reason to do what I say."

Her fingers brushed mine when she reached for the cup. I noted the way her breath caught, and her eyes flew up to my face. Keeping myself casual, I surrendered the drink and didn't react to the way she affected me.

Bellamy lifted the cup to her mouth and sipped at it. Jolting it away from her lips, she made a face.

"What?" I asked, standing, ready to fight some battle I didn't even understand.

"I burned my tongue," she said, sheepish.

I spun on Kenny. "You made it too hot!" I growled. "She fucking burned herself!"

"I-I'm sorry, Mr. Liam. The water is just in the kettle—"

"It's fine." Bellamy's voice floated past me. "I shouldn't have gulped it. Hot chocolate is supposed to be hot."

I narrowed my eyes on Kenny, and he grimaced.

I dropped back in front of her, resisting the urge to stroke her knee.

"Thank you," she said after a moment. "I feel better now."

There was a slight difference in her color, but not nearly enough to convince me she was better.

"Book her a room," I told Kenny. "Under my name. Use my info."

"What?" She gasped. "No!"

I ignored her and stared at Kenny. "Send a burger and fries up and more hot chocolate."

Kenny started to walk away, and I remembered something. "No mayo on the burger!"

I turned back. There was this funny look on her face.

"What?" I worried.

"You remembered I don't like mayo."

A million comebacks flitted through my mind.

Of course I did. You're the only person on the planet who doesn't like mayo.

Only girls don't like mayo.

Lucky guess.

I could never forget.

I didn't say any of them.

"I remembered."

We stared at each other for what felt like a mere heartbeat, but then Kenny was behind me, clearing his throat. I glanced around, annoyed, but he held out the keycard to her room.

I took it and glanced down, noting the room number. "Seriously?" I looked up.

62

He grimaced. He knew as well I did what the issue was.

"It was the room she was trying to reserve."

I tossed the card back at him. "Fix it. Now."

"Yes, sir." He rushed off.

"What was that about?" Bellamy asked, scooting toward the front of the seat, trying to place her feet on the floor.

God. She was adorable. Just as beautiful as she'd been eight years ago.

Hell, maybe even more.

"Careful," I said, cupping her elbow gently and helping her up.

"I'm fine." She began. "About the room…"

"Don't argue with me," I said, mild. "You're not leaving."

Her chin jutted out, but then she dipped her head, looking into the cup. "Just for tonight."

I made a sound, but it wasn't an agreement. Over my dead body would she walk out of here tomorrow.

I picked up her bag, and she reached for it as if she were worried I was going to take it away. An angry, uncomfortable feeling wormed inside me, twisting and making my fists clench. Inspecting every inch of her, it irritated me that those damn sweats she was wearing covered so much.

I felt the need to search her for bruises. Someone hurt her. I knew it.

"Relax," I said, calm. "I'll carry it for you. Bring your hot chocolate."

I started for the front desk, then stopped. She bounced off my back and made a sound.

I chuckled.

She glared.

"Take a cookie." I held out the napkin.

"I don't—"

"Bells." The tone to my voice was not as gentle and cajoling as before.

She took the cookie, and I went to get the keycard. When I approached, Kenny looked up, his attention divided between me and Bellamy.

"I gave her a suite on the west side, facing the slopes and your cabin. I hope that's okay…"

"Good man." I took the key. "Send up the food."

"Already called room service."

"Thanks, Kenny. I'll remember this."

He seemed equal parts glad and horrified by that fact. I took a moment to give him my usual stare, trying to drop some of the intensity I emanated.

His shoulders relaxed.

"C'mon," I said, placing a hand to Bellamy's waist. She side-stepped the gesture, which only made me want to do it again.

When the elevator opened, I held the door so she could step inside. We rode up to her floor in silence.

There were so many things I wanted to say, so many things I wanted to know. Underneath it all was a hard knot of the knowledge I'd gained downstairs.

Knowledge I didn't like at all.

9

Bellamy

I SHOULDN'T BE DOING THIS.

The thought pretty much became my heartbeat as I stepped out of the elevator and followed Liam down the hall.

Liam!

I didn't have a choice. I literally had nowhere else to go tonight. I was exhausted, which I'd just embarrassingly proved by passing out. In his arms.

It was probably better I didn't remember being in his arms because that was something that would haunt me for the next eight years.

I'd be lying if I said staying in the room under his name didn't make me feel safe. Safer than I'd felt since I fled Chicago. I'd barely slept on the bus ride because I'd been terrified they'd somehow find me and run the bus off the road.

It wasn't even that far out of the realm of possibility. I'd seen what they were capable of. More than once.

I shivered so forcefully my teeth knocked together. Liam glanced over his shoulder at me and frowned. I covered it up by stuffing the cookie into my mouth.

It was a good cookie. Chocolate chip. My favorite.

"Here," he said, stopping toward the end of the hall, scanning the keycard and pushing open the door. I hesitated in the opening, a sudden burst of fear overcoming me.

Peeking up around my hair, I asked, "Will you go first?"

He nodded briskly and then went inside. I knew he couldn't understand, but he moved in a way that reassured me. My stare clung to him as he flipped on the bathroom light on his way past, glanced into the mirrored closet, and went on into the rest of the suite.

He checked everything, including behind the curtains.

"Looks good," he said.

The door that adjoined to the room beside me was locked with more than one lock and one of those chains. The sound the chain made the night it was burst through at my father's ricocheted around my brain.

Liam stared between me and the door, a frown pulling at his face.

I yanked my gaze away and tried to smile. I couldn't. I couldn't pretend that door didn't one hundred percent freak me out.

As if reading my thoughts, Liam dropped my bag and moved. Within seconds, he slid the heavy dresser out from under the flat-screen and dragged it so it was directly in front of the door.

He wasn't even breathless when he finished.

"You're safe here." He promised.

Tears filled my eyes, and I turned away. "Thank you for vouching for me, for the room."

His voice was quiet, but it felt like a slap. "You didn't lose your ID, did you?"

Without looking back, I shook my head.

"What's going on?"

"Would it be okay if I took a shower?"

He materialized behind me, gently palming my shoulders and urging me to face him. When I kept my face down, he lifted my chin. "This is your room. You can do whatever you want in here. Okay?"

I nodded. "I'm going to shower."

His gray eyes darkened like the sky just before a downpour. My heart thundered and my fingers itched. Oh, to be in that storm. Oh, to be caught up by him.

"I can't shower until you leave." I pointed out. I was proud my voice sounded normal.

He chuckled, and a warm rush of shivers went down my spine. Inside my stolen sneakers, my toes curled. "I'm not going anywhere."

"Why not?" I demanded. "You said this was *my* room."

"And it is. But someone has to answer when room service knocks."

"Oh." I hadn't thought of that.

"Go." He stepped back, palmed my bag, and held it between us. "Take a shower. I'll make sure no one bothers you."

"Even you?" I asked.

He smiled. "Even me."

The beckoning of a private bathroom, hot water, and some soap was too great a call to ignore. Even though I shouldn't, I trusted him. I trusted I could take a shower and Liam wouldn't bother me.

I still locked the bathroom door. And pushed the trashcan in front of it.

What? It was all I had to work with.

At the very least, it would fall over if he made it through the lock and pushed open the door. It was an alarm system for beggars.

I turned the water inside the glass-enclosed shower to hot. Steam began to fill the bathroom almost immediately as I looked in the mirror. I jerked as though I'd been slapped. By my own reflection. I did not look good.

Circles beneath my eyes, tangled, limp hair, and blotchy skin. My lips were pale, something that was seemingly alarming, and the sweats seemed to hang off me more than they had just two days ago.

After stripping off the clothes, I stared at them in my hands. I would love nothing more than to toss them in the trash and never see them again. I couldn't. I only had these and what was in that bag. If I hadn't been so paranoid to pack a "getaway" bag, I wouldn't even have that.

For the first time ever, my paranoia didn't seem so silly.

Setting aside the clothes on the long counter, I filled my hands with the small freebies that hotels stocked in their suites—shampoo, conditioner, soap—and climbed beneath the spray.

A long sigh expelled from my lungs the second the hot water rained over my head. I stood there nearly melting for long, blissful moments. I could almost feel some of the worst of the last couple days dripping off me and circling down the drain.

A few tears leaked out, mingling with the water on my face.

After a while, I grabbed the shampoo. It took half the

tiny bottle just to wash my hair. Probably a sign I should cut it. I couldn't bring myself to do it, though.

I love your hair. The voice from the past floated through my head, matching the one I'd heard tonight.

Pushing away the thought, I focused on washing and enjoying the hot water. I knew I needed to form some kind of plan, but honestly, I was too tired to even think of it. All I wanted was some sleep.

And to feel safe.

You might never be safe again. Sticking my face beneath the spray, I tried to drown the thought.

I lingered too long in the shower. I was hiding, but I didn't care. I still couldn't believe Liam was here and in the next room. I thought I'd never see him again. And once I did, I certainly didn't expect the reaction I got.

Almost as if he was glad to see me. Like he cared.

Don't let him hurt you again. I reminded myself. *You have enough to deal with.*

Using a spare towel, I wiped the fog off the mirror. There was some lotion on the counter, so I smoothed some on over my arms and legs, then gently patted it into my face. My bag was on the closed toilet seat. The clothes and things had been in there for so long I barely remembered what was inside.

Except for the envelope. That I remembered with vivid clarity. It was still the exact same as the day my father shoved it into my bag.

I hadn't touched it since.

I'd never taken so much as a single bill out of the fat wad of cash inside.

I'd never planned on it.

But I didn't have a choice now.

It's sort of like he's watching over you now, even though

he's gone. It was a beautiful thought, wasn't it? The notion of a daughter who wanted to be a daddy's girl.

The cold truth was I wouldn't be here today if it weren't for him.

I'd be back in my old life, with the job I loved, a relationship with my mother, and using the name I was born with.

Nudging aside the envelope, I went through what was there. A few pair of panties, a bra, a pair of jeans, T-shirt, and a sweater. There was also a brush, some Chapstick, and a few feminine products. Ooh! And some deodorant. I never thought I'd be excited about that.

It was strange how having everything taken away, twice, had such an effect. Small things people took for granted every single day became big things to me.

I grabbed the brush and worked it through the entire length of my hair. It took forever because I hadn't done this in two days and because my hair reached the middle of my back. Once finished, I smoothed on some lip balm, the deodorant, and then looked at the T-shirt and jeans. My stare strayed to a white, fluffy robe hanging nearby. Once the undergarments were on, I slid the robe into place, belting it tightly.

When I opened the bathroom door, the scent of fries hit me in the face. My stomach growled loudly, and a wave of lightheadedness came over me.

Pushing it aside, I padded self-consciously out into the bedroom. Liam was standing at the window, hands behind his back, gazing out across whatever view was there.

The room service tray was on a table near the window, silver dome lids covering the plates. I had to walk past the sofa, coffee table, and bed to get to it.

Hopping from foot to foot, I stared at his back and hugged my bag.

"Food's gonna get cold," he said, not even turning around.

"You don't have to stay. I'm better now. Really."

He made a sound and pointed at the chair near the food.

He was *not* this bossy eight years ago.

How rude.

I told myself the reason I wasn't telling him where he could go with his bossy self was because of the ordeal I'd just been through, and arguing any further would just zap what little energy remained.

I was lying to myself again.

It was a horrible habit.

In a small act of defiance, I went to the table and sat in the chair beside the one he'd told me to sit in.

He laughed.

The sound brushed over me like a caress, and goose bumps rose along my arms. Why did he still affect me this way?

Liam turned from the window, taking me in with one sweeping glance. Then, deftly, he pulled the covers off two plates, one with a burger and one full of fries.

I sighed appreciatively.

"Hot chocolate is in the pot." He pointed at a small, white ceramic-looking kettle and a white mug.

I snatched a fry and groaned when the salty, fried goodness exploded over my tongue. Liam dropped into the chair across from me, his eyes heavy-lidded, his face neutral.

"This your first time back since..." his voice trailed away.

I paused in eating. "Since that time you had sex with me and then disappeared?"

He made a choking sound.

"I wasn't going to put it like that," he murmured, glib.

"The night you loved me and left me? The night you promised me something, then took off in the night?"

His mouth turned down.

"I didn't."

I laughed. It was a bitter sound. "It doesn't even matter." I started to get up.

He moved so swift I didn't even see him at first. Not until his palm spread out on my shoulder and gently pushed me back into the seat.

"I'm sorry. I—" He rubbed a palm over his face and sighed. "Just eat, okay? I didn't mean to upset you."

I leaned back, drained. Liam pushed the burger toward me. After a moment, I lifted it off the plate and took a bite. Then another.

Amused, Liam watched. "Good?"

I squinted one eye and tilted my head. "Good." Then I took another bite. Still chewing, I mused, "Would be better if they used ground steak and switched out the bun for something just a little softer on the inside."

His eyes widened in surprise. "What are you, a chef?"

"Used to be," I said, setting down the burger. An air of sadness washed over me. "Sorry. Sometimes I slip into a foodie without realizing it."

He smiled. "A foodie?"

I nodded and picked up a fry. "It's all very good. I really appreciate you ordering it for me." Thinking about that, I jumped up. "I'll pay you back." I went for the duffle, but Liam caught me around the waist and towed me back.

I sucked in a breath when my body was pulled against

his. For one brief moment, I relaxed into him. He smelled nice, sort of like pine... and snow.

"I'm not worried about your money," he rumbled near my ear. I swear I felt his thumb caress the side of my hip.

"Then it won't be a big deal when I pay you back for tonight."

He sighed heavily. The action blew his breath against my cheek. My eyes slipped closed for a second.

"Back to your seat," he said, giving me a gentle push.

I ate a few more fries, then paused while reaching for the cocoa. "Would you like some?"

Holy moly, was I raised in a barn? My mother would die if she knew I'd sat here this whole time in a robe, eating in front of him.

He smiled. "I already ate."

Then why do his eyes look so hungry?

After pouring some of the rich liquid in the mug, I wrapped my hands around it and tucked my legs under me, making sure the robe covered all my important parts.

Liam's eyes never left me. He was like a wolf in a cage, calmly watching his prey, as if he would know the exact moment to strike.

I thought he'd been intense at seventeen... It was nothing compared to the way he was now.

"So you, um, run BearPaw now?" I asked, trying to distract myself from the way he stared. From the way he made my insides jump around.

"Something like that."

"I thought you were a big-shot snowboarder, winning medals and sponsorships."

I knew my mistake instantly.

A huge smile spread across his face, sort of the way

the rising sun stretched across a rainy day. "You've been checking up on me."

I wanted to smack myself in the head. Internally, I groaned. Of all the things to make conversation about, I had to go and bring up my stalker ways?

Smooth, Bellamy. Real smooth.

I lifted my chin. "I saw an article a few years ago."

His eyes glimmered as if he knew better. I thought he might poke fun at me, but he didn't. "I got hurt about a year ago. Ended my pro career."

I gasped and sat forward. Hot cocoa splashed over the rim of the cup and splattered the pristine white robe.

"Crap!" I exclaimed and jumped up. That only resulted in *more* cocoa spilling on me. Muttering a few expletives, I set down the mug, held out my hands, and stared down at myself. "I can't believe I just did that!"

Liam's deep, warm chuckle filled the room. I glanced up, forgetting all about the robe.

"I should try and clean this up." I went from the room, grabbed a spare cloth, and started to soak up what I could.

In the end, I looked like a walking disaster. Which was exactly what I was.

Defeated, I trudged out into the room. I felt like crying. "This was as good as I could get it. I'll pay for the replacement."

"Housekeeping will get that out, no problem. I'm sure they've seen worse." He didn't seem concerned.

I glanced down at myself and frowned. "So much for wearing something comfortable," I muttered.

"What?"

I glanced up. "Nothing,"

"Don't you have some extra clothes in that bag?" he asked, quizzical.

"Yeah," I said, picking it up. "I'll just sleep in the T-shirt and wear the sweater tomorrow."

"You only have two shirts?"

"I was in a hurry when I left," I mumbled, embarrassed. Clearing my throat, I said, "I'll just go into town tomorrow and get a few things."

Liam pushed out of the chair, rising to his full height. He had to be over six feet tall the way he towered over me. He reached over his shoulders, tugging off the BearPaw sweatshirt he was wearing.

I slapped my hands over my eyes. "What are you doing?"

He laughed. "I have a shirt on under this."

I lowered my hands just in time to see him pull that off, too!

I gasped again, but this time I didn't cover my eyes. I couldn't. He was too damn good-looking. There was no stopping the way my stare glued to his bare torso and arms. He was cut. Actually, I think the proper term for Liam's upper body was *shredded*.

His arms rippled with definition, and the way he moved... My mouth ran dry.

I gaped, not even able to hide it.

The laughter died away, the humor in his face fading. I was rooted in place as he prowled closer, his glorious freaking chest on full display.

I swallowed numbly, unable to speak.

"Here," he said, his voice like sandpaper.

The kind of sandpaper that could buff me smooth.

When I didn't do anything, the corners of his mouth kicked up and he shook what he was holding in front of me.

"Bells."

I blinked. Glancing down, I saw him holding out his T-shirt. "What?"

"You can wear this to sleep in tonight."

"That's yours." It was a stupid thing to say. Of course it was his.

But I mean, it was *just on his body.*

"I'm letting you borrow it."

"You don't have to do that."

He made a frustrated sound and pushed it into my arms. "Take it. Go change."

My eyes went back to his chest, lingering. He didn't try to cover up or back away. He stood there under the weight of my eyes and let me stare.

After who knows how long, I snapped out of it and ran into the bathroom as if my robe were on fire.

It wasn't.

But my insides sure as hell were.

10

Liam

HELL'S BELLS.

This woman still had the ability to climb under my skin and shake me up unlike anyone ever had. Over the years, I told myself it was a fluke. A teenage thing. Hormones. That's why it never happened again.

I was twenty-six now.

It was happening right now. And it was Bells who stood in front of me.

Fuuuck.

I'd learned something since sitting in this room with her. The more things change, the more they stay the same.

I never knew what that meant. Actually, I thought it was a stupid saying people liked to spout to make themselves sound wise and shit.

I had no interest in sounding wise, but now I understood.

We were both so different. I could tell by the haunted

look in her eyes. The way she practically vibrated with the desire to run. The way she stayed.

As a teenager, Bellamy was trouble.

As an adult, Bellamy was *in* trouble.

It had to be bad for her to come here. She was still bitter and pissed off about eight years ago. Something I actually was baffled by. I couldn't push the issue, not right now anyway. If I did, she'd bolt.

I couldn't let that happen.

Where was her dad? Her mom? Why was she alone, starving, and with one measly bag of shit to her name?

Timid movement across the room drew my eye. I saw her hesitating in the bathroom door, almost as if she were dancing around, not wanting to come out.

"Get out here," I said. "Your food is getting cold."

She made a little sound, and I smiled. It was short-lived, however, because she stepped out wearing my T-shirt.

It was like someone killed me, then restarted my heart.

My hands slapped down on the arms of the chair and squeezed.

Holy shit. Desire and need slammed into me so hard and fast black spots swam before my eyes. I'd never wanted anyone or anything as bad as I did in that moment.

She came out, nearly tiptoeing, her bare feet sound-less on the carpet. I watched her tug at it as if it weren't modest enough. But it was. It hung nearly to her knees. The neckline was a little big and exposed the delicate arch of her neck and the creaminess of her collarbones.

She'd pulled up her damp hair, tying it in some kind of knot on her head.

She was thinner than I remembered, but I didn't care. My God, she was fucking beautiful.

If I'd been standing, possessiveness would have brought me to my knees. It was sharp and heavy. I honestly wondered if the load didn't lighten how the fuck I would bear the weight.

All at once, I got angry. So goddamn angry.

I lurched out of the chair and paced toward her then away.

"What's his name?" I demanded.

Her soft intake of breath made me close my eyes for a brief second. *Cool it.*

"Whose name?"

I made a rude sound. "Don't play stupid with me, Bells. Your husband." God, just saying that out loud made me want to punch something.

The fact that she was some other man's—

"Husband?" The bewildered tone in her voice made me pause.

I spun and pinned her with a stare. "You have a new last name. I know you're married."

Her mouth formed a little O.

"Is that who you're running from?" I pushed a hand through my hair. "Did your husband hurt you?"

"I…" Her words faltered.

I made an aggressive sound, and she flinched.

"Shit," I swore low and went to her.

She took a step back, but I reached for her anyway. I had to. She was standing there swallowed up in the shirt I'd just worn against my skin.

Fuck me, I might as well cream in my jeans.

"What are you doing?" Her voice shook.

I tucked her against my chest, wishing I hadn't put the sweatshirt back on. Wishing to hold her against my bare body. "I didn't mean to yell." I rubbed a hand up her back. "I'm not going to hurt you, Bells. You're safe here."

"I'm not safe anywhere," she replied.

The sound of her voice cracked my heart.

I held her a little tighter. I was shocked when, after a few moments, I felt her arms close around me, hugging me back.

My stomach somersaulted. A surreal feeling washed over me. I couldn't believe this. I couldn't believe she was here and I was holding her.

After a moment, she rubbed her face against my shirt and inhaled. I smiled.

Bellamy pulled away, and it was the hardest thing ever to let her go. I took comfort in the fact my T-shirt was draped on her body. Like some kind of statement.

As if somehow I was staking my claim.

She tipped her head back and looked at me, wary. "I'm not married."

"Come again?" My voice was hoarse.

"I'm not married. My name—"

"Have you ever been?"

She shook her head slowly. "Never."

I made a sound as if I'd just won some tournament and lunged at her. She squealed when I scooped her up around the waist, lifting her off her feet and twirling her in a circle.

She wasn't married. *She was mine.*

"Geez, you could show a little disappointment at my state of singlehood," she muttered when I set her down.

The urge to kiss her was so strong. So strong I grabbed her around the waist again and pulled her to me. She ducked her head, her forehead brushing the front of my shirt.

Taking a deep breath, I let her go, went back, and

dropped to the chair. "Come eat." My voice was strained, but hey, I'd managed not to kiss her.

"I'm not hungry," she mumbled.

"You just passed out because you haven't been taking care of yourself," I intoned.

Bellamy dropped into the chair and picked up her mug. "When did you get hurt?"

"About a year ago," I said.

She nodded. "That's right. You already said that."

I'd repeat myself for you a thousand times.

"What did you hurt?" Her blue eyes were beautiful. Empathetic.

"Tore my ACL."

She made a sound. "And you can't snowboard anymore?"

"Not for the pros. I still do it around here. I teach some lessons." I probably shouldn't do that at all, but fuck that. This was my life.

"You really loved it."

"I really did."

We fell silent. Talking about my bum knee wasn't fun.

"Liam?"

I made a sound.

"I'm really sorry to hear about this. It must have been hard."

The knot in my chest didn't feel good, so I tried to make light of it. "Not as hard as finding out you didn't know about this, too."

So much for thinking she'd come back for me.

She ducked her head. "It's been a rough year."

"What's going on, Bellamy? I know there's something."

She set aside her mug. "I'm really tired."

I wanted to push her. But I wouldn't. The dark circles under eyes and the pallor of her skin warned me off.

Right now, her being here and rocking my shirt was more than enough. I got up and went to the bed, yanking down the blankets in one move.

"What are you doing?" She was cautious.

"In you go." I pointed.

"I'll walk you out." She glanced between me and the door.

I laughed, shaking my head. "Subtle. I'm not leaving."

"Well, you aren't sleeping with me!" She planted her fisted hands on her hips.

I tried real hard not to smile. "Wouldn't dream of it."

A little bit of hurt flashed in her eyes, and I was a bastard because I was glad for it. I wanted her to want me even just a fraction of the way I wanted her. I cleared my throat and added, "At least not tonight."

Her eyes whipped up to mine.

This time I smiled, letting some of the desire and possessiveness shine through.

She ran for the bed and jumped in, pulling the covers nearly over her head. "You can see yourself out."

I threw my head back and laughed.

Then I returned to my chair.

Making a noise, Bellamy sat up, pushing down some of the covers to glare. "What are you doing?"

"Staying 'til you fall asleep."

Her mouth opened. Closed. Opened again. "But why?"

"Because you want me to."

"You're ridiculous."

"You didn't disagree."

She fell back on the bed with a groan.

I grinned and settled my hands over my middle. "Go to sleep, Bells. I'll watch over you."

She rolled onto her side, gazing out the window above the table. "The snow here is prettier than anywhere I've ever seen."

She was barely visible beneath the blankets. Time and again, my eyes would go back just to make sure she was still there.

The sound of her yawn filled the room.

I reached over and flipped off the light.

It wasn't long before the her steady, even breathing filled my ears.

I sat in that uncomfortable chair until the sun began to lighten the sky. I'd doze on and off, only to wake to make sure she was still okay.

Eventually, I forced myself up, staring down at her while I stretched.

She looked so innocent. She said I'd hurt her. She'd hurt me.

I probably shouldn't be here right now. I shouldn't be thinking all these thoughts I've been having all night long.

I always did things I shouldn't.

After tugging the blankets around her just a little bit farther I turned and left the room, silently shutting the door behind me. Before stepping away, I made sure the lock was definitely engaged.

I wasn't even partway down the hallway when someone stepped out of one of the rooms in front of me. Instantly, I jerked to a halt, feeling I'd been caught doing something wrong.

It was stupid. I was a grown-ass man. I could do what I wanted.

I answered to no one.

And I didn't even do nothin'!

Alex glanced over his shoulder. The second his eyes saw me, they widened and a huge grin broke out over his face. He made a show of looking me up and down.

"Same clothes. Rumpled. Bleary-eyed," Alex listed, then snickered.

I glowered at him. Shoving his shoulder, I said, "Get moving."

"Mr. No Girls Tonight is doing the walk of shame this morning," he crooned.

I stopped abruptly.

Alex turned back. The look on my face erased the look on his. "Liam?"

"It's not like that," I snarled.

His piercing blue eyes widened. "Then what is it?"

My chest felt tight. Seeing her last night. Seeing her sleeping this morning... I shook my head. "Bellamy is here."

"Bellamy..." Alex mused. "Why do I know that—" My best friend's head whipped up. "*Bellamy?* As in the girl that got away Bellamy?"

My lip curled. "I hate it when you call her that."

"Oh *shit*," he said, part amusement, part shock.

I groaned. "I know."

He retreated to where I was. In front of me, he leaned in, speaking low. "And last night you had a piece of that?"

My growl echoed along the hallway. I grabbed him up by the front of his wrinkled shirt. "What the fuck did you just say to me?"

"Whoa." He held up his hands. "Too soon?"

I shoved him back, and he stumbled. "Get the fuck outta my face."

"I'm kidding. You know I'm just kidding."

"She's not a joke." I insisted.

"Yeah." He nodded, smoothing out his shirt. "Yeah, I can see that."

I started walking. As I went, I glanced over my shoulder to make sure she hadn't somehow heard us. The hall was empty, and it kinda pissed me off. I'd been hoping to see her standing there.

"What's she doing here?" Alex asked, falling into step beside me.

"I'm not sure yet," I murmured, thinking about the way she looked last night. "But something's up. She acted like she didn't want to be here, but…"

"But?" Alex lifted a dark brow when I didn't finish.

I glanced at my best friend, frowning. "It was sort of like she didn't have a choice."

"What're you gonna do?"

"Something," I muttered.

"Something," he echoed.

I gave him a bland look. He shrugged.

When we got downstairs, I slapped him on the back. "You go. I have to make a stop before I head to my place."

"Hey, L?" he asked.

I turned back.

"You know whatever you need, I'm here, right?"

"Yeah, Alex. I know. Thanks, man."

"Anytime," he replied, then left the lodge.

I went to the front desk, picked up one of the phones, and dialed down to room service. "It's Liam," I said when they answered.

"What can I do for you this morning, Mr. Mattison?"

"Just Liam." I corrected. I always did. Mr. Mattison was my father and it always would be.

The man cleared his throat. "Liam."

"I need a pot of hot chocolate, some OJ, water, some flapjacks, eggs, and toast all sent up to room 440."

"Right away, sir."

"Charge it to me."

"Liam?" he asked, as if he hadn't heard.

"To me. Charge it to me."

I felt his surprise. I'd never done anything like this before. I didn't explain. I didn't fucking have to.

"I'll let the staff know this is priority."

"Thank you," I said, then replaced the phone.

On my way to my place, I glanced back at the lodge. Soon as I showered and changed, I'd be back.

Bellamy

The knocking on my door brought me out of a dead sleep.

Horrible memories assaulted me. My pulse sped up so fast I worried it actually might make my heart explode.

For a moment, I was disillusioned and unsure of where I was.

Then it all came back. BearPaw. My room. *Liam*.

Immediately, my eyes flew to where he'd been when I fell asleep. The chair was empty now, and an ache I didn't care to acknowledge bloomed in my chest.

Another firm knock sounded on the door. Pressing a hand to my chest, I stumbled out of bed and went on unsteady legs toward it. There was a peephole, but I cowered away from it, afraid of what I might see.

The last time I had an unexpected visitor, he tried to kill me and I ended up a fugitive from my own life.

For the second time.

"Room service!" a woman called from the other side of the door.

I gripped the neck of my shirt. A familiar scent of pine and snow wrapped around me. Instinctively, I inhaled.

"I didn't order room service," I called out, suddenly a little braver than before.

There was a slight pause. "Liam Mattison called down and placed the order."

Liam ordered me food?

Suspicion clouded over the desire to be warmed a little by the gesture.

"Leave it outside the door. Please," I called out.

"Of course," the woman replied.

A few moments went by, and I heard nothing. My eyes stayed latched on the door handle, expecting it to turn and open.

After I got tired of standing there, strung out, I crept closer and peeked into the peephole.

No one was there.

My palms were clammy when I undid the lock and cracked the door. There was a room service cart there, and the scent of pancakes floated to my nose. In a burst of movement, I pushed the door wide, grabbed the handle on the cart, and pulled it inside. The second the cart was fully in, I threw myself on the door and locked it up.

Wheeling the trolley over beside the bed, I dove beneath the covers and pulled them around my bare legs. The scent of breakfast made my stomach rumble, and I glanced at the plates dubiously. How did I know Liam was actually the one who sent this?

What if those men had found me? What if everything on that tray was poisoned?

The phone rang, and I nearly fell off the side of the mattress.

Groaning, I snatched the stupid thing up because it was loud and obnoxious. "Hello?"

"Did they deliver breakfast?" His voice was like a warm rush over my senses.

My scalp tingled, and I didn't stop the smile that formed on my lips.

"Liam?"

"Are any other guys having room service delivered to you?"

"Umm…"

He growled into the line, and the tingles turned into a dull ache.

"You still wearing my shirt?"

I glanced down. I was indeed still wearing it. "Nope," I said. "Took it off the second I got up. It's itchy. And it smells."

His rich chuckle made my eyes slide closed. "Liar."

"You really sent me breakfast?"

"Pancakes, eggs, toast. OJ, hot chocolate… the works." As he spoke, I leaned over and lifted a few of the lids. It was everything he said.

"That was…" I murmured, staring at the food, a little misty-eyed.

"Selfish," he proclaimed.

"What?" I squeaked.

"Eat up, Bells. I'll be back in a little while, and you're coming with me."

I made a sound of alarm. "I can't go anywhere with you!"

"Why the hell not?"

I stuttered, unable to form one coherent argument.

He laughed low. "I'll see you in a few."

I sat there with the dial tone in my ear for a few moments before hanging it up. Now that I knew the food wasn't sent here to kill me, I grabbed a fork, poured too much syrup on the pancakes, and pulled the plate into bed.

The remote was on the bedside table, so I switched on the flat-screen and found a news station. I wondered if perhaps any kind of reporting was being done about what happened at my apartment.

I ate almost all the pancakes, half the eggs, and drank some cocoa, and in that entire time, nothing was reported about me or anything going on in Chicago. I knew I was a long way from home, but this wasn't local news. Hell, there was even a story from a small town past Chicago about a seeing eye dog!

I could view the lack of news coverage in two ways:

1. No one knew anything about my "disappearance." Therefore, no one was looking for me, and my location here was unknown.

Or

2. No one cared enough to realize I was even missing.

I was going to go with number one. Hopefully, my quick escape and then no-hesitation to hop a train to the next town and then a bus here left a cold trail to follow.

Having enough of the news, I switched it to the cooking channel and watched it for a short while before dragging myself into the bathroom. Thank goodness there was a complimentary toothbrush with paste because my getaway bag of essentials was seriously lacking in dental hygiene.

I washed my face, put on some more lotion and lip balm, then pulled my hair out of the bun I'd tied it in before falling asleep. It was still damp in some places where it had been tucked under, so I pulled out the hairdryer and blasted the long, dark-blond strands for a few minutes while using the brush to smooth some of it out.

When I was done, I ran my fingers through it and felt satisfied it wasn't a tangled mess, and it fell over my shoulders and down my back, slightly tousled.

I didn't really want to take off Liam's shirt. It wasn't itchy. Or smelly. In fact, the fabric was that just-right, worn-in softness, and his scent was something I wished I could bottle. I tugged it off anyway, folded it neatly, and laid it on the end of the bed so I could return it.

The entire time I dressed, I thought about what had happened and what I was going to do.

The only thing I knew for sure was witness protection promised me safety and they failed. I thought maybe after a full night's sleep, some food, and a hot shower, things would look a little clearer. Or at the very least, some inkling of a plan would be brewing in my mind.

I had nothing. Nothing but fear.

Another thought assailed me, one so formidable I sank down on the bed, my knuckles white from the way I squeezed my hands. What if the men who found me also found my mother?

What if, when they couldn't find me, they went after her instead?

Tears came fast and slid over my cheeks silently. My crying had no sound. I barely even felt the wetness. I was too numb with terror.

I shouldn't have run. I should have let that man shoot me in my kitchen. I'd be dead, and this whole thing would be over. My mother would be safe.

It was my fault she was in this mess to begin with. *If only I had listened to her...*

A knock on my door made me shriek. Gah, I seriously needed to work on my jumpiness.

Pressing a hand to my chest, I yelled, "Who is it?"

"Liam."

I scrubbed at my face, trying to get rid of the evidence of my tears. Blowing out a shaky breath, I glanced through the peephole. He smiled into it as if he knew I would look.

A little giggle escaped me, and I slapped my hand over my lips. This was no time to laugh! My life was in shambles, and my mother could be in danger.

I had no way of knowing… *What have I done?*

Unlatching the door, I began to pull it open. Liam surprised me by grabbing the edge and keeping it partly closed.

"What are you doing?" I worried.

"Warning you."

The bottom fell out of my stomach. "Did they find me?" I worried. "Oh God, I should go."

I started backing away from the door.

Liam cursed low and pushed it open all the way.

All at once, a flurry of movement and a burst of activity barged into my room. Liam moved fast, grabbing me around the waist, steadying me.

Seconds later, I understood why.

Deep barking filled the space. Automatically, I grabbed at Liam. His hands curled a little tighter around me, drawing me closer. "It's just Charlie."

Taking that as his introduction, a giant, hairy dog leapt on me. The sound of his nose sniffing away as though he were patting me down was so loud it was all I heard. My eyes widened as I took in the ginormous St. Bernard with brown ears and a black-and-white face. He looked just like that dog from the movie *Beethoven*.

"Use your manners, Charlie," Liam told him.

The dog dropped down, but his body wiggled and his huge tail beat the air.

I laughed and let go of Liam instantly. "Look at you!" I said, kneeling to pet him.

"Watch it. He's a walking slobber machine." Liam chuckled and shut the door. The sound of the lock being thrown knocked my tension down a notch.

Charlie licked my chin with his giant, sloppy tongue, and I laughed. He had a huge, furry head, and my hands buried behind his ears to scratch. He made a loud groaning sound and sat down.

"Is this your dog?" I asked, glancing at Liam.

He was watching us with a soft expression, his lips tilted up just slightly.

"Yep. Charlie. Got him right after I moved home. He loves the snow as much as I do."

"You have your own built-in coat," I told Charlie, rubbing his chest.

The dog flopped down on the floor and rolled, offering his belly.

Liam laughed. "Well, you're in."

"In?"

He nodded. "Charlie only shows his belly to people he likes."

"I like you, too, boy," I said, scratching his belly.

He licked me again, and I squealed. He definitely was a slobber machine.

"So you were warning me about him?" I asked, still feeling a little tightness in my diaphragm.

He nodded. "Charlie tends to barrel into a room. I didn't want him to knock you on your ass."

"I didn't know you had a dog."

"There's lots of things you don't know about me,

Bells." The admission was quiet, sort of secret, and it made me swallow.

Liam cleared his throat. "I wasn't sure if you liked dogs or not, but Charlie was mad I left him alone most of the night, so I figured I'd let him come along."

"Most of the night?"

He nodded, his gray eyes turning stormy.

He was with me all night? My stomach dipped.

I stood up from the floor, and Charlie jumped up, shaking out his coat. A string of slobber literally smacked into the wall.

"Dude," Liam told him. "Not cool."

Charlie didn't seem to mind and went over to the cart and started sniffing at my leftover breakfast. He was so big he could snatch it off the plates if he wanted. I noticed the way his eyes moved to Liam as he sniffed.

"You know better," was all Liam said.

Charlie sat down with a huff but continued to stare at the food.

"Thanks for breakfast," I said because I had no idea what else to say.

"You look better this morning." I shifted a little as his eyes perused my jeans and T-shirt, landing on my hair. "Your hair is longer."

I nodded.

"I like it."

The compliment made me feel warm in ways I hadn't in a very long time. All the fighting I did with the length when it got tangled or was a pain to wash didn't seem so annoying anymore.

"You ready to go?" Liam asked.

I straightened. "Go?"

He nodded. "I have a lesson. Thought you might want to come. Watch Charlie for me."

I glanced at the dog, his tail beating against the floor. "I don't think it's a good idea."

He raised a brow. "You got something better to do?"

God, he was so nice to look at. His light-brown hair was slightly mussed. The scruff on his jaw looked almost golden. It was such a contrast to his stormy eyes. Like the man had a little bit of heaven and a little bit of hell right there on his face.

He was dressed in a thick sweater this morning. The kind with a neck that zipped. The collar was turned up, framing his jaw. Beneath the hem, a white T-shirt stuck out, and his jeans molded to the front of his thighs.

The boots on his feet were big and sturdy. Perfect for traipsing around in the snow. The leather was wet as though that was exactly what he'd been doing.

"Do you live in the resort?"

"No. I have a cabin on the other side of the slopes. Charlie needs room to run, and I like my space."

"Just you and Charlie live there?" I couldn't help but ask.

A slow smile lifted the corners of his lips and put a little mischief in his eyes. "Just me and Charlie."

Didn't mean he didn't have a girlfriend, though. I mean, just look at him. Even when I was sixteen, everyone at the resort drooled over him and vied for his attention. That was when he was a boy. Now he was all man.

His smile turned into a full-on show of teeth. "I'm single."

"Oh. Good."

More of his teeth flashed.

I wanted to smack myself in the forehead. "I mean… I didn't… mean." I groaned. "What I meant was that's good because I don't think your girlfriend would approve of you basically putting me up in the hotel last night."

"Or tonight," he intoned, stepping closer.

I stepped back. "Tonight?"

He nodded.

"I can't stay tonight. I have to go."

"Go where?"

"Uh." I backed up until I felt Charlie nudge me with his nose. Without thinking, I reached behind me and patted his head. "That's really not any of your business."

Liam's eyes narrowed.

The dog nudged me again, so I grabbed a piece of the toast I hadn't eaten and slipped it to him.

"You're going to spoil him," Liam grumped.

"He's hungry." I gave him another piece.

"Get your coat," he replied. "I have to be downstairs."

"I don't have a coat."

He frowned. "We'll get you one in one of the shops."

I grappled for another reason I couldn't. In the end, I felt my shoulders sag. "I really shouldn't leave this room."

He studied me for long moments. The weight of his stare was enough to make me squirm.

"It's very clear to me you're running from something. Or someone. Someone who obviously scared you pretty bad."

I didn't say anything. Didn't confirm or deny.

Liam closed the distance between us and stroked over my cheek with the pad of his thumb. "Come out on the slopes with me, Bellamy. I'll stay close. So will Charlie. I won't let anyone get to you."

Damn him. Damn the way he made me feel. I knew better. I absolutely knew better.

But Liam's power was impossible to deny.

12

Liam

CHARLIE LOPPED ALONG BEHIND BELLAMY LIKE SHE WAS A new toy. Probably because of the food she slipped him.

Or maybe because that was just the power of Bellamy.

In a way, his immediate devotion was sort of proof that no matter what kind of trouble she was in, she was innocent. Dogs sensed these kinds of things. They could tell if a person was a good seed or a bad one.

I'd already known she was good.

But it was sort of nice the dog proved it.

Her eyes were extremely watchful as we moved through the resort, almost overactive. The girl was making me feel on edge, and I never felt that way. A wave of concern rolled over me for her safety, for dragging her out of her room. What if I shouldn't have? What if she was better off hidden away?

What kind of life was that?

Not the kind she should have.

Besides, I was very worried that if I let her out of sight too long, she'd disappear. Bellamy wasn't the only one who'd kept an eye out. I'd done the same with her over the years. Granted, her life wasn't plastered on the sports channel. She didn't have reporters vying for her attention and printing stories.

I didn't know too much about her life, other than she lived in California and went to college.

I tried to look her up after my injury, but it was as if she'd vanished without a trace. It pissed me off, and I knew a small part of me mourned her as the rest of me mourned the loss of my career.

Bellamy was here now. I could take that second chance. This time I wouldn't screw it up.

"Here," I said, taking her elbow and gently nudging her toward one of the ski shops at the resort. Everything was attached to the main building by a series of hallways or breezeways. She allowed me to steer her into the store, but I felt the nervous energy wrapping around her.

Leaning down, I whispered, "Relax, Bells."

Then I patted Charlie on the back. "Stay with Bellamy."

He was an incredibly perceptive dog, having belonged to the ski patrol before his handler tragically died in a car accident. After that, Charlie had stayed with Sharon until I showed up busted and pissed off.

Sharon brought him to me one day, and that was pretty much it. I felt better having him around, and I liked to think he felt a purpose again, helping me back on my feet. And at least with me, he got in a lot of snow time, something he loved.

Bellamy smiled when the dog pushed up against her leg and walked along beside her.

"Liam," Robin said, materializing out of a rack of equipment. "So nice to see you."

"Hey, Robin," I said, stopping to smile. "How's it going?"

"Better now that you're here," she replied. She was an attractive woman with dark hair and eyes. She'd been working at the lodge several years before I came back. She ran this shop, and she did a good job at it. "Are you here for some equipment? You need new gloves already?"

I chuckled. "Nope, making these last." I glanced across a few racks where Bellamy was browsing.

Browsing = hiding.

"We need a coat and some snow gear," I said, pointing at Bells.

Robin glanced between me and Bellamy with surprise in her eyes. "Helping out a guest? How sweet."

I wanted to correct her, to lay claim to Bellamy right then. I knew if I did, news would whip through this resort at lightning speed.

"That's me. Sweet as sugar," I said instead.

I didn't know what was going on with Bellamy, and I wasn't sure if she wanted anyone to know I knew her. I figured some anonymity might be wise, for her protection.

The reply, though, made Bell's eyes roll to the back of her head.

I suppressed a smile.

"All right, then. Let's get some things pulled."

I cleared my throat, and Robin glanced over. "Lesson starts in thirty."

"I do love a challenge," she purred and then got to work.

Ten minutes later, I stepped up beside Bellamy, who

was loaded down with a black puffer coat with a zip-out fleece lining, waterproof, lightweight snow pants, thick socks, gloves, and a scarf.

Robin had run into the back to find a hat Bells liked but was only stocked out here in green. She was willing to take it, but I wasn't. I wanted her to wear blue. It would match her eyes.

The second Robin was gone, Bellamy glanced up at me. "I can't afford all this right now, Liam."

I made a sound. "Don't worry about it."

"I am worrying about it. This is not your responsibility. *I'm* not."

My eyes cut to her. I felt my jaw work. "I'm making it my responsibility."

"I don't want you to be involved."

"Sweetheart, I got involved the second you passed out in my arms."

"Shoulda let me fall on the floor," she grumped.

I laughed.

"Seriously, I'll just go back up to my room."

"It's the dead of winter. You're in Caribou. You can't walk around in jeans and a sweater the entire time. You'll freeze to death."

Her eyes cast downward.

I opened my mouth to say something, but Robin appeared. "Last one in blue!" she said victoriously. "And it has the BearPaw logo on it."

"Perfect." I took the hat from Robin, noticing the large box in her hand.

She cleared her throat. "I noticed your shoes, thought you might want something more... weather appropriate?"

Bellamy glanced down. "You mean something that's not ugly as sin and a size too big?"

"That, too," Robin muttered.

I followed both women's gazes and grimaced. How had I not noticed those godawful things on her feet earlier?

You were too busy looking at the rest of her.

The sneakers looked at least five years old, worn in some spots and filthy in others. The right foot had a tear in the side, and one of the shoelaces looked as though someone had chewed on it. Speaking of laces, they were tied tightly, double knotted, and when Bells lifted her foot, the shoe kind of swung, proving the fact that if they weren't tied so fucking tight, they'd fall right off.

Anger rushed through me like a forest fire under a strong gust of oxygen. I don't know how she ended up like this, but whatever the reason, I hated it.

"Size six, right?" Robin asked.

"How did you know?" Bellamy seemed surprised.

Robin laughed lightly. "It's my job. Here we go." She set down the large box and pulled off the top. "I didn't have black, which seems to be your preferred color." She glanced at all the dark selections Bells had chosen.

Bellamy's cheeks turned pink.

"But hopefully you'll like these." She lifted one of the tall boots out of the box and held it out.

Bellamy's eyes went wide. She reached toward the shoe, her finger stroking over the light-brown fur sticking out of the top. "They're beautiful," she murmured.

"They're Sorel. Waterproof, weatherproof, and lined with fur. These are in light brown and feature sturdy blue laces. The varied shades in the fur really bring it all together."

The part that hugged the foot wasn't leather, but

some kind of thick rubber material in black, and they had a white sole.

Bellamy dropped her hand away from the boot and lifted the box to check the price. I could almost hear her head explode when she saw.

"We'll take them. Everything," I said.

Robin beamed. Bellamy made a choked sound.

"Put it all on my tab. Okay?"

Robin was the one to choke now. "*Your* tab?"

I nodded and started gathering up all the merchandise. "C'mon, Bells. I'm gonna be late."

I knew she wanted to argue, but she wanted out of there more, so she followed close behind, clutching the giant box of boots.

"Thanks, Robin. You're the best," I called over my shoulder on the way to the front.

"Bye!" she replied, shock still ringing in her voice.

Once outside the shop, I couldn't help but laugh. "Did you see her face?"

"It probably looks a lot like mine." Bellamy warned.

I glanced down and grimaced. She was pissed. Figures she'd be the only woman on earth to get pissed when a guy took her shopping.

"You can pay me back. Okay?"

Her teeth sank into her lower lip, but she nodded.

I blew out a breath.

I walked quickly to the instructor quarters, noticing she had to practically run to keep up. The second time she nearly tripped on those damnable shoes, I slowed my pace.

"What's with the shoes?" I asked, gruff.

She was silent a moment. I gave her the side eye.

"I stole them out of a gym locker. Didn't have time to shop," she practically snapped.

"Whoever you stole them from was probably relieved. That shit is awful."

Her eyes flew to mine, shocked. Then all at once, she started to laugh. I joined in, and then the pair of us were standing outside the instructor quarters, staring at each other, laughing.

Charlie barked.

"C'mon." I opened the door and motioned for her to go ahead.

There wasn't anyone around, so I pointed to a small changing room and dumped all her new stuff in there. "Suit up."

While she was changing, I opened my locker and pulled out everything I needed to get dressed, too. When I was tugging on my instructor badge and nametag, the door opened and she stepped out.

Charlie rushed her, greeting her as if she'd been gone for a week instead of a few minutes. She laughed, not bothered at all by his excitement, and patted him on the head with her gloved hand.

"Everything fit okay?" I asked, clearing my throat.

My God, she was fucking beautiful.

I'd missed her.

I didn't even realize how much.

Sure, we sometimes joked that she was "the one who got away," and sure, I wondered sometimes what might have been... But this—this was a completely different feeling.

"I like the boots," she said quietly.

I glanced down at her feet and smiled. The fur sticking out around her legs was pretty adorable. "They're a lot better than those other things."

She giggled.

My gear swished when I walked over to her, snagged

the blue hat out of her hands, and pulled it down over her head so it rested just above her eyes. My hands lingered on her cheeks before they fell away completely. "I knew it."

"Knew what?"

"That the blue would just make your eyes even more beautiful."

She ducked her head, and I lifted it back up. We stood there for long moments, just searching each other's eyes, not saying a word.

Bellamy drew in a shaky breath, and I pulled back.

"C'mon. I need to be out there."

I grabbed up my clipboard and snowboard.

"You're going to be teaching a lesson?"

I nodded. "I have a few today. They're classes."

When we stepped outside, the cold winter air blasted us. I liked the way it slapped over my cheeks, sort of like a personal wakeup call every day. I breathed deep, letting the icy tendrils of air fill my lungs.

Charlie barked and bounded through the powder, kicking it up when he could.

Bellamy laughed, watching him. I glanced down. Her cheeks were already turning pink from the cold.

"I have some time between each class. We can get some lunch later."

She didn't say anything. Her eyes wandered past me to a group of people up the hill. "Is that them?"

I followed her gaze. "Yeah. Hang out nearby, okay? Charlie doesn't need a leash. He'll stay with you."

She nodded, and I smiled.

The urge to lean in and kiss her was so strong. I resisted, though. "See you in a bit."

"See you."

I went to teach my class, glancing back to make sure she was still there.

She was. For the entire lesson, she stayed nearby, Charlie her shadow. Every once in a while, I would get distracted because I would hear her laughter in the wind. I'd turn and look to see her and my dog rolling around in the snow.

Yeah, I had no idea what made her run here or why she so desperately needed to hide.

But the more I was around Bellamy, the less I even cared.

13

Bellamy

THE AIR WAS CRISP. THE SNOW WAS PURE. A DOG'S FUN was genuinely innocent.

Being out here was like a fresh start. A fresh start I wanted so desperately my chest ached with it. Supposedly, I'd gotten a "fresh" start a year ago, but it never felt that way.

I ended up feeling like a dirty secret. Like an entirely new person that only shared the same silhouette of who I used to be.

With the blue hat Liam insisted on pulled low on my head and the long strands of my hair sneakily tucked into my coat, I felt pretty disguised. Everyone out here was dressed alike, and without my blond hair to give me away, it was as if I were just another person on vacay at BearPaw.

I couldn't help but think of my father and the time we spent here together. It had been the only real time I'd gotten to spend with him.

It seemed silly I missed him. I mean, yes, he was my father, but I could count on one hand the amount of times I'd seen him in my life.

Was it him I missed or just the idea of a father?

I had no illusions about what a great man he was or even a great father. In fact, I knew he wasn't great at either. If his absence in my life wasn't proof, the way his life came to a violent end was.

My eyes strayed to Liam. How confident he looked in front of the line of people he was instructing.

I could count on one hand the number of times I'd seen him in my life as well.

Oddly, it was less than my father. I missed Liam, too. Something deep inside me might even argue I missed him more than my dad. Eight years of missing someone I barely knew.

The heart doesn't measure time, though, does it?

The heart has its own way of equating value. And it seemed my heart had a soft spot for men who didn't stick around.

I glanced around, off to the right where the ski lift was running. People on skis and snowboards all stood in line. Laughter floated down from the cars overhead as they soared up the mountain.

As I stared, I was transported back in time. To eight years ago...

It was early. So freaking early. I didn't even drag myself out of bed for school at this hour. Yet here I was, pulling on all the brand-new snow gear my father had bought me downstairs. I glanced at the door that adjoined our rooms, thankful we didn't have to share just one. That would be totally embarrassing.

And it wouldn't have made what I was doing possible. Once I had all the layers piled on—seriously, I could not imagine doing this every day; back in Cali, it sometimes felt like a chore to put on sandals instead of just flip-flops—I headed out.

The slopes opened early for all those people who liked to get in some runs (as they called them in the brochure) before they had to work or fill their day with one of the other million activities here at the resort.

I'd thought my father was insane when he showed up and announced we were going to some tiny town in Colorado for a vacation. Who vacations in the snow?

It really felt like the twilight zone when my mother agreed to let me go.

I'd been skeptical, nervous even, but now that I was here, I loved it. This place was gorgeous. I'd never seen so much snow and so many trees in all my life.

There was just one problem. This California girl did not know how to ski. At all.

That was why I found myself standing there with a pair of skis that felt like clown shoes attached to my boots as I stared up at the ski lift, a machine I was supposed to sit in while it dragged me over the terrain on a wire.

Yikes.

Clearly, I didn't think this through. I might have to admit defeat.

As I stood there, at war with myself, someone skidded past, throwing up a wave of snow against my legs. I craned my neck, following the person on the snowboard as he curved around and stopped behind me.

When he lifted the goggles off his face, I was momentarily dumbstruck. He was freaking gorgeous. Clear, smooth skin that seemed sun-kissed even in this snow. Strong brow, defined jaw, and a straight nose.

His eyes were gray.

Not that in-between color either. You know the one where

the color isn't quite blue and not quite green.

True gray.

Like a cloudy sky. Or a floor of pebbles in a river.

"You're supposed to get on it. Not stare at it," gray eyes told me, a cocky smirk curving his mouth.

"I think I like my feet down here. On the ground."

He smiled. "First time?"

I swallowed, glancing down at his lips. They were kissable. Sooo kissable.

I couldn't speak, so instead, I nodded.

"You're out here pretty early for a first timer. Most of us on the slopes at this hour are regulars."

"You're a regular?"

"Of course. I have mad skills."

My stomach fluttered a little when he smiled like that. "I came out because I wanted to practice a little. I'm here with my father, and..." My voice faded. Why was I telling him this? He was a stranger.

"And?" He leaned in as if he were really interested.

"And I wanted to impress him. I didn't want to look like a newb." I glanced down at the snow. "It's stupid."

"Not stupid."

Surprised, I glanced up. He grinned at me, and I found myself grinning back. "Stupid if you're too terrified to even get on the lift."

"Maybe you won't be as scared if I ride with you."

"What?"

He nodded and motioned for me to follow him. "C'mon. If you ride with me, I'll be your first." Even with the goggles and hat on his head, I could see him wagging his eyebrows.

"I think I'll pass," I said, glancing up at the car floating overhead.

"I'll hold your hand." He offered.

Glancing between him and the lift, I decided to go for it.

Using the poles, I pushed off, sliding instantly down the small slope toward the lift entrance. Once I got going, I couldn't stop.

"Watch out!" I yelled, but he didn't move. Instead, he planted himself right in front of me and caught me around the waist.

"And you're worried about the lift? I think you should be more worried about the skis strapped to your feet."

Embarrassed, I pulled back, but my skis had slid up over his board, and I couldn't just take a step back. I would have fallen if he hadn't tightened his hold.

"I'm Liam," he said, our noses mere inches apart.

"Bellamy."

"You're up!" the lift attendant called.

Liam managed to untangle us and direct me in front of the coming seat. Standing beside me, he took hold of my elbow. "Now," he said right when the bench arrived.

We both sat, and the cart kept moving, sweeping us off the ground. Liam pulled a bar down in front of us as I clutched at the poles and stared over the side.

"Here," he said, taking my poles. Once they were gone, he reached for my hand.

I knew gloves were a necessity out here in the frigid temps... but I wished there wasn't a glove between us.

"Don't look down. Look out."

"What?" I glanced at him. For a long moment, I swear I got lost in his eyes.

"Look out," he replied, taking my chin with his free hand and turning my face so I would see the sweeping view.

I gasped. Up here, everything looked so pristine. So fantasy-like. The snow was like a white blanket enveloping everything, even the deep-green trees. Fat snowflakes floated from the sky, brushing against my cheeks and creating a while haze over everything.

"It's so beautiful," I whispered.

"See what you would have missed if you'd stayed down there on the ground?"

"Thank you."

"Next stop is ours." He gestured to the approaching platform.

"Already?"

His chuckle was enough to melt the snowflakes still falling out of the sky. "Unless you want to ride all the way up to the black diamond course. And judging from what I saw on the ground, you should probably stick to the bunny hill."

I smiled, sheepish. "You're probably right."

"When it comes up, you have to get up quick."

My teeth sank into my lower lip, and I concentrated as we met the platform. Liam and I stood quickly, but I still wasn't quick enough. How could anyone be with these death traps on their feet?

I didn't get flattened by the still-moving car, though. Instead, Liam hoisted me off to the side.

"Thanks," I said when we were out of harm's way.

"How about a free lesson?" He gestured to my skis and handed me the poles I'd actually forgotten about.

I glanced at the snowboard he was so confidently perched on. "You can ski, too?"

"Since I could walk."

"Don't you have something else you'd rather be doing?"

His teeth flashed. They were as white as the snow. "Keeping you from killing yourself or someone else on those things? I think that's pretty important."

I laughed.

"C'mon. Give me thirty minutes and you'll be outskiing your dad."

He spent thirty minutes teaching me how to ski.

He spent thirty minutes carving out a place in my heart that I had no idea would still be there eight years later.

The sound of flirtatious laughter brought me out of the blast from the past. Charlie nudged my hand and whined. I scratched him behind the ear as I glanced around toward the sound.

It didn't take long to find it.

It was right in front of Liam.

The lesson must have just ended because people were going off to do their own thing. A few people hung back, adjusting their equipment. Liam had a clipboard in his hand and a black knit hat pulled down over his head. Snowflakes were sticking to it and lying on his broad shoulders.

The girl laughed again, and my back teeth came together.

She had blond hair. It fell it wet waves from under her hat. Her eyes were covered with a pair of mirrored sunglasses, and her ski outfit was hot pink and navy. I knew by the way she was leaning toward Liam she was flirting with him.

I heard the low timbre of his voice, but couldn't make out the words. He didn't lean toward her as she did him, but he wasn't running away either.

It shouldn't bother me.

It did.

I was here to hide. I hadn't even wanted to see him. I had so much going on. The last thing I needed was to get involved with a guy who literally broke my heart at the age of sixteen.

Walk away, Bellamy. Just walk away.

My feet obeyed. I started walking.

But not away.

Toward the girl who was standing there looking like a life-size Barbie, trying to flirt with a man who most definitely was *not* hers.

14

Liam

Yesterday, this girl looked so much like Bellamy.

Yesterday, when I saw her in the snow with her damp blond hair, it was like a punch in my gut.

Today was different.

Today, as I stood here and watched her, she looked nothing at all like Bells. She was so much not Bellamy that I wondered what the fuck I'd been thinking yesterday.

I did get one thing right, though. I wasn't into her yesterday, and I sure as fuck wasn't now.

I was partly impressed she was still trying, though. After I got up and walked out at the Tavern last night, I thought for sure she'd gotten what I was throwing down. Here she was, though, back for another lesson. Back to flirting while her friend stood a short distance away.

She was either hella stupid or had a set of balls on her the size of melons. How unfortunate for her both of those things were not attractive.

"I'm so bummed you had to leave early last night," she said, segueing into that from whatever she'd been talking about. "You look a lot more rested today. Maybe we can try again tonight?"

She reached out and laid her gloved hand on my chest.

I was so disinterested it might alarm me if I didn't know why. Usually, I was ready for a good time, and being a famous pro athlete turned expert instructor got me a lot of snow bunnies. I didn't want a snow bunny now.

Unless Bellamy decided to become one.

I smiled down at Heather (that was her name, right?) and moved to pull her hand away from my chest when Charlie barked and charged out of nowhere. He barked again and plowed between me and Heather, knocking her back onto her ass.

"Charlie!" I called as he jumped up, putting his two front paws on my chest. He was a big dog, close to two hundred pounds. If he wanted to be somewhere, he barreled right in. "Bad dog," I told him, even though I wasn't even mad. He licked my face.

I pushed him down, and he wagged his tail as if he were proud of himself.

Heather was sitting in the snow, her eyes wide.

"Sorry about that," I said, giving her a smile. I reached down to help her up, something I knew she was reveling in. Even after I had her back on her feet, her hands clung to my arms.

"Is that your dog?"

I started to reply, but a voice cut in.

"I'm sorry," Bellamy called as she approached. "I tried to stop him, but he was too excited to see you."

Her voice was not apologetic at all.

I chuckled and slid a knowing glance in her direction. Not acknowledging my eyes, she lifted her chin and regarded Heather.

Seeing the two women together now, I wondered what the fuck I'd been thinking. Bellamy was so much more beautiful.

"I hope he didn't hurt you. Charlie is just a big puppy."

"Who are you?" she asked, brushing some of the snow off her.

"I'm the dog nanny."

I made a choked sound, and Heather glanced at me sharply. "You have a dog nanny?"

I nodded. "Just look at him." I pointed to Charlie, who was bouncing around some poor skier. "He clearly needs supervision."

Bellamy giggled.

My stomach fluttered a little bit with the sound.

Heather's eyes turned calculating, and mine narrowed. I had no idea what she was thinking, but I knew that look. I'd seen it a lot in the past few years. This girl was threatened by Bell—my *dog nanny*—and I knew she was going to let out her claws.

Careful, bitch. My charming, athletic façade will give way to an evil Jack Frost if you so much as look cross-eyed at her.

Without thinking, I moved, shifting closer to Bellamy, bringing my side right up against hers. It was a silent message.

One this girl didn't seem to receive.

"Well, maybe the nanny can take the dog on an overnight so we can finish what we started last night." She spoke to me but looked at Bellamy. Her eyes were cold, her air haughty.

I started to step forward, to completely block Bells

from sight. This was a situation I could diffuse with one strike of my icy tongue.

Bellamy put out a hand on my chest, silently telling me to back off.

I made a sound, but she stepped forward. "And what exactly did you start with Liam last night?"

"Oh, do you need me to spell it out for you?" Heather stuck out her lower lip in a pout.

I snarled.

"I think maybe you do," Bellamy said, stepping in front of me but backing up so her back came right up against my front. My hand folded around the material of her coat, pulling her a little more firmly against me. "Because I'm confused. He couldn't possibly have started anything with you last night because he spent the night in my room."

Guess Heather wasn't the one with claws. And Bellamy was jealous.

So freaking jealous.

I could probably live off this for years. *Years.*

Heather's eyes widened, then flashed angry. "Like he'd spend the night with you."

I felt the slight tensing in her body. It wasn't visible, but having her pressed against me made it impossible not to notice. The barb hurt her.

That pissed me off.

I moved swiftly around her, my body completely blocking her from view.

"Actually, I would. I'd spend every night with her if she'd let me. Let me make myself *very* clear here." I spoke low, intensely. "I'm not interested, Heather. Not now. Not ever."

She gasped as if she couldn't believe the words that

just came out of my mouth. I stood back, folding my arms across my chest, and stared.

"Whatever," she spat and turned to go.

Her friend was watching with a puzzled look on her face. When she reached her side, Heather spoke low, and the other girl stared back at me, shock on her features.

I waved.

Then I dismissed them completely. Pivoting, I stared at Bellamy. "You're so jealous."

"Am not," she spat.

I laughed.

She made a sound. "I was trying to help you out. That girl was as dumb as a box of rocks. You could do better."

I stepped close, putting a hand on the side of her waist. "Like you?"

Her swift intake of breath was her only reaction. Her eyes bounced between mine, vulnerability in the blue depths.

Alex chose that moment to ski up. And Charlie bounded over with a bark. These interruptions could go for a long walk off a short pier.

"Who's this?" Alex mused, taking in the pair of us.

Bellamy turned toward him, her eyes widening. "Alex?"

A slow smiled spread over his face. "In the flesh!" Then he glanced at me, back at Bells, then to me again. "Damn, Bellamy got hotter."

I growled and shoved him. "Shut it."

He laughed. Then he came forward and scooped her up into a hug. "Long time no see, girl!"

Bellamy laughed.

I envied the easy way he just reached out and hugged her. The easy way he made her laugh.

It made me want to punch him.

"You look…" Bellamy mused after he put her down. "Grown up."

"Milk does a body good," he quipped and held up his biceps.

"You don't drink milk." I reminded him.

"She didn't need to know that," Alex whispered.

Bellamy giggled. "Still the same smartass, I see."

"Some things never change." Alex confirmed. "Like the heart eyes my boy's giving you."

Bellamy's cheeks, already pink from the cold, turned a blazing shade of red.

I gave Alex a hard warning stare. He winked at me.

"You got something in your eye?" I asked.

"You still live here?" Bellamy asked Alex.

"'Course," Alex replied. "BearPaw is home."

"Are you an instructor, too?"

"Yep. I'm just as good on a pair of skis as our boy is on a board."

"Almost." I corrected.

"Well, I was never pro," he muttered.

"That's really great that you two are still friends after all this time," Bellamy said, her voice kind of wistful. It made my guts knot up.

What the hell had she been through?

I should have kept a closer eye on her.

"Best friends." Alex slapped me on the shoulder. "Since diapers."

Bellamy dropped down in front of the dog and started petting him, telling him he was a good boy.

"You two want to grab some food?" Alex asked.

"I have another lesson in thirty." For the first time in a long time, I wished I could skip out on it.

"Bellamy, then." Alex glanced down at her.

A grumbly sound rolled out of my chest. "She's staying here with me."

One of the other instructors was walking by, and Alex called out to him. "Hey, Brant! You mind taking our boy's next lesson in thirty?"

Brant glanced down at his clipboard. "I can do it. But I can't do any of your afternoon ones. I have my own."

I nodded. "I can handle those."

"Sure thing, then."

"Thanks, man. I appreciate it," I said, going over to shake his hand.

"No problem, Liam. You've covered for me lots of times. I can finally return the favor."

After he walked off, I turned back to see Alex leaning down to Bellamy. "All he does is work. He works so much sometimes he does other people's work. Guy needs a hobby."

Bellamy's eyes slid to mine.

Something warm passed between us. Something that made me want to skip lunch and go back to her room.

"Come on, lovebirds. I'm starving."

On his way past, I grabbed Alex by the coat and pulled him close. "Lay off," I growled quietly.

He chuckled. When I didn't join, his eyes narrowed on mine. "What's going on, L?"

"Nothing. She's just been through a lot, okay? Take it easy."

"So no commenting on the way you both look at each other?"

I let go of his coat and shook my head. "Definitely not."

He laughed. "She's not so willing to pick up where you two left off, is she?"

I gave him the finger.

The whites of my best friend's eyes doubled in size. "*Ah, shit.* Liam's gotta work for something."

I gave him the finger again.

It was going to be a long lunch.

15

Bellamy

I forgot how much I liked it here.

Over the years, I convinced myself I only looked back on my two weeks at BearPaw with rose-colored glasses because I had a wonderful time with my father here.

I told myself I was so crushed by Liam because he was my first taste of love. Teenage hormones made him irresistible to me, so when everything happened, it felt worse.

I started lying to myself young. It was proving to be a horrible habit to break.

Truth wasn't easy, even to admit to yourself. Especially when the truth was something you didn't want to hear.

Spending the morning basically frolicking in the snow with a big, fluffy dog, under Liam's watchful eye, made me remember all kinds of things. Feelings.

Feelings I thought were only that severe because I'd been sixteen.

I was twenty-four now, and the rush of emotions swirling inside me was overwhelming. Just as intense as they ever were as a teenager. Sometimes when I caught Liam looking at me, the feelings of desire, of attraction… of crackling chemistry were so strong they battled back the fear I had for my own life.

You know a man had a powerful pull over you when you started to forget someone was trying to kill you.

I'd become a girl of skirting around confrontation. Of letting myself be defeated even when I wanted to fight. I gave up so much, walked away from my entire life. I found my way to BearPaw to hide. As a last-ditch effort to get away from my demons.

So what did I do?

Nearly got into a fight with the first girl I saw talking to Liam.

Actually, she wasn't talking to him. She might as well have just taken off her coat, shirt, and bra and stood there with her ladies flapping in the winter wind. It would have been *less* obvious.

Ho-bag.

I'd acted borderline crazy, but he stood there and backed me up.

Oh, the feelings that caused to swim inside me. If I wasn't careful, I'd become an ocean and drown in Liam.

I was getting far too attached. It had barely been one day, yet I found myself gravitating toward him when the dark fear in me tried to sink in its claws. What was more? Liam seemed to sense it. It was as though he knew exactly when I needed a little extra shielding. A little extra assurance.

Oh my God, it had been *so* long. So very long since I'd felt even remotely secure.

I'd never known a man who made it impossible to

breathe but at the very same time was like a surge of oxygen directly into my lungs.

Seeing Alex was another jab to my kidneys. His easygoing, long-term relationship with Liam was a reminder of something I never had, something I probably wouldn't ever again.

Lunch had been fun. Sitting there in the back booth of the lodge with a giant bowl of cheesy potato soup, right beside the window with a view of the slopes. Liam slid onto the bench beside me, his leg pressed along mine. I didn't pull away. The jittery way he made me feel was addictive. Instead, I just pretended I didn't feel him. Like his strong leg muscle wasn't impossible to notice.

I didn't talk much. I just listened to the two play off each other. They were funny, and even though they insulted each other more than anything, I could see the bond they had. They might not be blood, but they were family.

As I dipped my crusty, warm bread into the soup and stared out at the snow, I thought about my family. My mother.

How I failed her.

The fear Liam somehow dulled inside me came back. It came back so hard and so strong I could barely finish eating.

"Is something wrong with the soup?" Liam asked, using his finger to swipe my spoon back and forth along the rim of the bowl.

"It's so good," I said. "I must just still be full from breakfast."

He frowned.

"Well, I'll eat it if you won't." Alex reached across the table for my bowl.

Liam slapped his hands away.

"Wasting food is a crime," Alex mumbled, pulling his hand back.

I laughed and pushed the bowl toward him. "Have at it."

Alex glanced at Liam, then cautiously reached for my soup.

After Alex and Liam cleaned their plates (and mine), they slid out of the booth. Liam held out his hand for mine. I surrendered, the breath in my chest hitching when his warm fingers closed around mine.

"I gotta get back. The snow bunnies are probably wondering where my fine ass skied off to."

"I'm sure they're all looking." I confirmed.

"Bellamy, girl," he said and pulled me in for a hug. "Good to see you."

"Thanks," I said, pulling away. "It was nice to see you, too." I meant it. Even back when I was sixteen, I'd liked Alex.

"You should stick around for a while. I'll take you into Caribou, get you some chocolates."

Chocolates? I glanced at Liam.

He laughed. "Alex's parents own the local chocolate shop in town."

"Mmm." Alex agreed. "They sure do know how to make some chocolate." He motioned to himself.

Liam groaned. "That joke is so old."

Alex winked at me, then held up his hand as he headed out. "See ya!"

"He looks so much older... but he still acts seventeen," I wondered out loud.

Liam cackled. His palm hit the small of my back. "C'mon. I have some more lessons this afternoon."

"I think I'm going to go back to my room," I said, my feet stalling.

Liam turned fully to face me. He was so big he blocked out the rest of the room. "What?"

"I'm, uh, tired." I hedged. "You go, do your job."

He crossed his arms over his chest. "What's wrong?"

"You were quiet at lunch and you barely ate."

"I told you I was still full from all the food you sent up this morning, and how is anyone supposed to get a word in edgewise with you and Alex at the table?"

He grunted. "Don't lie to me."

"I'm not lying." I started past.

He caught me around the waist and towed me up against his body. My lungs froze. This no-breathing thing around him was really getting to be a problem.

"Bellamy."

I lifted my chin, answering his call.

"What's wrong?"

My body went slack against his. I didn't slide to the floor, though, because he was holding me, giving me strength when I was all but out. "I just want to go to my room."

"You can't leave."

I glanced up. "You think I'm leaving?"

"I think you're going to run from me again. I can't let you."

"I never ran from you. You ran from me." My throat felt tight, my lungs burning. I started to fidget against him.

"Breathe," he instructed.

I took a gasping breath. The tension in my lungs went away.

Shocked, I asked, "How did you know?"

"Because I have trouble breathing around you, too."

"Please. Just let me go to my room."

Liam eased me back on my feet. Once he was sure I

was on solid footing, he stepped back. "Fine. But promise me you'll be here later. Promise you'll have dinner with me."

"I—"

"Promise," he growled.

"I promise."

He took my hand and towed me along at his side, through the lodge in the opposite direction of the elevator leading to my room. "What are you doing?"

"Taking you to get Charlie. You don't mind if he hangs with you this afternoon, do you? He'd probably like the company."

"Of course." I agreed. "I like Charlie."

"He likes you."

Once Charlie was in my care, Liam walked us both to the elevator and made sure we got inside. He towered right in the opening. The doors didn't even budge, as if they knew better than to close before he was ready.

"Take care of my girl, Charlie," he told the dog.

"I'm not—"

Liam leaned in and kissed my forehead, making me forget I was talking. "I'll be up to get you for dinner, Bells. If you need me, call the front desk. They know how to find me."

Numbly, I nodded.

The second he stepped back, the doors chimed shut and the car slid up. I patted Charlie on the head and blew out a shaky breath.

In my room, I curled up on the bed with Charlie (who definitely was a drool bucket) and stared out the window, watching the flurries blow around in the wind.

I couldn't stop thinking about my mother. If what I had done somehow made her a target and if she would be as easy to find as me.

By the time the sky started to dim, I'd worked myself into a pretty good panic. I couldn't just sit here anymore. I couldn't hide or even think about my own safety if hers was at stake.

When Liam knocked on the door a little later, I didn't even hesitate opening it and pulling him inside.

"Bells?" he asked, searching my eyes. "What is it?"

"There's something I need you to do for me."

16

Liam

"CONSIDER IT DONE," I ANSWERED WITHOUT A SECOND OF hesitation.

Bellamy's eyebrows rose. "Just like that?"

Stroking the backs of my fingers over her cheek, I whispered, "Just like that."

"What if I wanted you to kill someone?"

"Then he probably deserves to be dead."

Her eyes nearly fell out of her head, and I couldn't stop the chuckle vibrating my throat.

"You can't be serious."

I bent down, bringing us eye to eye. "Look at me. Do I look serious?" My gaze was unflinching, nearly unapologetic.

She gasped. "No wonder I can't breathe when I'm around you. You're crazy."

I felt my eyes darken. The only part of me that moved was my arm, curling around her waist and tugging her into my front. "You make me crazy."

"Liam."

Straightening, I brought her body with mine. Using my free hand, I rubbed my thumb along her lower lip. It was red as if she'd been chewing on it earlier.

"What's wrong, sweetheart?"

"I can't tell you," she whispered.

"Do you ever wonder?"

"Wonder what?" Her words were breathless. Everything beneath my skin hummed.

"Wonder if our kisses now would be just as electric as they were eight years ago?"

"No."

I blinked. "No?"

Her throat worked. She was so damn close I actually heard her swallow. "I know they would be. I can feel it."

Groaning, I dipped my head, holding my mouth just centimeters from hers. When I spoke, I let my lips whisper against hers. "Are you going to let me?"

Her voice quivered. "We shouldn't."

"Are you going to let me?"

A shiver shook her body. I gathered her even closer. "Yes."

One slight movement brought us together. It was the greatest rush I'd ever known. Greater than roaring down a mountain, greater than nailing a jump everyone told me was impossible. It was even greater than the time I'd gotten so much air it felt as though I were flying.

Nothing compared to how Bellamy's lips felt against mine.

Nothing.

The softest sound I'd ever heard filled my senses. Dipping low, my arms closed around her and lifted. Bellamy's arms wound around my neck. The hat I had on my hair was suddenly gone, and her fingers buried themselves in my hair.

One arm went under her ass, supporting her, and her legs clamped around my waist.

I moved, pinning her between the door and my body as my tongue licked into her mouth and glided around like it owned the place.

She was warm and wet. The little sounds she made vibrated into my mouth, and I swallowed them down as if I'd never eaten a meal.

Her hands kneaded my scalp as I fucked her mouth with my tongue, and little shivers raced down my neck and spine because, fucking Christ, her hands were fucking magic.

Without lifting my mouth, I turned my head the other way, kissing her with relentless passion, spurred on by the undeniable chemistry that whipped through this room like a lightning storm.

I pressed against her so close I felt her nipples turn hard against my chest. My dick was throbbing. It was so hard I almost hurt. But it was a hurt I would live with the rest of my life as long as she let my mouth stay on hers.

My palm rubbed across her ass. Bellamy tugged my upper lip into her mouth and sucked. I moaned, and she released it, licking over the same spot with her tongue.

I muttered something completely incoherent, and she replied with equally unintelligible words. I went on kissing her, running my hands over her outline and letting the sweet torture of her body bring me to the brink of madness.

When at last I forced my mouth away, it was all I could manage. I kept her pinned between the door and me, chest heaving, lips tingling. My forehead lowered to hers as her hands slowly left my scalp and dragged down the back of my neck.

"There's more," she whispered, her voice so raspy it would have startled me if I wasn't so goddamn languid. Fuck, it was almost as if I'd just gotten laid, but our clothes hadn't even come off.

"What?" I whispered, leaning down to kiss her shoulder.

"There's even more chemistry now."

I groaned and laughed at the same time. "Jesus. You're right."

"Put me down now, Liam."

A strangled sound ripped out of me. "You can't say my name like that and expect me to put you down."

Her chest heaved some more, and I went back for her lips. This time I kissed her softer, but the result was still the same.

By the time I let her slide down the door, I was damn near shaking with need. I had to get out of this room and away from the big bed just begging for me to lay her across it.

After a few moments of trying to compose myself, I turned to her and nearly lost it all over again. Her hair was mussed. Her lips were puffy, and the glassy look to her blue eyes was what wet dreams were made of.

She needs you right now, Mattison. Get it together.

Clearing my throat, I said, "How about you let me take you dinner? You can tell me all about what you need, and then I'll do it."

"Still just like that," she echoed.

"Oh, baby." I brushed my palm down the length of her hair. "Even more so now."

1 7

Bellamy

I said yes when I should have said no.

He kissed me senseless… and when the world slowly came back into focus, *I knew*.

I knew it wouldn't be eight more years of Liam carved into my heart.

It would be a lifetime.

18

Liam

"I'm not so sure about this." Bellamy worried, standing beneath the lit-up wooden awning at the entrance of the lodge.

I turned so I was standing in front of her, using my body as a buffer for the harsh night wind. Winter nights here in Caribou were not for the faint of heart. Bellamy was a California girl, so this type of wind had to feel bitter.

"You don't want to go into town?" I asked quietly as I snuck a glance at her lips.

I wanted to kiss her again.

I wanted to kiss her a thousand times.

"It's not that." She hedged, her eyes moving up to connect with mine.

"You're afraid," I murmured, stepping closer.

She nodded once.

"The restaurant is a small, local place. It's already

dark outside, and I'm driving, so no strange cabs or buses."

"How'd you know I came here on a bus?" she asked, suddenly suspicious. Her wide eyes glanced around uncertainly.

"Uh, I didn't. But I do now." She came here on a bus? Alone.

What the actual fuck...?

She blew out a breath. "I'm sorry. I'm jumpy."

I tilted my head. "We can go back up to your room. I'll order room service."

I could almost hear the debate going on inside her mind. A gust of wind rushed in, and the ends of her hair blew sideways, covering part of her face. I shifted again, stepping so I was in front of the new wind pattern.

Bellamy brushed the hair from her cheek. "The restaurant is small?"

"Very. And they have tacos."

"Can we come back here after?"

"Of course."

"Okay. I want to go."

The sound of my truck was distinct as the valet pulled it beneath the awning. Sliding my arm around Bellamy's waist, I said, "C'mon."

The valet came around the front with a smile. "It was a pleasure, Liam."

I chuckled. "Thanks."

Bellamy's eyes fell on my truck, and her steps faltered. "That's your truck?"

"Never seen anything like it, have you?" the valet interjected.

"I don't think I have," Bellamy replied, still looking at it.

"It's just a Chevy," I said and urged her forward.

The valet laughed. "And you're just a ski instructor."

"I am!" I yelled over my shoulder.

More laughter sounded from the valet post. I pulled open the passenger door and stepped back.

Bellamy glanced between me and the truck.

"How about some help?" I knew the smile on my face was wolfish.

"Maybe just this once."

"Foot here," I said, pointing to the runner. She stepped up, and I lifted, depositing her onto the orange and black leather seat.

"I guess having big tires like this makes it easy to drive in the snow," she said, gazing at me.

"Sure does." I leaned around her, palmed the seat belt, and fastened it. "Be right back."

Jogging around to the driver's side, I jumped in and adjusted the vents so they were pointed toward her. Then I flicked on the heated seats.

"Why are they staring?" Bellamy asked, gazing through the tinted window at the valet guys.

I laughed. "It's the truck, sweetheart. The guys always paper, rock, scissor it to decide who gets to pull it around."

"I guess it's not just a Chevy?" she asked.

I chuckled and pulled away from the curb. My eyes flicked over the custom leather interior. Most of it was black, but the seats were trimmed in bright orange and so was the dash and steering wheel. The monitor built into the dash was touchscreen and everything was state of the art.

"It's a Chevy Colorado Extreme. Basically a Chevrolet Colorado model with a ton of upgraded specialty parts and bonuses to make it suitable for rugged outdoor use. Perfect for an extreme athlete like me." I paused to give her a wink. She rolled her eyes. "Technically, this truck isn't in production, so it's not available for purchase. It was created by Chevy as a show truck. Chevy caters a lot to the Thai market, and this was built for that."

"But we aren't in Thailand."

"Nope. But I was once. Chevrolet was a major sponsor of mine when I was still a pro boarder. I used to travel for them a lot. I did an ad campaign a few years back and visited Thailand with them. I saw this beauty during that time and commented how much I loved it."

"And they gave it to you." She surmised.

"It was considered a gift from the country."

She made a choked sound. "The *country* of Thailand sent you a *gift?*"

"They like me."

She laughed and shook her head. "You have to be making this up."

I shrugged. "Nope. That's why all the guys at the resort get a hard-on for driving it. Because it's like driving something that doesn't even exist."

"Well, it is a pretty truck."

I snorted. "It's not pretty. It's *extreme.*"

"Well, I like that it's orange."

I laughed.

"Although, I thought we were trying to blend in tonight. You know, not draw attention. This truck is an eye magnet."

"Meh. Everyone is used to seeing it around here. They know it's mine."

Bellamy turned and stared out the window. It was dark, but as soon we came down off the mountain where BearPaw was perched, the streets lit up from the shops and string lights in the trees lining the road.

I pulled into a spot behind the restaurant and killed the lights and engine.

"Stay there," I instructed so I could go around to her side and help her out. The parking lot was slightly icy from the snow we had several days ago. It would melt during the day but refreeze when the sun went down. "Careful," I told her, making sure her feet were firmly on the ground before letting go to shut the door.

We walked around to the front of the little place that had a multicolored fabric awning over the door. On the underside were some string lights that illuminated up the red front door.

"I haven't had Mexican in a while," she murmured as I pushed open the door.

"Liam!" a round woman with dark hair and red lips exclaimed and rushed around a wooden podium.

"Rosa." I spread my arms and smiled. She came forward, and I folded her into a hug. "Looking beautiful as always."

"Oh, you," she said, swatting me in the chest. Her eyes slid to Bellamy. "He's a charmer, this one."

"Yes, he certainly is." She agreed.

Now why didn't it sound like a good thing when she said it?

"Table for two?" she asked, tucking a menu under her arm.

"Something in the back?" I asked, hopeful.

"Ah, yes. Private." Rosa led us to a corner booth in the back of the place. The tabletop was still damp from where it had been cleaned. I took the seat that looked out over the room, leaving the one for Bellamy that would hide her from view.

I didn't even know what I was protecting her from,

but it didn't matter. It felt like the most important thing I'd ever done.

"I don't think I've seen you around Caribou before," Rosa said to Bellamy after handing me the menu.

"Um," Bellamy replied, not sure what to say.

"She's a guest at the resort. Thought I'd show her around the town while she was here."

"Ah, yes. Very good. Well, enjoy your dinner."

When she was gone, Bellamy slumped against the tall, wooden back of the booth. "You're a regular here?"

"They make good tacos."

"You aren't just a ski instructor, Liam." She sat forward, her eyes studying my face. "You're a town celebrity."

I shrugged. "My family has always been famous in Caribou. You know that."

"Yeah," she said, a dark note creeping into her tone.

"Why you say it like that?"

"It doesn't matter." She tugged the menu out of my hands and perused it.

I grabbed the top and pushed it down with one finger so I could look at her face. "It does matter."

"Liam!" The waiter approached. "Good to see you. Will you be having the usual?"

"You know it," I said, sitting back. "But I'll just take a coke to drink. No beer tonight."

The waiter nodded and turned to Bells. "And for you, señorita?"

"I'll have the same as Liam."

"Very good." He took the menu and went off to put in the order.

I tapped the tabletop in front of her. "Bells, we need to have a talk."

"We've been talking."

"A serious talk."

The color seemed to leech from her face. "I know you want to know what's going on with me."

"Yeah," I said. "I damn sure do. But I'm not talking about that."

She blinked. "You aren't?"

"Nope. I'm more interested in knowing what happened between us eight years ago."

She made a face. Her eyes became shuttered. "Pretty sure you were there, Liam. Or do you not remember? Was I just another notch to add to your belt?"

Anger rumbled through me like thunder in a storm. "You were *never*."

"Pretty sure when you sleep with someone, tell them you think you love them, and then disappear, that's exactly what it means."

I frowned. Was that really what she thought? "I didn't disappear." Thinking back to that morning, I said, "You never showed up."

She whispered, "Oh, I was there."

A rush of memories and emotions came over me all at once. Suddenly, I was transported back in time to that morning eight years ago. To the last time I saw Bellamy.

The sun hadn't even begun to rise when I glanced at my clock. For the first time in my entire life, I actually felt there was more to life than a mountain filled with snow.

The thought alone was shocking. Feeling it almost made me numb.

Rotating my head to the side, I glanced over at the blonde beneath the covers with me. We'd slept with the fireplace on all night. The warm glow in the room gave her dark-blond locks and golden sheen. Her light-colored lashes swept over her cheeks, making her look innocent and so damn beautiful.

I didn't want to go.

I didn't matter, though. I didn't have a choice. I'd worked almost my entire life for this. My parents worked for it. Getting here wasn't easy, and finally, finally, I had the contract in my hand and the promise of a career I knew could make me a star.

The past week changed me. I knew it. I felt it. It was practically unexplainable, and I knew no one would believe me if I tried.

They would all say I was too young to feel like this. That I was thinking with my cock and not my head. Giving up years of work for a girl who didn't even live here was stupid and irresponsible.

I might even agree.

But I loved her.

It didn't matter I'd only spent a week with her. It didn't matter I wasn't even eighteen years old yet. People had been treating me like an adult half my life. It really wasn't that surprising that I would act like one.

She stirred, her head lolled toward me, and one of her eyes cracked open enough to see I was staring at her. She smiled softly, and her body rolled, following her stare.

"What time is it?" she whispered.

"Not quite time to get up yet, but soon."

Her hand moved beneath the quilt, found mine, and I threaded our fingers together.

"I wish I didn't have to go."

Blue eyes settled on mine. Their weight made me feel a little steadier. A little surer. "I wish you didn't either."

"We'll make it work, okay?"

"You promise?" she asked.

I went forward and kissed her intimately, rolling her onto her back and pushing her down with my weight. Her skin was bare against mine and warm from sleep. Unable to stop at her lips, I kissed across her jaw and down her neck, sucking the skin as I went.

Lifting my head, I gazed down into her eyes. "I love you, Bells."

Her breath caught.

"I know it's crazy. But that's how you make me feel. Half crazy. But I love you. I've never felt like this about anyone ever."

Tears glistened in her eyes, and she cupped my face and smiled. "I love you, too, Liam."

Not long after, she had to sneak back to her room and I had to get ready.

I knew the car was waiting downstairs and I didn't have time, but I found my father anyway.

"I can't go," I said.

He jerked up, his eyes wide. "What?"

"I know this is crazy, Dad, and I'm sorry. But I can't go today."

"Son." He stood from his desk. "I know you're nervous, and it's scary you will be away from me and your mother—"

"That's not it." I cut in. "I'm in love. I can't leave her behind."

He made a sound. "The girl you've been with this last week?"

I nodded. "Her name is Bellamy. I'm in love with her"

My father chuckled. "I'm sure it feels that way now, son. But—"

"Don't you dare tell me I'm too young. Or my hormones are out of control," I snapped.

His brow furrowed, and when he looked up, concern shone in his eyes. "I don't think you're too young. I wasn't much older than you when I met your mother. We were young and crazy. Just the two of us building a resort from nothing."

"Then you understand," I said, the tension coiled inside me starting to let go. I started to feel some peace.

"I do." He reached out and put a hand on my shoulder. "I also understand that you signed a contract, Liam. You're a pro athlete now. People are counting on you. They're putting their faith and resources into you. Being a man is honoring your commitments."

My shoulders slumped.

"I'm sure this girl—"

"Her name is Bellamy."

"Bellamy is very special. And if so, then this isn't the end. She'll be there for you, supporting you just like the rest of us."

"I won't get to see her."

"Not often. But if you two are really meant to be, you will find a way to make it work."

I felt as if my heart had been hanging together by threads, but this conversation severed all of them. I was no longer a man with one heart.

I had two.

One that beat for Bellamy and one that beat for boarding.

"Go find her. Tell her good-bye."

"She's meeting me down at the car."

"Good." Dad nodded. "Tell her you'll call her. You'll email."

I nodded.

"Now is the time to follow your dreams, Liam. If you don't, you will regret it for the rest of your life."

I knew he was right. Of course he was.

We said good-bye in his office. It wasn't hard because I knew him and Mom would be at my first competition.

I went downstairs and waited. Nervous energy filled me. But so did determination. I wasn't going to choose today. Not between my two hearts.

I was going to have both. I would make it work.

"Liam!" the feminine voice called out.

I pushed off the car and spun, a smile dying on my lips. It wasn't Bellamy that rushed toward me. It was Kelsey.

It didn't seem to matter how many times I told her I wasn't into her. It was like she had selective hearing. She thought because she was popular and beautiful and we grew up together that she had some kind of right to me.

"Hey, Kelsey," I said, stepping back.

"I came to wish you luck!" she exclaimed.

Before I knew what that meant, she threw herself at me. Locked her arms around my neck and kissed me. I was so shocked it gave her a chance to thrust her tongue in my mouth.

The second I realized what the fuck she was doing, I shoved her off, holding her at arm's length away from me. "What the hell?" I spat and wiped my mouth with the back of my hand.

"I'll see you when you're home next," she said and then pranced away as though she were proud of herself.

I went back to waiting.

Waited some more.

I waited until my manager got out of the car and told me I had to go.

She never came.

Bellamy never came to say good-bye. For years and years, I wondered why.

The sound of two cokes hitting the tabletop of the tiny Mexican restaurant snapped me back to reality.

I gasped and looked up.

Bellamy was watching me with a funny expression on her face.

"You saw." I panted. "That morning, you saw."

She didn't seem confused at all, almost as if she too had been sitting there reliving that morning.

Slowly, Bellamy nodded. "Yes, Liam. I saw."

147

19

Bellamy

HE GROANED. A LOW, KEENING SOUND THAT ACTUALLY sounded painful.

"Liam?" I worried, reaching across the table, unable to just sit there. Compelled to comfort him.

He watched my hands slide close, snapped his stormy gaze up to mine, and moved. The tall, wooden backing on his booth shuddered under the pressure of his movement. In one smooth measure, he slid onto the bench beside me, his body pushing mine to the side.

"What are you doing?" I gasped.

Even when we were talking about how he crushed my heart, I still couldn't breathe when he touched me.

His torso rotated toward me. His wide hands came up, holding my face firmly so I couldn't look anywhere but at him. "I didn't kiss her."

"I saw you." I tried to pull away.

"She threw herself at me, and I shoved her off. I didn't want Kelsey. I didn't want anyone but you."

His admission slammed into me. "Don't play games with me." I warned, my voice shaky.

"I swear to fucking God, Bellamy. You can ask my father. I went to his office just before to tell him I couldn't go. I told him I loved you and that I had to stay."

My mouth opened, but no sound came out. No air got in. If his hands weren't still pinning me in place, I'd have fallen back.

"Breathe," he murmured, reminding me.

I sucked in some air.

His eyes turned tender. The storm clouds receded, leaving behind a sterling gray. Liam dipped his head and pressed a soft, quick kiss to the corner of my lips.

"I waited that morning. I waited so fucking long. My manager was livid. I shoved Kelsey off and went back to waiting… and you never came."

"You kissed her."

"No." He shook his head. "She kissed me."

I started to shake my head. I couldn't believe what I was hearing. To know something as absolute for eight years, something that changed me forever, and then find out that absolute wasn't so concrete as you thought…

If I'd only said something. If only…

"I was going to assure you I'd make it work. I was going to vow it."

I made a sound.

His eyes bounced between mine, his stare so open and sincere.

"I thought you lied to me," I whispered. "I thought you'd said what I wanted to hear to get what you wanted."

"No, baby. I wouldn't."

"I'd heard all the rumors about you. Everywhere I

went, the staff was talking. Gossiping. I'd seen that girl around. I'd seen her hanging on you. I—"

"I tried to call you after you went back to California."

"I didn't answer."

"I know."

"You gave up," I whispered, sorrowful.

"I did."

Abruptly, he let go of my face and tugged me into his chest. I fit perfectly. His body formed around mine like a glove. I shuddered as I was battered with emotions and feelings.

"I never should have given up." He moaned into my ear.

Clutching the front of his T-shirt, I buried my face. Liam pulled me away, and I tried to curl back into him.

"Bells."

I lifted my chin.

"I never stopped loving you. *Never*. Even when I tried."

"Me either," I murmured, rubbing the place above my heart.

Liam palmed my chin with one hand and pushed it up, descending upon my lips in a single motion.

If I hadn't believed his words, his kiss couldn't lie. It was the kind of kiss that left you naked, the kind that whispered directly into your heart. His arms clutched me so close it was as if we were one body. His fresh snow scent rose and wrapped around me, making me feel claimed and protected all at once.

It was a completely inappropriate kiss for a restaurant.

For anywhere with more than just the tow of us. I kissed him back equally, not giving a damn where I was or who could see.

I'd almost died more than once in my life, and I thought for sure I'd never see him again. I thought I would never feel this way.

But here he was. In my arms. Crawling under my skin. Owning every single beat of my heart.

The sound of a throat clearing broke into the haze.

It cleared again.

Liam lifted his head, looked over his shoulder.

When his body tensed, mine did, too. My hands curled back into his shirt. He moved so he was blocking me completely from whoever was standing there.

"Your tacos are ready," the waiter said, his voice a little disbelieving but also kind of awed.

I couldn't help it. I giggled.

Liam's broad shoulders shook under his silent laugh.

"Set 'em down right here, friend. I just worked up a hella appetite."

I gasped.

Oh my God! That was terribly embarrassing!

The waiter chuckled. "Guess it's a good thing you have a back booth."

Liam cleared his throat. "Yeah. Sorry about that, man. No disrespect was meant. I just, ah, got caught up in the moment."

"Sometimes passion cannot wait," he replied graciously. Once we had everything we needed for the tacos, he slipped away, into the back.

I fell over into Liam's side. "Go back to your seat!" I hissed, shoving him.

He didn't even budge. Not one inch.

"Hell no. I'm staying put." As if to prove his point, he kicked up both his long legs up beneath the table and used his former seat as a footrest. Then, he slung out one arm across my shoulders. "Eat up, Bells. These tacos are bomb."

He proceeded to shove half a soft-shelled taco into his mouth and groan.

My stomach was still flipping and flopping all over the place. My hands were still trembling and my mind still in shock over what he'd said.

"It's gonna be fine, now, Bells," Liam told me, settling a little firmer against me. "Now that I know what happened, I can fix it."

"It's not that easy," I murmured, glancing at the food. It looked pretty damn good. The pico de gallo looked homemade.

He paused in chewing and glanced at me. "The hell it isn't," he announced. "I'm not making the same mistake twice."

My heart fluttered, sort of the way a hummingbird's wings did. So fast. So furiously.

"Things are different now," I said, laying my head against his shoulder. "I'm different."

"You still feel perfect to me."

I sighed.

He took a sip of his drink, then spoke. "I know you're talking about whatever made you run here. And I don't give a damn about that either."

"People want me dead, Liam," I said quietly. So quiet I was hoping he might not hear.

He heard.

The taco in his hand fell onto the plate with a slap. He angled himself to look down, still keeping me tucked under his arm. "Come again?"

I nodded, not willing to say the words twice. "It's not safe for you to be around me."

"I lived the last eight years of my life without you. I

couldn't move on no matter what I tried. It was fucking miserable, Bells. I'm not doing it again. Never again."

"You might not have a choice."

He laughed. It wasn't a friendly, warm sound. It was cold. Cold as the snow he lived in. Maybe even colder. "Nothing and no one will take you away from me again."

I didn't say anything. I mean, what could I say to that? I was torn between spilling everything and saying nothing to try and protect him.

The first rule of witness protection was to say nothing.

Liam already knew too much.

"Eat your taco's, sweetheart," he said, going back to eating. "You can tell me about every single flavor you taste."

I didn't think I was going to be able to eat.

But I did.

I ate almost the entire plate, and then Liam finished the rest. He wasn't kidding. These tacos were the best I ever ate.

I knew Liam thought we could just pick right up where we left off. But we couldn't. It was impossible.

And when he finally realized that, we would both know heartbreak all over again.

2 0

Liam

"Ask me."

"What?"

"Since I pretty much controlled the conversation at dinner, you never got the chance to tell me what that something was you needed me to do."

Bellamy looked like a hot little snow bunny sitting in my truck. Black leather seats surrounded her, a black coat wrapped around her body, and those damn boots with the fur sticking out of the top felt like a tease to something I really, *really* wanted. Eight years ago, her hair was long. The kind of length I could tangle my hands in and pull her close. The kind that spilled over my chest when she lay on me.

It was even longer now. The same honey strands that sometimes turned gold under certain light. I loved it. I wanted to take two handfuls and wrap it around my fingers over and over again.

Her skin was still soft and smooth, and her blue eyes could still haunt a man's dreams.

"I don't really think this is the place to talk about that," she replied.

Oh, that was right. We were having a conversation. Sometimes words failed me when I looked at her.

I reached into the cab, palmed her waist, and lifted her out. The second her feet hit the pavement, I caught her hand, pushing my fingers through hers. The valet appeared instantly, grinning from ear to ear.

"I won," he announced, holding up his hand to show he'd thrown a rock in their most recent rock, paper, scissors match.

I laughed and held out the keys. "Be careful with her, okay?"

"Of course, Liam," he replied. "As always. She will be parked in your designated spot."

"Thanks."

Bellamy looked up at me from beneath her blond lashes. "Not many people around here call you Mr. Mattison."

I made a sound. "That's my dad. Not me."

"They all love you."

I made another sound.

"Are you really taking over the resort?"

I paused and slid a glance to her. "Supposed to."

"But that's not what you want?"

I groaned. "We're talking about something *you* want right now." I reminded her.

The lodge was pretty quiet, something that was kind of surprising because it was one of the most popular gathering places at the resort. But then I remembered there was some kind of show in one of the other buildings. I was kinda glad for the peace.

Tugging Bells's hand, I walked to the table with hot cocoa and cookies to pour us each a cup. Once I was done, I handed hers over, and she smiled.

I watched her lift it toward her lips, then frowned, quickly snatching it back out of her hands.

"Hey!" she said, surprised.

I took a sip of it and grimaced. Then I handed it back. "Hold this."

"Of course. Let me hold this drink you made *for me* for you," she muttered.

I chuckled. "I like your sass, woman." Popping the top off a can of whipped cream, I filled the top of her cup with it and then stuck in one of those super-skinny red straws. They were meant for stirring, but everyone I knew used them to drink out of.

"Wait 'til that melts in there a few. Then it shouldn't burn you." I went back to my own cup and added some of the whipped cream to it.

I felt her eyes, so I turned and lifted a brow. "Yes?"

"You tested my drink to see if it was too hot?"

"You burned yourself last time." My eyes went to the front desk, then back. "That guy's lucky I didn't fire his ass."

She gave me a stern look. "You can't fire someone for giving them a cup of hot hot chocolate."

"Are you trying to seduce me?"

"What?" she wondered, her eyes going confused.

"Because it's working."

"You're utterly ridiculous."

"Utterly," I mocked. I put on my best pout. "I burned my tongue for you."

Gasping, she set down the cup and grabbed my face. I liked the way her hands felt rubbing against my stubble. "You did? Let me see."

I stuck my tongue out. "Ight tere," I said, pointing.

She made a sound and leaned up on tiptoes to study the minor burn. I was getting quite the kick out of the undivided attention.

Until she kissed me.

Bellamy leaned right up and kissed the spot on my tongue that I told her was burned.

My heart collapsed.

All fun and flirting went out the window. My eyes dropped to hers, and she must have felt the change over me because her hands fell away from my face.

"You kissed me."

"It's not the first time." She pointed out.

"It is in eight years."

She kissed me. And I don't mean kissed me back when I kissed her. I mean She. Kissed. Me.

She swallowed. "Does it hurt very bad?"

She meant my tongue. "Not anymore," I rasped, not talking about my tongue at all.

"Liam, breathe," she instructed.

I inhaled.

I wanted to grab her and run. To lock us in her suite —no, my cabin—and not come out until I made up for every single year she was gone.

I knew I couldn't. I had to almost relearn her. The thought was absurd because my heart insisted it knew her better than anyone. But I wasn't seventeen anymore. I was a grown man, and as much as I wanted to listen to my heart, I had to also consult with my head.

Besides, making up for lost years wasn't something that could just be done in a bedroom.

After handing her the cup, I held out my hand. "Come with me."

I led us to the other side of the massive crackling fireplace. There was a small loveseat right by it, and I pulled her down on the cushion beside me.

"What do you need?"

After glancing around and realizing we had the privacy she wanted, she answered, "I need you to call my mother."

"You can't call her yourself?"

"No."

I don't know how that one-syllable word could sound broken. But it did.

My hand covered her knee. "You want me to get a message to her?"

She nodded and bit into her lower lip.

Gently, I reached up and tugged the flesh from between her teeth. "What kind of message?"

Blue eyes lifted to mine, wide, soft, almost pleading. "I just want to know if she's okay."

I nodded. The center of my chest felt tight. "Of course I'll call her, sweetheart."

Bellamy surged forward and grasped my hand with both of hers. The way she gripped them and stared at me cause my pulse to quicken. "I need to tell her to be careful. I need to warn her."

I puzzled. "Warn her?"

She nodded. "If the men can't find me… they might go for her."

"What the hell is this about?" I demanded. "You need to tell me. I can help you."

"I've already told you way too much."

"Like hell! You haven't told me shit."

"Don't you cuss at me!" she demanded.

"Now, sweetheart, you know it's nothing personal. I'm just worried about you."

She rolled her eyes. "Placating is just as bad as

159

cussing."

I grinned swiftly. The moment passed, though, and the gravity of this situation washed back over us. "I just wish you trusted me enough to tell me."

"It's not that." She glanced down at where her hands still held mine. "I just…" Her lips pressed together. Then finally she said, "Can you just call her? Please?"

I couldn't—*wouldn't*—deny her anything. "What's her number?"

Releasing my hands, she reached into her jeans and pulled out a ripped piece of paper with BearPaw's logo on it. The phone number was written across it in pen. Instead of taking the paper, I cupped her hand and the paper between both of mine. She was shaking.

I didn't like it.

"I'm scared for you to call her. Scared for you not to."

"Why?" I asked, rubbing my hands against hers, trying to give some warmth to her icy fingers.

"I shouldn't get you involved. What if they're watching? What if they come for you?" I started to shake my head, but she cut me off. "But I need to know. What I did… I put her in danger."

The way she slumped, as if she were exhausted and defeated at the same time, was too much for me to watch. I lifted Bellamy into my lap and settled back into the cushions. Her body relaxed into mine immediately, her cheek falling against my chest.

Possessiveness rumbled through me. The need to shield and protect had never been so fierce inside me.

"It's okay now," I murmured, gathering her closer and stroking her hair.

"I'm not sure it ever will be again."

A moment later, she lifted her head and gazed at me. "Sometimes I think I should just go back home. Let them find me. Then this will be over once and for all, and she'll be safe… and I won't have to run."

The mere suggestion that Bellamy surrender to whatever the fuck was going on was a hard no inside me. An *I will bring down this fucking town* no.

I couldn't stop the sudden heaving of my chest, but I tried not to go ape shit. I mean, she was sitting on me for comfort.

"You're not going anywhere. You're staying here, with me."

"I don't understand why you're still single." Her palm rested on my chest. "Why, after eight years, has no one claimed you?"

Emotion rumbled inside me. "Because you claimed me the day I saw you standing beneath the lift, looking green with fear." I palmed the side of her face. "You claimed me, Bells, and never let go."

She kissed the side of my jaw. My eyes drooped, my heart rate slowing to a thud. When she lifted, I lowered, and her lips brushed over mine.

It wasn't a long kiss. The second it was over, she tucked herself back into my chest and sighed. I sat there for a long moment, just staring over her head into the fire. I felt raw. Ripped open and bleeding. But I didn't want a bandage. I didn't want this intensity to ever dull. I always wondered what it would be like to see her again.

Sometimes I thought about it. Hoped for it even.

I never imagined it would be like this. As if the bond we formed eight years ago had strengthened, not weakened.

If it was this strong now, without us even trying, what would it be like when I gave her my all?

After I quieted the raging storm inside me, I pulled the phone out of my jeans.

"Let me see the paper, Bells."

"I don't think you should use your cell."

"It's a private number," I told her. "If I use one from the lodge, it will come back directly to BearPaw."

She seemed unsure, but I was. I took the paper and dialed the number. Just before I hit CALL, Bellamy's hand settled over mine. "Ask her about her roses."

"Her roses?"

She nodded. "It's sort of a code between us."

"It's winter."

"Just ask," she implored.

I lifted the hand covering mine and kissed it. Then I sent the number through. Bellamy's body was rigid as she listened to the rings. After the third one went unanswered, her hand fisted in the front of my shirt.

"Hello?" a woman answered on the fourth ring.

Bellamy nearly collapsed against me.

"Hi, Mrs.—"

Bellamy jolted up and shook her head adamantly.

I cleared my throat. "Hey, it's Liam. I was just calling to see how you're doing."

Relief flooded Bellamy's eyes, and she nodded.

There was a brief pause on the other end of the line, and I honestly expected the woman to just hang up. She didn't.

"Oh, how nice of you to call. I'm doing just fine. And yourself?"

Big fat tears rolled over Bellamy's cheeks, and I wiped one away as I spoke. "I'm doing good, too. Just, you know, catching up with old friends lately."

The woman paused again.

"I was wondering how your roses are doing? I know how much you love to garden." God, I hoped she actually did like to garden.

There was a small catch in the woman's voice when she replied, "M-my roses are doing beautifully. I'm so looking forward to spring when they all bloom."

Bellamy sniffled and fell into my chest. Her shoulders were shaking, and really, I had no idea a phone call could be so fucking difficult.

"I'm sure they are the prettiest on the block," I said. I had no idea what else to say.

"You said you're doing well?" she asked, but I knew instantly it wasn't me she was asking about.

Bellamy pulled back and nodded. Tears stained her face. "Yes, been busy, but everything is fine."

"That's good to hear," she murmured. "I've missed talking to you."

Bellamy touched the phone, pulling it closer as if hearing her voice was the most precious thing ever.

"So have I. I should call more often," I said.

"Yes, please do. Call anytime."

Bellamy sniffled and signaled for me to wrap it up.

"I've got to get going, but please take care of yourself. The winter months can be very long."

"I will. You take care, too. It was so good to speak with you, *Liam*."

After the call ended, Bells took my phone and hugged it to her chest, lay against me, and cried quietly.

I rubbed her back because I didn't know what else to do.

After a while, I asked, "How long has it been since you've seen your mom?"

"A year and a half."

"And your dad?"

Her breath caught, and her trembling increased. "Almost two years."

Did that mean she'd been alone all that time? With no one?

I wanted to demand answers, but she was already upset enough. "C'mon," I said, standing and taking her with me. "Time for bed."

I carried her up to her room, let us in, and fended off an overly excited Charlie, who had hung out here while we ate dinner.

After putting her down, she's grabbed my shirt off the end of her bed and hugged it to her chest. "You can't have this back," she mumbled and started toward the bathroom.

I chuckled. "I wouldn't dream of taking it."

I put on the Cooking Channel (she seemed to like it) and turned off all the lights except for a small lamp. When she came out of the bathroom, she looked vulnerable and sexy with my shirt falling around her legs.

Without saying anything, I pulled the covers back and gestured for her to get in. She trudged over and slipped beneath. I moved to cover her, but she glanced over her shoulder. "Will you lie here with me?"

I kicked off my shoes and slid in behind her, drawing her against my body. Charlie jumped up on the mattress, and I started to tell him down, but she squeezed my hand not to. The dog settled on the other side of her with a great huff.

Her giggle filled the corners of my heart, and she scratched behind his ears.

After a few minutes, she settled more firmly into my embrace. "Thank you for calling her. I feel so much better knowing she's okay."

I kissed the back of her head and snuggled her tighter.

She fell asleep in my arms, and I lay there and

wondered how I could fix whatever was going on. It was hard to find a solution for a problem you didn't know.

I drifted off at some point and awakened when the sky was just beginning to lighten. It was hard to slip out of the bed. I almost didn't, but I knew if I stayed, I wouldn't be able to keep myself from her body.

I knew I could have her, that if I started touching her, she probably wouldn't stop me.

I held off, though. Having her body wouldn't mean as much if I couldn't have the rest of her, too.

21

Bellamy

I WAS RUNNING OUT OF UNDERWEAR.

After a few days of being here at BearPaw, my getaway stash was dwindling. And I was sort of super tired of only having a pair of jeans as pants.

I wondered about my apartment. About my things. Was it all still there waiting for me to come back? Would the place still have bruschetta remains everywhere? Was the stove still on?

Or maybe the men had come back, hoping I would be there. Maybe they'd trashed the place as a message.

I wondered if the police knew I was missing. Maybe someone from work called them when I stopped coming in. Or perhaps they didn't care since I wasn't social and hadn't bothered to make friends with any of my co-workers.

I watched the news every morning, never seeing anything about me. But that didn't necessarily mean no one was looking. It didn't mean I was safe.

I was starting to feel safe, though. Just a little bit every day. Every day I got just a tad more comfortable, started to feel a tad more at home.

I didn't even miss Chicago. Well, aside from my underwear and the rest of my wardrobe. And maybe that bottle of wine I'd gotten that night.

It was odd I was hiding here. I felt more like me than I had in years. In a place I vowed to never return to. A place I'd come to as a last resort. I didn't plan to stay. Now, I didn't want to leave.

Eventually, I was going to have to go. The night I fled my apartment, I pretty much became a ghost. A fugitive from killers. A woman who would never be able to settle again.

I could go to the police. I could go back into witness protection. They'd tell me I was safe. Change my name, my identity, and move me across the country.

I'd be a sitting duck. And I'd be miserable.

It seemed no matter what choice I made, I was screwed. At least I knew my mother was safe.

For now. The whisper in my head was not welcome. I heard it anyway.

What I wouldn't give to go back to eight years ago on that morning I saw Liam with that other girl. I wished I hadn't run away. I couldn't help but wonder what might have been.

I wondered that a lot.

The knock on the door made me smile, something else that changed since I got here. Instead of cringing and hiding, I anticipated seeing Liam's face.

Still, I was no fool. I went to the door, bouncing from side to side on each foot. Charlie jumped and fidgeted beside me, then glanced up and whined.

I laughed. He knew who it was, and he was just as excited as me.

"Who is it?" I called out, even though Charlie's reaction already told me.

"Like you don't already know," Liam intoned.

Charlie barked, and I opened the door and stepped back. The giant St. Bernard bounded through the doorway and nearly plowed Liam over.

Liam laughed and scratched Charlie as his tail beat.

"Your dog missed you," I said.

Liam grunted and came into the room. "Since he's practically been living with you, I might argue."

Charlie brushed up against Liam's side, leaving a giant string of drool in his wake.

I laughed.

Liam caught me around the waist and pulled me into him. "How about you? Did you miss me?"

"Maybe," I said, ducking my head.

He picked me up, my feet dangling over the floor like I was a ragdoll. "I don't like that answer."

He made my heart sing. I giggled. "I just saw you a few hours ago."

He shook me gently. "Try again."

"Aren't your arms getting tired?" I wondered.

"*Bellamy*," he growled.

"I missed you."

He brought me close, and my legs wrapped around his waist. Our lips fused, and I melted into him like butter on a slice of hot toast. His fingertips found the hem of my T-shirt and pushed up until his palm was flat against my back.

I purred against his tongue, and he stroked it deeper, angling his head so he could achieve optimum penetration. My fingers coiled in his hair, as the rest of the world slipped away.

Between my legs, the last clean pair of panties I had grew damp, and I shifted my weight subconsciously, trying to satiate a hunger only he brought out in me.

I felt his fingertips dig into my back, drag down my spine, and flirt quite scandalously with the waistband of my panties.

Liam pulled his mouth away and swiftly sat me away from him. I swayed on my feet, and he came back, using his hands to steady me.

He'd slept in my room every night since the night he called my mother. The night I'd asked him to hold me. I didn't have to ask anymore. It was as if he knew. I hadn't slept so peacefully in so long. It was almost shocking how much clearer my head was in the morning after an actual night of restful sleep. Add that to all the meals he kept having sent to my room and the lunches I ate with him and Alex every day... It was almost a complete change in me.

Food, sleep... feeling safe.

I would never take those things for granted ever again.

We never did more than sleep, though. He would hold me, and I would drift off. He never stayed the entire night, though. And he never kissed me in bed, unless it was on the forehead.

The kisses like we just shared, they were coming more frequently. The need for him bubbling in my blood was soon going to boil over.

I knew I shouldn't, but oh my, I wanted to. I wanted him.

"Why aren't you dressed?" he asked, suddenly noticing I was still only wearing his T-shirt.

"You don't like my outfit?"

He lifted an eyebrow. "You know damn well the answer to that."

I smiled, sort of feeling like an overfull cat.

He groaned beneath his breath and rubbed his hand over the back of his neck. "You test my patience like no other."

I blinked innocently, secretly thrilled. I hoped he felt even a fraction of the desire he inspired in me.

"I have lessons," he said, his eyes lingering on my body.

I flopped down on the side of the bed and fed Charlie a piece of toast.

"No wonder he wants to stay here when I creep out at the crack of dawn," Liam muttered.

"Why do you?" I asked, pausing, toast in midair.

"Why do I what?"

"Why do you leave early in the morning? Are you afraid the staff knows you're sleeping up here?"

His eyes flashed with shock. A couple strides brought him to where I sat. He kneeled on the floor in front of me, angling his body between my knees. Before he spoke, he ripped the toast out of my hand and tossed it to Charlie, who gulped it down in one swallow.

Small shivers rushed up and down my arms and legs when he placed his hands on my knees. He was always so warm. "I don't care who knows I'm up here with you. Hell, I'll go downstairs and call a staff meeting and tell them all right now."

"I don't think that's necessary," I said dryly.

"You're right. It's not." He grinned. "'Cause they're all already gossiping like some reality show, and they think I don't know it."

A flicker of embarrassment went through me. "I'm

sure I can imagine what they're saying." Swallowing, I looked at things as I'm sure they were being perceived by the staff here at BearPaw.

The beloved athlete, their soon-to-be boss, the town sweetheart since birth... and here I was, dressing in the same outfit day after day, showing up with too-big, janky stolen shoes and no coat. My room was in his name. He sent food up every morning, and I ate lunch with him every afternoon.

I trailed along to his lessons and basically shared custody of his dog. They all probably thought I was using Liam.

And if I was being one hundred percent honest with myself, I kinda looked like a whore.

The thoughts made me jolt up. I would have rushed away from him, but he kept his hands on my knees and pushed me back down. "Where do you think you're going?"

"This is wrong." I fretted. "I really need to go. I've already screwed up my life, my mother's life... I can't do it to you, too."

Liam frowned, and I used the opportunity to slip away from him. Rushing to my bag, I pulled out the envelope of money my father had given me. He hadn't lied that day almost two years ago. He said the money was clean, that he wanted me to have it.

The police checked. The money was indeed earned by my father. Legally.

And he'd given it all to me.

I'd probably wonder until the day I died if he would have had enough to buy himself out of trouble if he'd used it. My lawyer told me once it wouldn't have been enough...

But I would still always wonder.

It was only a few thousand dollars, but it was still a decent stash, especially for a girl who needed to run away and start over. I counted out a thousand and whirled to give it to Liam. I gasped and fell back because he wasn't across the room anymore, but right behind me.

"Easy," he murmured, reaching out to steady me.

I brushed away his hands and shoved the cash between us. "Here."

"What the hell is that?"

"You said I could pay you back for everything." I shook the money at him. "I'm not sure if this will cover it all. Those boots..." My voice trailed off as my gaze lingered on those beautiful, too-expensive boots he'd bought me.

He made a sound and knocked my hand aside. "I'm not taking your money."

"You have to!" I exclaimed.

"Why?" he intoned. He was a stubborn mule!

"Because I take care of myself."

"No."

I gasped. "No!"

"No."

"Take the money, Liam," I growled.

He folded his arms over his chest and narrowed his silvery eyes on me. It was quite intimidating, and I was starting to feel a little shaky. I hated the feeling. Being weak.

I knew I wasn't. Not really. But to be honest, confrontation wrecked me. Since that day I hid between two walls and watched two men confront my father... to death.

"Please," I said, my voice hoarse. My arm was still extended between us, holding out the cash.

Liam sighed and took the bills. Then he folded them

in half and grabbed my still-extended arm, tugging me gently into him.

The next thing I knew, he'd picked me up and sat down the bed with me in his lap. The money lay forgotten beside us, and he lifted my chin with the back of his hand. "Why are you suddenly so intent on giving me a stack of money?"

"I was always going to give it to you."

"Why now?" His voice was patient. Kind.

It was almost my undoing.

"Because I look like a whore!" I exclaimed.

He drew back, shocked. "What?"

"I'm staying in this nice suite under your name, wearing clothes you paid for and eating meals you send up or charge to your account. You said it yourself. Everyone is talking… and it looks like I'm taking advantage of you."

He jolted up, bringing me with him. Then he set me on my feet. "You are *not* a whore," he spat as though the mere suggestion disgusted him.

"Liam, just take the money. Please."

"Get dressed," he said, his voice hard.

"Liam—"

"Dressed!"

Charlie went to the corner and lay down. Clearly, the deadly calm yet severe tone was one he knew not to mess with.

I made a face at Liam, and he came over and pulled the T-shirt off my body in one swift movement.

I gasped and moved to cover up my bare chest.

He gaped. "Why the hell are you not wearing a bra?"

"I don't sleep in a bra, you jackass!" I said, flinging my arms out, giving him a good view of the girls.

He averted his eyes.

I started crying.

It was my last straw. Oh my God, the amount of emotion that bubbled up inside me was almost too much. I felt as if I were being ripped apart by emotions that were sharper than knives.

I spun, feeling my hair float out around me in a curtain. My vision was blurred as tears fell from my eyes. Rummaging around in my bag, I searched for my bra and T-shirt, only to realize they were hanging in the bathroom. Keeping my back turned, I reached for the sweater lying nearby to cover up before I went into the bathroom.

"Bells," Liam's voice was so soft. It made me cry harder.

The bastard.

He reached for me, and I jerked away. "Don't touch me."

"Hey," he said again, ignoring my demand. His fingers curled around my upper arm and tugged me around.

I snatched up the sweater and held it front of me like a blind.

He yanked it away and threw it on the floor. "Stop."

"Stop covering up what you clearly don't want to see?"

A rough noise ripped from his throat, and I was pulled into his chest. My body slammed up against his, my entire naked torso.

Hell. All I had on was panties.

Reaching down, Liam carefully brushed the long strands of my hair back over my shoulders, removing any concealment I might have left.

"Why are you doing this?" I whimpered.

"I didn't mean to yell at you, sweetheart," he murmured, grazing a finger over my collarbone. "And I sure as hell didn't mean to make you feel embarrassed for being… naked under my shirt."

"I'm not naked," I muttered.

He smiled but quickly tried to conceal it.

"I've been wanting to see you like this since I saw you standing in the middle of the lodge that night."

I snorted.

"I'm serious. I've been trying to take it slow."

"Slow?"

He nodded. "That's why I get out of bed every morning. I don't trust myself to be in this bed when you wake up looking all sleepy and sexy with mussed hair, wearing my shirt."

"You don't have to say that."

"I'm not just saying that, Bells." His voice was a little sardonic.

I gave a little huff, and he grabbed my hand, guiding it to the front of his jeans.

I drew in a breath. My eyes flew to his face. Liam was stiff as a board.

"I'm pretty sure the raging hard-on I have isn't just me pretending."

I gave it a little squeeze, and he moaned.

"Liam." I wetted my lips with the tip of my tongue.

He pulled my hand away and kissed the back of it.

"I want to rip those panties off you and do things that will make you walk funny and tremble for a week," he murmured, stepping forward, making me walk back. "I want to hear my name fall off your lips when I make you come. I want to touch your entire body a million times over, then do it a million times more."

I drew in a shaky breath as my back hit the wall. Liam curved his arms around me so I wasn't leaning against the wall, but I was pressed against his chest and leaning into him.

"It isn't that I don't want to see you, sweetheart. It's that I'm genuinely afraid that when I do, I won't be able to control myself."

My nipples were hard. My panties, which had started to dry, were slick again. His voice was like a damn aphrodisiac.

I shifted, brushing my erect nipples against his chest. A small sound broke from between my lips. He hands flexed against my back.

"So you want me?" I whispered.

He laughed, a rich, throaty sound. "You have no fucking idea how much."

"I think I might," I whispered.

Liam lifted me just like he had when he first came in the room. My legs wound around his waist and my back hit the wall. Using his hips to pin me in place, he moved back so he could stare down my body with heated eyes.

A flush bloomed across me, and my head hit the wall.

Liam lifted his hand, allowing it to hover over my breast, and looked into my eyes.

I nodded.

His hand covered me instantly, completely cupping the soft mound. His palm rubbed over the nipple, and I sighed. He stroked and massaged my breast before moving to the other one. I began to pant and move against him restlessly.

He whispered my name and lowered his head. I gasped on first contact, the way his warm mouth surrounded my nipple. He sucked and teased until I was straining against the wall. Chuckling, he pushed me back and went at the other breast.

My skin was taut and throbbing. Between my legs, I

was dripping. Tingles of pain shot down from my chest and ended in my core.

I rocked against him, agitated and not really even realizing why.

Liam drew back. His lips were slick and his eyes were heavy. I shoved off the wall and kissed him passionately. I could feel his rigid length straining to get closer, and I tried to move down so I could match up my body with his.

He made a sound and pulled me back up. I whimpered.

He chuckled. "We don't have time for that right now," he murmured, kissing me again.

"You started it," I grumped.

"And I'm going to finish it."

My back hit the bed, and a pillow was pushed beneath my head. Liam grabbed another pillow and pushed it beneath my butt, angling my hips up. As he lowered beside me, his lips sucked my breast into his mouth again, and I spasmed up off the bed.

He pushed me down, still sucking as his hand trailed down my body toward my panties.

I titled up toward his hand, giving an answer before he even asked.

He laughed low and moved on to my other breast, delving his hand below the only fabric on my body.

I bit into my lower lip to keep from crying out as my hand found the back of his head and held him to my breast.

Liam's finger flicked over the swollen, sensitive bud, and my legs began to tremble. He made a sound, lifting his head. I glanced at him, not really seeing.

A finger slid inside me, and my eyes slid closed. He began moving in and out, occasionally twirling his finger around my clit. The sounds I made were unavoidable. It felt as if I'd lost all control of my own body, my own senses.

Liam was in control now... and he was a *very* good driver.

He moved up my body a little, his weight settling a little more into my side. Two fingers slid into me, and his lips latched onto mine.

I cried out when he pushed his fingers deep and did something inside me, something that made me cry out again.

Liam swirled his tongue in my mouth, using his thumb to press down on my bud, and did that thing with his fingers again.

I shattered beneath him. I broke into a million pieces, and it had never felt so good.

I cried out his name, and he swallowed the sound. He kept touching, milking more out of my body, and the tremors went on and on.

Eventually, I fell back, completely boneless, completely awed.

Liam gently withdrew his fingers and stroked my core over my panties for a few minutes before pulling away.

Cracking one eye open, I glanced up, and he chuckled. "Feel better?"

I made a sound.

He kissed me again, letting his tongue linger inside my mouth. When he sat up, I stared at his body, at the way his hair was mussed from my hands and his cheeks were flushed.

God. He'd been so beautiful at seventeen.

Now he was just devastating.

He was chiseled and honed. He looked rugged from

all the outdoor sports and slightly rough around the edges from experience.

I loved him.

I never stopped.

I never would.

"Hey," I murmured, stroking his back.

He glanced around. I pushed up, climbing around him and into his lap, letting my legs fall on either side of his hips.

His erection was still going strong. Boldly, I brushed my hand against it. He stiffened, and a hiss came out of his mouth.

"That looks painful."

He caught my hand. "You don't have to."

I raised an eyebrow. "What if I want to?"

His eyes searched mine.

"Are you going to tell me no, Liam?"

He surrendered before he could even say the words.

I pushed against his shoulders, forcing him back against the bed. Pushing the shirt up on his stomach, I licked across his defined abs and inhaled the fresh scent of his skin.

"You smell like snow."

"That's because I live in it."

"I like it."

He made a sound, and I licked down his stomach again.

It took a minute to work his jeans down over his pulsating erection, but I did it and managed to sneak in some teasing caresses. Before pulling his boxers down, I rubbed up his length and grabbed on to give it a squeeze.

Liam seized the pillow and pulled over his face to muffle the sound that escaped him. I had to admit... knowing his face was covered made me a little bolder.

Before he tossed aside the pillow, I pulled down the waistband and licked over his tip.

He shuddered, and his hips rose off the bed.

I licked him again, then sucked just his head into my mouth. More sounds were muffled by the pillow, and I smiled.

Once all the fabric was gone, I lifted his thick cock off his body and began pumping it as I drew one ball into my mouth, then the other.

Even though I wanted to play and taunt him, I was too impatient.

Instead, I perched above him, held up his rod, and slid my mouth down over it. His silky flesh glided over my lips and into my mouth so easily. He moaned, and I sucked deeper, taking him until his tip hit the back of my throat. I repeated the action over and over until he strained upward.

Changing course, I pulled the tip into my mouth and sucked, using my hand to pump him. His salty flavor coated my tongue, and I wanted more.

I began sucking deeper and faster.

His hand dug into my shoulder and then tightened more. I heard the pillow slap against the headboard when he tossed it away.

"I can't hold it anymore," he ground out.

I sucked deeper.

"*Fuuuck*," he swore and began to pulse, emptying into my mouth.

I swallowed his pleasure, gentling my mouth, but not yet willing to let go.

His hand fell away from me. His body melted into the mattress. I lifted my face but gave him a final stroke with my hand.

"Come here," he growled, pitching upward and dragging me up his body.

He kissed me deep, not caring a bit I still tasted like him. He kissed me until I ripped my mouth away and gasped for breath.

"I fucking needed that." He groaned.

I ran my fingers through his hair. "You should have just said so."

He made a rude sound. "I was trying to do the right thing."

"Feels pretty right to me," I whispered, lying against his chest.

"You're damn right it does."

After a moment, he got up, pulling me with him. "C'mon. I need to be downstairs."

I grimaced and adjusted my still soaked panties. "Think you could take me shopping in town? I need some clothes."

"Sure thing. I'll take you later today."

After I pulled on the jeans and sweater, I pulled my hair into a messy knot on my head. I needed hair products, too. I was all about the natural look, but I drew the line at cavewoman status.

"Bells." He took my hand, drawing me around. Cupping my face, he gazed into my eyes. "I didn't mean to make you cry."

"You didn't. I just… My feelings were hurt."

"Yeah, because I fucking hurt them."

I shook my head. "I don't want people to think of me like that… I—" My voice faltered.

"What, sweetheart?"

"I want people to know you mean a lot to me. That I would never use you." My eyes stared into his. "*You know that, don't you?*"

He made a sound and drew me to him. Hugging me close, he spoke above my head. "I know."

"Please take the money, Liam."

"I don't want your money."

"It's important to me."

He cursed, and I smiled into his chest.

"No one thinks of you like that," he said, pulling away.

"How do you know?"

His eyes narrowed and flashed like steel. "Because if anyone said anything remotely close to that, I'd fire them and make sure they didn't work in this town again."

I shivered because I knew he had the power to do it.

"Besides..." He went on more casually, his usual charming self. "Everyone likes you."

"They do?"

"Of course. C'mon." He held out his hand, and I surrendered mine. Before he could pull me away, I swiped up the money and handed it to him.

He made a face, sort of like he just ate something rotten. "Half?"

It seemed it was all I'd get him to agree to, so I gave him half the amount and then pushed the rest into the pocket of my jeans.

It wasn't exactly what I wanted, but it was something.

He glanced at his watch before closing the door behind me and Charlie. "We have just enough time for the stop I need to make before we head outside."

"What stop?" I asked.

"You'll see."

22

Liam

BELLAMY THOUGHT PEOPLE THOUGHT SHE WAS A HOOKER.

I was taking care of this shit right now.

That cockamamie idea never even occurred to me because it was fucking ridiculous. But now the thought was out there. I saw the pain in her eyes.

Sure, people were talking. I'd been seen with her since she got here. I very rarely was seen with the same girl more than twice. Alex accepted her, too, something else I was sure had tongues wagging. Lunch with the same girl *and* my best friend?

They were probably already planning the giant town wedding.

Jesus A. Christ.

I never worried about what other people thought before. Quite frankly, I couldn't give a rat's ass now if it was me they were thinking and talking about. But it wasn't just me now.

There was Bellamy.

And I was going to make it abundantly clear exactly what was going on and exactly the kind of respect everyone would damn well show.

Down in the lodge, I crooked my finger at the couple employees who were bypassing us down the hall. Their smiles turned wary, but they reversed direction and followed me anyway.

Bellamy gave me an odd look, but I ignored her.

At the front desk, the attendants stood a little straighter as I approached. "Liam?" the girl to the right said.

I made a motion with my finger. "Round up the staff. The ones around anyway. I want a word."

Bells gasped. "What are you doing?"

I lifted an eyebrow and said, "Setting the record straight."

"Oh my God!" she hissed. "This is not what I wanted."

I grunted. "It's what I want. I insist."

She turned to the employees behind me. "I am so sorry. Just go back to work."

"They don't work for you, sweetheart," I said gently. I'd already made her cry once today. That was pretty much my lifetime limit.

The man standing there nodded at her apologetically.

She groaned.

Once the girl behind the counter hung up the phone, she discreetly nodded toward me. A couple were coming in the front, luggage behind them. I pointed to Kenny. "Stay here and man the front. Shelby can fill you in after."

"Yes, sir," he said, glancing at Bellamy.

I had to hold back a snap ordering him not to look at her. It was irrational, but Kenny needed to keep his eyes in his head.

Clearly, after what happened upstairs in the bedroom, the possessiveness inside me was making me downright beastly.

Back behind the front desk was a room where guest mail came, an extra computer was hooked up, etc. Behind that room was a breakroom for the employees. Out in the hall, I opened the door and motioned for the few people following to go ahead. Once they were inside, I glanced down at Bellamy.

She narrowed her eyes as if issuing a warning.

I kissed her.

Inside the room, about twelve employees stood around, including the bartender and Sharon. It was a very small fraction of the people who worked here, but it was enough to send word spreading through the resort like wildfire.

I closed the door behind us and let go of Bellamy's hand.

Stepping forward, I cleared my throat. Everyone waited quietly, sort of warily. "Relax, guys," I said, offering a smile. "It's not like I'm lining up a firing squad."

"You don't normally call meetings," someone said.

"You never do." Someone else piped up.

"Just let him speak." Sharon shushed everyone.

I gave her a grateful smile.

"I just wanted to address all the talk going around about Bellamy here." I gestured to Bells. She turned as red as a tomato. "I know everyone is talking."

A few people looked embarrassed, a few intrigued.

"In case anyone is wondering, Bellamy is my girl-friend. Her room is under my name here out of respect for her privacy. She's still paying all the bills, and I hope you all treat her as a guest, because that's what she is."

"Of course." Sharon nodded.

Someone in the back raised their hand. I had to hide a snicker. I felt like a teacher. "Yeah?"

"With all due respect, you've never had a girlfriend."

I shifted so I could stare at the woman speaking. "Just because you say with all due respect doesn't mean you can ask whatever you want."

She flushed.

People glanced around uncomfortably.

Bellamy stepped up beside me and smacked me in the stomach. "You called a meeting to make some announcement, and then you wonder why people are curious. Don't be a turd."

A few laughs turned into coughs.

Sharon just outright laughed. "I like her."

"Fine," I muttered, then offered the girl a smile. She relaxed and smiled back.

"You're right. I've never brought a girlfriend around here before. I've known Bellamy for years. She's not someone who just showed up and now we're together. It's been a long time coming."

People turned curious glances to her. It was the truth. Plus, it would take some more suspicion off her. People didn't need to know she ran off eight years ago and I let her. Let them think I'd met her during my time away as a pro snowboarder. Yeah, there had been flings since I'd been home, but that was none of their damn business.

"Anyway, the point is Bellamy is part of the BearPaw family now. She's *my* family now. You all know how much my father and I value respect and loyalty. That now extends to her. If anyone has a problem with that, you can see HR and pick up your last check."

Bellamy squirmed uncomfortably. She was just going to have to be uncomfortable because I meant this.

Sharon was the first to step forward. She reached out her hand, introduced herself, and then pulled Bellamy into a hug. At first, my girl was surprised, but then she hugged her back.

A few more people came to introduce themselves, and then I told everyone to get back to work, only after telling them to let their fellow employees know.

The door was barely shut behind the last person when Bellamy swung on me. Her hands fisted on her hips, and the look on her face was fiery. "What the hell did you just do?"

My reply was mild. "I made sure everyone knows you aren't just some girl."

"You announced that I'm your girlfriend!"

"You don't want to be?"

"You don't announce it first and then ask *after*!"

"That wasn't a no."

She tossed her hands up in the air. "You are impossible!"

I started toward her, but she held her hands out, palms up. "Oh, no you don't. Keep your magic paws off me!"

I bit back a smile. "Now why would you want me to do that?"

"'Cause I can't breathe or think when you touch me!"

I opened my mouth, but she made a sound. "No trying to charm me either, mister."

I closed my mouth and stared at her. She was pretty cute.

"I've barely been here a week. A week, Liam! Now you go and tell everyone we're together... that we're... we're *family*."

"You are my family," I said quietly. "That won't ever change."

She groaned. "Liam."

"That's all it took last time. One week."

"We're adults now."

"We still have the same hearts."

"My life is complicated."

"I don't care."

With every rebuttal I made, I took a step forward. I don't think she realized I was getting closer; she was too busy spazzing out.

She stopped pacing and looked at me. "If you knew, you would care."

"Then tell me."

She shook her head and stared up at the ceiling. "What am I doing?"

I caught her around the waist, and she stiffened.

"How'd you get over here?"

I smiled. "Do you want to be my girlfriend?"

"It's not that simple."

"It is."

"Maybe in your caveman mind," she muttered.

I laughed.

"I seriously can't believe you just did that." She glanced at the door.

I pulled her face around and stared into her eyes. "Did what? Made sure everyone knew you were important to me? Made sure you got the respect you deserved? Let everyone know in no uncertain terms that if push came to shove, I would choose you every single time?"

She sighed. "How do I fight that?"

"You don't." On the tail of that, I repeated, "Do you want to be my girlfriend?" Actually, I wanted her to be more than that, but I had to start somewhere.

"I wish I could." The wistfulness in her voice made my feet tingle.

"How about you make that a yes?" She started to speak, but I put my lips against hers, quieting the words. Still holding my lips against hers, I whispered, "Until you can prove to me you can't be one."

Her lips moved against mine. "I don't want to prove it."

I know. That's exactly why I said it.

She nodded.

I pulled back. "Is that a yes?"

"Yes."

I picked her up and spun her around. Charlie jumped around us and barked.

"I never worked so hard for anything in my life."

"If you thought that was work, then you've had a life of leisure, my friend."

I laughed and set her down.

"Thank you," she said quietly. "For making sure no one thought I was taking advantage of you."

"I really don't think anyone thought that. It was probably the other way around." I laughed low. "But you're welcome."

I took her hand and led her toward the ski instructor quarters, Charlie loping along beside us. A few employees stared as we went past; a few more poked their heads out of their offices.

Word was spreading.

Good.

Inside the quarters, I picked up the clipboard with the schedule and flipped through. Then I picked up the phone and made a couple calls, arranging for all my afternoon lessons to be covered.

When I was done, I turned to see Bellamy sprawled out on the floor with Charlie. "What was that all about?" she asked.

I opened my locker to get dressed. "I cleared my afternoon. I'm taking you to town."

She pushed up on her elbow. "You didn't have to call out of work."

"I've barely taken any time off at all since I started working here. It's fine."

"Are you sure?"

I finished zipping up my coat and pulled her to her feet. "Positive."

I watched her get her coat and pull on her hat and gloves. Charlie stood beside her and wagged his tail. That damn dog was just as in love with her as I was.

"Ready to go outside!" she asked him enthusiastically. He leapt up and nearly knocked her over.

"Whoa," I said, rushing to catch her. "Careful."

She just laughed.

We went outside, and she went off to walk through the snow and play with Charlie while I worked.

I smiled to myself, watching her, noting the way some of the employees watched her as well. Pride swelled in my chest because she was mine.

And now everyone knew it.

23

Bellamy

MY BODY WAS HUMMING, PROBABLY FROM THE FULL-ON concert happening inside my heart.

I shouldn't have crumbled, but Liam made me crumbly. How could I look into his silvery, stormy eyes and tell him I didn't want to be with him? I did. I wanted that more than anything in the world.

Which was exactly why I should have stuck to my guns and not let it go that far. I didn't want to hurt him, but I was sincerely afraid that was where this was going.

He told everyone, out loud and without any hesitation, I was his family. *Family.* I really didn't know how badly I wanted that until he'd said the words. To be part of something. Of someone. To know I wasn't alone.

There's a reason you're alone. I reminded myself.

Everything felt so uncertain. I was torn between two lives: one I wanted and one I needed.

Wants and needs, my mother used to say. *What you want isn't always what you need.*

There was a fine line between those two things, wasn't there? A line I felt blurring more and more every day.

The longer I stayed here, the blurrier it would become.

I'd been thinking a lot about everything, about what I should do and where to turn. I had a few options, but all of them scared me.

I knew it was wrong to want to stay in this holding pattern just a little while longer. It was sort of like giving a shot to an alcoholic. Just that little bit could send them over the edge again. The more I had of Liam, the more I would want.

The more it would hurt when I had to leave.

"What's going on in that head of yours?" Liam asked from the driver's seat.

"The town is just as pretty during the daytime, even without all the lights in the trees," I commented, gazing out the window.

He made a sound like he didn't believe that's all I was thinking, but he didn't really want to call me out.

"Where to first?" he asked, driving slowly down the main street in town, Caribou Boulevard.

"I'd like to get some shampoo and a few necessities like that," I answered. "And I need to get some clothes. I'm sick of these jeans."

Laughing low, he pulled into a parking spot at the end of the street. "We'll head into the Trading Post here on the corner. They should have everything but the clothes. Hell, Hal might even be stocking those, too."

I looked not far down the sidewalk to the store with a large wooden sign that stretched across. TRADING POST, EST. 1930.

"Is that like the local Wal-Mart?" I asked.

Liam grinned. "Kinda, but don't call it that in front of Hal. If you want one of those big box stores, I'll drive you into the next town over. They've got some bigger stores."

"No," I said quickly. "This is perfect." The less people, the better.

After Liam helped me down out of his monster truck (it wasn't really, but it was big), I inhaled. The sweet scent of chocolate filled the air. "That smells so good."

"That's The Confectionary." He pointed across the street. "Alex's parents' candy shop."

"Mmm," I said appreciatively.

"I'd take you in there, but Alex would be pissed. That's definitely a shop he'd want to show you."

"He's proud of them," I said, feeling a small lump of emotion in my throat.

"Oh yeah." He agreed, placing his hand on the small of my back to guide me toward our first stop.

It felt like a blast from the past when a bell rang as we opened the door and walked inside. A few people nearest the door paused in what they were doing and looked up. A few greetings to Liam were called out.

"Everyone." He smiled and gestured toward me. "This is Bellamy."

"Hi, Bellamy," they all said in near unison.

I waved.

Liam draped his arm over my shoulder and guided me farther into the store. I told myself the jumpy feeling in my belly was because new people were staring, not because I felt slightly giddy that I was out in public and he had his arm around me.

I felt sixteen again.

"That girl stuff you want is over here," he said, pulling me along.

"Boys use shampoo, too." I pointed out.

He grunted. "I have one soap in my shower that does everything. Girls have like twenty products for each part of their body."

I turned toward him, stopping. Poking him in the chest, I said, "And just how would you know how many products women have in their showers?"

He blanched. "Uhh…"

I giggled.

Liam lunged as if he was going to attack me but instead wrapped his arms around my waist and kissed the side of my neck.

Pressing his forehead against mine, he said, "I haven't been a choir boy."

"I kinda figured."

"You're the only one who matters, Bells."

I whispered, "I know."

Pulling away, I started down the shampoo aisle. "By the way, I'm getting you shampoo and conditioner. I don't care what your *one* bottle says. It's not good for everything."

A man was walking past Liam, and he leaned in and commented, "Women. Always trying to buy us shit we don't need."

The man belly laughed and patted Liam on the shoulder. "Just agree, son. It saves time."

Liam appeared behind me with a wicker shopping basket with two big handles. It was charming, and I looped it over my forearm and picked up a bottle of familiar-looking shampoo. Then I realized it was the kind I'd used when I was under protective custody and the cops did all my shopping.

I set it down so fast I knocked over the ones behind it.

"Shoot," I swore beneath my breath.

"It's okay, Bells," Liam said, reaching over my shoulder to fix it. Before pulling back completely, he dropped a kiss to my cheek.

More butterflies ensued.

A man from the back of the store called out to Liam.

"Hey, Hal!" he called back. "I'll be right back," he said and jogged off to talk to the owner.

I enjoyed my time checking out the products and making my selections. I chose some detangling shampoo and conditioner, some lightweight styling cream, and added a wide-tooth comb from the bargain bin to my bag. Then I picked up some body cream, a few razors, and cheap shaving cream. It was made for men, but it worked the same as the "girl" stuff, and it was like a quarter of the price. Geez, these companies put a pink cap on it, make it smell like flowers, and then want to upcharge you by like seventy percent. They must be high from all that fake scent they're dumping into stuff.

After that, I grabbed a fresh toothbrush and full-size toothpaste and a vanilla-scented lip balm. I missed my face moisturizer from home, so I grabbed something similar and picked up a bottle of face wash.

I don't care what Liam said. One bottle of soap was *not* for everything.

After adding a few more things to the bag, I turned into the next aisle, which happened to be filled with candy.

Liam stepped up behind me, leaned over my shoulder, and pointed to a bag of Red Vines. "You still like those things?"

He remembered.

"You still think Twizzlers are better?"

He smiled. Then he grabbed a bag of Vines and a bag of Twizzlers, tossing them into my basket. "Yep."

His hand slid beneath the handles resting against my arm and tugged up. "By the weight of this basket, I can say with one hundred percent certainty that you definitely have a soap for every part of your body."

"I got you some stuff, too," I returned sweetly.

Liam groaned and tossed the bag over his shoulder.

After I paid for my items, Liam stowed the bag in the truck, and we wandered down the sidewalk, hand in hand.

People greeted Liam and gazed at me with interest. He introduced me more than once as his girlfriend.

As apprehensive as I felt, it was overshadowed by pride. Pride in being here with him, pride that he was so willing to make sure everyone knew he was mine.

(Well, he probably saw it as staking his territory, but I preferred to see it the other way.)

There were a few other shops where I managed to find some bargains on some clothes. Nothing fancy. Stuff that was warm and a pair of jeans that weren't as loose as the ones I'd been wearing.

"Please tell me we're done," Liam said when we stepped out of the last boutique.

I laughed. "Almost." I promised. "One last store." I pointed across the street.

Liam followed my hand and smiled slowly. "Now that's the kind of store I wouldn't mind helping you shop in."

I smacked him in the stomach. He made a sound, but I know it didn't hurt. "You aren't coming in there with me."

"Why the hell not?" he demanded.

I hid a smile. He sounded like a surly five-year-old. "Because what I have on beneath my clothes should have a little mystery."

Leaning into my ear, he whispered, "I saw what you had on this morning."

I felt my cheeks heat and desire unfold in my belly when I thought back to this morning. Liam laughed secretly, took my hand, and led me across the street.

Traffic actually stopped for him.

Forget the actual traffic lights hanging above. No. The people here deferred to Liam Mattison.

Once we were safely across, the traffic pattern started up again.

Liam followed my stare out onto the street. I glanced at him with a knowing look. He shrugged.

"Stay here," I ordered.

"I'm gonna see it all anyway," he intoned meaningfully.

"Stay," I instructed. He was right. He was probably going to see it all anyway.

He laughed but sat down on the bench outside the store. I couldn't help but think the shop placed it there on purpose, as if maybe a lot of women sentenced their significant others to it while they shopped for panties.

The inside was scented like roses, and my stomach flipped a little because it made me think of my mother. As I wandered around looking at the tasteful displays and drawers of undergarments and nightgowns, I reminded myself that my mother was safe. I'd just heard her voice.

Things change.

The thought made me stop and stare down at my feet. I didn't think this worry for her would ever go away. Maybe I should reach out to her. Maybe the risk of being together was smaller than the one of being apart.

I never knew what the right choice was. It was exhausting.

In the back of the store, I found a nice display of cotton and lace panties. I wanted something cute, but I wasn't the type to choose anything overly sexy. I went about selecting a week's worth, then turned to look for another bra. The one I had was fine, but it would be nice to have at least one more. I found a rack of buy one get one half off and chose two.

I thumbed through a rack of nightgowns but ended up passing because if I bought one of those, then I wouldn't need Liam's T-shirt.

On my way to the register, an odd feeling climbed up my neck.

My footsteps slowed, and I tried to brush it off. I even went as far as to turn between two large racks. I told myself to calm down, that thinking of my mother had me spooked.

The entire time I stood at the register as the girl rang up each item, the knot in my stomach grew harder and harder. Off to the side, someone dropped something, and I jumped so forcefully I knocked over a display of lip-gloss on the counter.

"Oh my gosh!" I exclaimed, hurrying to right the stand and pick up the mess. "I'm so sorry."

"Happens all the time," the girl said.

Halfway through putting away the lip-glosses, I turned and glanced over my shoulder. No one was there.

My heart started to hammer as I handed over some cash, and I realized this was the same feeling I'd gotten in the grocery store that night I was attacked. Like I was being watched.

What's worse? I felt I was being watched as I was buying underwear.

shudder

"Thank you," the sales girl said, and I jolted again.

"I'm sorry," I stammered and handed her the few remaining glosses I had yet to stack. Soon as my hands were empty, I grabbed the bag and bolted for the front door.

Through the windows at the front of the store, I saw Liam standing on the sidewalk, laughing. A little of the fear inside me eased, but then it jacked up tenfold. What if the men found me? What if they were watching right now?

What if they knew Liam was with me!

"Liam!" I gasped, rushing outside, nearly face plating on the pavement.

"Whoa." He gasped as two figures rushed toward me.

I screamed.

"Bells!" Liam's voice cut off my shriek. "Hey, I got you." I was lifted against his chest, secure arms locked around me.

My eyes flew around, seeking out anyone who looked suspicious.

All I saw was Alex.

"You all right, Bellamy?" He worried. Then his eyes widened. "Is there some creep in there hassling all you bunnies while you shopping for lacey things?"

A low growl built in Liam's chest.

"We've got to handle this," Alex told him.

They started marching toward the door.

"Stop!" I pleaded. "There's no panty perv in there."

"Panty perv?" Alex echoed. "That's some creativity right there." He held out his fist so I could bump it, but Liam shoved it away.

"What's wrong?" Liam asked.

I stepped away from him and took a shuddering breath. "Nothing. I—" I glanced around again, noting nothing out of the ordinary. In fact, I didn't even feel like someone was watching me now. I shook my head. "Nothing. I think I'm just tired."

Alex stepped forward and tried to peek inside my bag. "What'd you buy in there?"

"You are not seriously trying to look at my girl's underwear." Liam snarled.

Alex glanced at me and winked. Swinging around to Liam, he said, "Panties! Ah, that's what they sell in there? Nasty."

Liam rolled his eyes.

I laughed.

"C'mon, Bells." Alex draped an arm over my shoulder. "What you need is some chocolate, and I know just the place you can get it."

"It's Bellamy to you," Liam intoned, trailing along behind us.

"Don't worry. I bought him some rash cream at the store. He should be less grumpy by tomorrow," I whispered—*very loudly*—to Alex.

Alex cackled. "I think I'm gonna like having you around." He glanced over his shoulder to look at Liam. "I heard all about your employee meeting. I feel left out, bro." He put a hand over his heart. "I mean, to be left out of such an important announcement." Alex turned to me. "My man off the market, and I wasn't even there to watch the death of his singlehood."

I giggled.

Liam pulled Alex's arm off my shoulders and replaced it with his. "Your time is coming, A. And when it does, I'm going to do all this to you."

"Now why would I want to go and get un-single?" He wondered.

Liam glanced down at me and winked.

A rush of heavenly scented air burst forward and twirled around us. My stomach growled.

"They have hot chocolate, too," he said against my ear.

"Bellamy." Alex swept his arm out toward his parents' store. "May I present The Confectionary."

"If it's half as good as it smells, then I'd say this place has my vote for favorite shop in all of Caribou."

"C'mon. My parents are dying to meet you." He grinned. "They're definitely interested in the girl who's making Liam settle down."

I glanced at Liam, and he smiled.

"Fair warning." Alex went on. "My mother is going to insist you're too skinny, feed you everything, and then give you a giant bag to take home."

Liam laughed. "He's right."

The two guys went forward. Alex opened the door, and Liam went ahead. Before I followed suit, another tingle of something creepy-crawled up the back of my neck. I whipped around quickly and stared down to the end of the block.

I could have sworn I saw someone disappearing around the corner.

24

Liam

SHE WAS TOO QUIET.

Glancing across the interior of the Extreme, the feeling that something was off grew a little stronger. She was almost somber, watching out the window as I drove.

I reached across the seat and took her hand, folding it in mine. "You're not just tired."

Bellamy turned toward me. The blond strands of her hair fell over her shoulders like long ribbons. "I ate too much chocolate."

I laughed a little. "Well, according to Alex's mom, you didn't eat enough."

She groaned. "You guys weren't kidding about that."

"Nope."

"That place is amazing, though. It's like this little sugar world in the middle of a snow mountain. I love it in there."

I made a sound of agreement. "Yeah, it's pretty amazing." I paused. "You know, I've been playing around with the idea of opening a small shop at the resort to sell their candy. Maybe see if they would develop an exclusive flavor or chocolate for us."

"That's an amazing idea," she said, turning her body toward me. "Why haven't you done it?"

"Because my father's still in charge."

She was quiet a beat, then said, "And you think by bringing this idea to the table, it will just prove his point that you are capable of running BearPaw."

I glanced at her out of the corner of my eye, then back at the road. "I never said that."

"You didn't have to."

"Just like you didn't have to say you aren't just tired," I countered.

"We're talking about you right now." She sniffed.

"How convenient," I retorted.

"Did you ask Alex's parents what they think about having a location up at the resort?"

Shaking my head, I answered, "Not yet. It would be a no-brainer, though. Some of our guests don't venture down to Caribou. They stay in the resort because we make sure everything they need is there. This would be a chance to get their candy in the hands of new customers."

I felt her watching me, so I glanced over. "What?"

She smiled. "How many other great ideas like that do you have in your head?"

"Just a couple," I muttered.

Bellamy laughed and kissed the back of my hand. "Are you afraid you can't be passionate about snow-boarding if you're running an entire resort?"

That hit a soft spot. A spot no one else realized was still there. One I barely liked to acknowledge myself. My voice was quiet. "It's hard to give up on what you love."

"Yeah, I can understand that."

The empathy in her tone was very real. I felt it all the way into the pit of my stomach. I gave her hand a squeeze. "You mean how you used to be a chef?"

She nodded, gazing back out the window.

"You've only been here about a week, Bells. I don't think your career will vanish that fast." I paused. "Unless you burned everything you cooked."

She gasped and smacked my arm. "Blasphemy!"

"All I'm saying," I teased, "is that I've yet to eat any of your cooking. I've yet to even see you in a kitchen."

"Is that a challenge?" Her tone was wry.

"If it will get me fed? Hell yes."

She giggled. "I'd love to cook for you." Her sigh was sad. "I miss it so much."

I wasn't sure what to say to that. I hated she missed it, but I also was glad she'd had to run here.

"I gave up being a chef a lot longer than a week ago," she told me reluctantly. Her face turned back to the window. The sky was darkening already and there were heavy clouds that promised snow.

"How long's it been?"

"Almost two years."

I frowned. That was roughly the same amount of time she'd been without her mother.

What the hell was going on here?

"So what did you do before you came here?"

She shrugged. "I worked in a law office. Filed a lot of papers."

"That's like the complete opposite of being in a kitchen."

"I know." Again, her tone was wistful and sad.

"What happened today?" I kept my voice gentle. What

I really wanted to know was what happened today, last week, and two years ago.

She was quiet a moment, then, surprisingly, she answered, "You ever get the feeling you're being watched?"

Something inside me went absolutely still. Was someone watching her? The thought made me feel sick and murderous at the same time.

"Watching you how?" I asked carefully.

Bellamy tucked my hand a little farther into her lap, covering it with her free one. "I just got this feeling. A creepy feeling like someone was around… watching me."

"When you came out of the store?"

She nodded.

Inwardly, I cursed. I should have paid more attention to our surroundings. To her.

"I didn't see anyone, though, so it was probably just paranoia."

I pulled under the awning of the resort and put the truck in park, letting her idle. "But?" I pressed.

Bellamy locked eyes with me. "But it was the same feeling I got that night. The night I ran here." A shiver racked her shoulders, and an uneasy feeling snaked around within me.

Reaching across the cab, I cupped her face and leaned close. "I'm not gonna let anything happen to you, sweetheart."

She cast her eyes downward and shook her head. "Don't say things like that, Liam. Sometimes bad things happen no matter what."

I pushed up her chin and nearly flinched at the ghosts I saw in her blue stare.

"Ah, baby," I murmured and leaned in to touch my lips to hers.

She sighed and leaned in, and I deepened the kiss.

When I pulled back, I tried to reassure her. "You're with me now, Bells. I'll watch out for you."

She smiled sadly, pulled away, and climbed out of the Extreme without any help.

We walked in silence up to her suite, and then that silence was obliterated by an over-exuberant Charlie. I left Bellamy and overgrown pup on the floor to use the bathroom, and when I came back, they were still rolling around on the carpet.

I laughed. "I'm ordering dinner. What do you want?" I was starving. She might be stuffed from chocolate, but I needed a steak.

"Baked potato soup," she answered. "And Charlie wants a hamburger."

"He has dog food."

"Pleeease," she said, peering up from the floor with a big grin on her face.

Charlie barked.

They were working against me.

I laughed. "Fine."

A short while later, we were eating—well, *I* was eating. Bellamy was feeding Charlie the damn hamburger they suckered me into.

When my cell rang, Bellamy jolted upright, which told me she was still feeling jumpy from earlier in town. I picked up the phone, planning to silence the ringer when I saw who it was. "It's just my dad," I told her, wanting to make sure she knew nothing terrible was on the horizon.

She looked relieved, then went back to doting on the dog.

"Hey, Dad," I answered.

"Liam, we need to talk."

I sat up a little straighter. "Is everything okay?"

"Everything is fine, but I would like you to come to my office."

"I'm kinda busy right now," I replied, shoving another bite of steak into my mouth.

"Yes, I can hear you chewing, son." He sighed.

I grinned at the phone, though he couldn't see.

"When you are finished with your dinner, come to my office."

I glanced in Bellamy's direction. She was watching me from the floor. It didn't feel right leaving her tonight. I felt like she needed me.

"I'll come first thing in the morning." I compromised.

"Tonight would be better."

Bellamy stood from her seat beside Charlie and nodded. "Just go."

I frowned.

"I'll be waiting, Liam," he said and disconnected the call.

I pulled it away from my ear and looked at it. "He hung up on me," I grumped.

"Your father wants to see you?"

I grunted. "Yeah. I'm supposed to go to his office."

"Did he say what for?" she called out as she went into the bathroom to wash her hands.

I raised my voice over the sound of running water. "No, so it must not be that important."

When Bells appeared around the corner, I said, "I'll see him in the morning."

"Why not tonight?"

I hesitated. Then I smiled, lopsided. "'Cause I want to be with you."

Bellamy came over, took my fork, and put it on the plate, then proceeded to straddle my lap. I palmed her ass and pulled her more firmly against me. "Well, hello," I purred.

She ran her fingers through my hair and linked them at the base of my neck. "I'm fine, Liam. Your father wants to see you. You should go." There was a little bit of something in her voice.

I wasn't quite sure what it was.

I arched a single brow. "What if I'm not fine?"

Her hands parted, sliding up until she held the sides of my head, leaned in, and kissed me softly. She definitely wasn't making a very good case for me to leave this room.

"I'll be here when you get back." She spoke against my mouth. Too soon, she sat back, putting unwanted distance between our mouths.

"Come back here," I growled and clutched her sides.

She giggled and pushed me back. "I'd love to see my father one more time. If yours wants to see you, you should go. I won't get in the way of you and your family, Liam."

I'd love to see my father one more time. The words were like a right hook to my midsection. I remembered her dad. Joe was his name. He seemed like a nice guy. Whenever Bells was around him, she glowed as though she were very eager for his attention.

Looking back at it now, as an adult, there seemed to be something a little desperate about it. How I'd met her in the snow early in the morning. When she'd been practicing so she could impress him.

Daughters shouldn't have to "impress" their fathers.

My hand slid up her side to rest on her neck. My thumb brushed mindlessly at her collarbone. "Where's your father now, sweetheart?"

She swallowed thickly. Her hands clenched between

us, and she shook her head. Her cerulean eyes met mine, imploring. "Go see your father."

I was afraid it would hurt her if I didn't. As if me turning down this opportunity to see my father would somehow wound her heart.

"Why don't you come with?" I murmured, stroking the side of her hair. "You can finally meet him."

"I'd like that. But not tonight. Tonight, he's asking for you."

I let out a growl. "Fine. I won't be gone long."

"Maybe after, you could stay the entire night." The heat in her eyes was unmistakable.

My cock, which was already at attention, jerked. I wanted to stay. All night. Every night. "Of course I'll stay," I murmured, pushing off the back of the chair and bumping our chests together. My arms wrapped around her, and my forehead touched hers. "But I want you to know that we don't have to have sex. I'm okay with waiting."

"What would we be waiting for?"

I kissed the tip of her nose. "I just want you to trust me, sweetheart. I want you to feel safe with me."

She sighed. "Liam. I've never felt safer with anyone ever."

Then why haven't you told me why you ran here? I thought it was just a thought. You know, something that stayed in my head, for my brain only.

Apparently, the question spilled out, filling the room and making Bellamy draw back.

Her brow furrowed. "You think I don't trust you?"

"That's not what I meant."

"Then what other reason could I possibly have for not spilling my guts." She climbed off my lap and moved away from me. "Is that what you're thinking?"

I stood. "No. I told you what I was thinking. I want you to feel safe."

"Did it ever occur to you I want you to *be* safe?"

"What?"

She tossed her arms up. "This is why I was hesitant to get involved. This is why I tried to resist you."

"You tried to resist me?" I echoed.

She made a rude sound. "Yes. I did a shitty job. You're just too…" She waved her hand around in my direction. "You."

"Thank you?"

A choked sound erupted from her throat. "I'm trying to be serious, Liam!"

"So am I."

She sank down on the edge of the bed, and the mattress dipped slightly toward the floor. "From the minute I looked at you, there's been no one else." Her voice filled the room. It was quiet, but it was all I heard. "I tried to move on. Dated a couple guys."

I made a sound. I didn't want to hear about them. I hated anyone who touched her when I wasn't around.

She glanced up, a ghost of a smile appearing for just a moment. "It's always been you. Even when I told myself it wasn't. Even when I told myself I hoped you weren't here when I got on that bus…" She laughed humorlessly. "I try to lie to myself. I'm so bad at it."

I moved in front of her and dropped onto my knees.

Her head lifted enough to meet my eyes.

"I hoped you would be here. When I was staring into that gun… all I saw was you. You were the first thought that came into my mind. You were almost the last thought I would ever have."

A gun? Jesus.

"I'm here, baby," I all but crooned, wrapping my hand around the back of her neck. "I'm here."

"I love you."

My heart stopped. My lungs stopped. I was pretty sure the entire world stopped.

"Liam?" she whispered, peeking up from beneath her blond lashes.

My voice was rough and hoarse. "What did you just say?"

"I love you. I always will. No matter what."

I cleared my throat. Then cleared it again. I mean, I knew… *I knew* how she felt. I felt the same. We'd pretty much said it, but not those three words. Not so clear cut.

I opened my mouth. Nothing came out. I couldn't find the words that were right there on my fucking tongue.

"Breathe, Liam," she murmured.

I inhaled. As oxygen filled my lungs, the words I'd been searching for tumbled right out. "I love you, too, Bellamy. So much it literally scares me."

Her breathing hitched, and I pulled her off the bed, down onto the floor, and into my lap. I kissed her fast and deep, hunching into her, around her, trying to get as close as humanly possible. Fuck. I could crawl under her skin, and it still wouldn't be enough.

Her ankles linked behind my waist, and I kissed with all the pent-up feelings I'd been holding inside. Rolling, I pinned her into the carpet, my body moving against hers impatiently.

Charlie loped over, breathing over us. Without lifting my lips, I reached around and pushed him back.

He retreated. Even he knew I wanted to be alone with her.

My hips thrust against her, and a sound of rough

impatience ripped out of me because there were too many layers between us. Too many clothes.

"Liam," she murmured against me. "Liam."

I lifted just enough. Her face was blurred through the haze of emotions. "Yeah?"

"We can't right now. You have somewhere to be."

"I'll go tomorrow." I lowered my mouth. She turned her head, and my lips brushed her cheek. Not one to be put off, I trailed kisses over her cheek, down her jaw, and then nibbled to her ear.

She moaned and clutched me to her, then pushed me back. "You have to."

The only thing I *had* to do was get inside her.

She pushed me again, and I made a frustrated sound. Her palm caressed my cheek. "Your eyes look like the sky before a snowstorm."

"I want you, Bells."

"I want you, too." Her thumb traced my lower lip. "*After* you meet with your dad, okay? Later tonight."

"I've been waiting eight years. Eight. Long. Years."

"A couple hours are nothing compared to that."

I took a deep breath and pushed up. Then I bent, helping her to her feet. There was no ignoring the massive tent in my jeans.

She brushed her hand over it, and I moaned. "If you do that again, I will have you naked and under me in seconds."

"I do trust you," She told me quietly a few moments later, after stepping away.

"I know."

She shook her head. "Remember when I said I'd be your girlfriend until I gave you a reason I couldn't?"

"Bellamy…" I warned.

She was fucking crazy if she thought she could tell me she loved me and then turn around and walk away.

I wasn't letting her go.

"This is the reason, Liam. The reason I haven't told you. The reason I shouldn't have come here. I love you so much, and I want you to *be safe*. Above everything else. Even above your happiness… and mine. I don't think you can be safe when I'm around."

"You're wrong," I argued.

"I hope I am." She relented. "It's why I'm still here." She made a sound and turned away. "That and I really don't think I can lose you twice."

I went to her, wrapping my arms around her from behind. Against her ear, I made a promise. One I would kill to keep. "You're not going to lose me. Not ever."

Her arms covered mine, and I rocked us back and forth for a few quiet minutes. After a while, she brushed at her cheeks and sniffled. "You should go. Your father is waiting."

I really didn't want to go.

She turned in my arms, smiling up at me. "I'll be here when you get back."

"Swear it," I demanded.

"I swear."

I kissed her again, allowing my tongue to linger on hers.

"I'll be back," I said, pulling away. "C'mon, Charlie," I called. He got up and rushed to my side. "I'm gonna let him get some exercise and put him outside before we come back up for the night."

She nodded. Her lips were swollen from our kisses.

"Lock up behind me," I instructed.

Bellamy followed me to the door, and I gave her one last lingering look before stepping out into the hall.

"I love you," I told her. I would never be able to say it enough.

"I love you, too."

I could never hear it enough.

I waited until I heard the door lock before I moved off down the hall.

25

Bellamy

I WAS A COWARD.

Part of me was okay with that. Not very *girl power-ish* was it? Thing was it was the coward part of me that kept me here. That kept me with Liam.

I couldn't regret that. Not ever.

I might never be the poster woman for strength and courage. I didn't even want to be. I just wanted to live my life.

My life. Not the life of Bella Lane—a woman who lived a bland existence, worked in a stodgy law office, lived alone with no family and afraid to make any real friends. A woman who would sometimes sneak off to the corner grocery store to get some good ingredients and make a meal for one because it was the only way I could feel alive.

I'd felt more alive in the past week, living out of a bag, with one ill-fitting pair of jeans and underwear I had to wash in the bathroom sink than I had in the almost two years.

I needed to tell Liam.

To come clean about everything. My father, witnessing his murder, the trial, witness protection… and running for my life. It wasn't fair of me to confess my love when he really had no idea what the hell he was dealing with.

I was no longer a sixteen-year-old girl with daddy issues.

I was a grown woman on the run from murderers.

Funny, though, how both those versions of me loved the same man.

And that's why you have to tell him. A man like Liam, a man that inspires this kind of love, deserves the truth.

Maybe it was a copout that I continued to say nothing because I wanted him to be safe.

Oh, I did want that. More than anything.

But keeping him in the dark was sort of like leading him into a cage with a hungry tiger, then turning on the light.

I went to the window and leaned my forehead against the cold glass. It was snowing outside. Small, icy flakes rained from the sky, giving a fresh coat to the blanket already glistening on the mountain.

If I was going to stay here, then I had to be honest.

I puttered around the room a little while, unpacking the items I'd purchased today, folding the clothes, and placing it all on top of the dresser.

Most of it was basic, everyday wearable items. There was something different about them, though. They weren't all black. I'd gravitated toward some colors. I hadn't worn a lot of color in a long time.

I'd always just picked up black. I always told myself it

would help conceal me, and perhaps it matched my heart after everything…

But today, I bought blue. And green. And pink!

I didn't want just black anymore.

Watching my father being beaten and murdered flipped a switch inside me. Almost being murdered and going on the run flipped it back.

I used my new products in the shower, taking time to shave and moisturize. Knowing that Liam was spending the night made me want to take extra care with my appearance, something else I hadn't thought about much in recent years.

After pulling on his T-shirt, I brushed out my hair, and since I had some new hairbands, I took the time to put it into two fishtail braids that fell over my shoulders. The braids fell past my breasts and took forever to finish, but once they were secured and I puffed them out a little with my fingers, I smiled.

Worth the work.

Flutters of anticipation were no stranger as I waited for Liam to come back for the night. I couldn't wait to be in his arms. To feel him against me. In me. Around me.

I really did try to move on from him all those years ago.

About a year after that morning, I was with someone else. I went to the bathroom after and cried silent tears. It felt wrong. So wrong.

After that, I didn't get intimate with anyone until this guy I'd been dating for six months. At that point, it was pretty much do it or get left. Maybe I should have let him leave, but I didn't.

I didn't cry after, but that night, I'd dreamt of Liam. And I spent the next day trying not to read every article online about him. I continued to date him. We were together for almost two years. He eventually broke up with me because he said it felt as though I was always somewhere else.

He was right. I was.

It almost seemed unreal I was here at BearPaw and that Liam was back in my life. Never in a million years had I thought this would happen.

I climbed between the covers and turned on some made-for-TV movie and glanced out at the falling snow again. He'd been gone a while, and I was getting anxious to see him.

Almost as if I'd conjured him up myself, he knocked on the door.

I jumped up as he knocked softly again. My heart was pounding, fingers tingling, and my eyes desperate for his face. I ran to the door, the soft fabric of his shirt caressing my thighs as I went.

The anticipation made me stupid. The passion I felt clouded my judgement.

For the first time in I don't know how long, I pulled open the door without calling out first, without glancing through the dreaded peephole.

The smile on my face fell instantly, faster than it took the shirt to settle around my legs. With a shriek, I moved to slam the door.

But it was too late.

I should have paid more attention today in town. I should have heeded that creepy sensation of being watched.

I didn't.

And now it would cost me my life.

26

Liam

THE DOOR TO MY DAD'S OFFICE WAS AJAR. NOT ALL THE way open, just enough for Charlie to stick his head in and shove it open wide.

I heard my dad chuckling before I even made it through.

"Charlie!" he called out. "How's it going, my good man?"

I smiled listening to my father talk to my dog. It was as if he thought of Charlie as one of the guys. I guess he was in a way. Charlie had helped pull me out of a deep depression, a depression that still held deep inside me with its dark tendrils. Sort of as if it was lying in wait.

Charlie became a part of the family this past year, not just to me, but to everyone around me. They all knew the giant drool-monger helped me in ways no one else had been able. If for no other reason than to give me a purpose. It was hard to wallow in self-pity when there was a dog tugging on your sheets to get up because he had to piss or dragging in a leash because he wanted to walk.

"He's doing great, Dad. He just ate a hamburger," I said, coming into the office and shutting the door.

Dad laughed again, and I smiled because Charlie had his head lying in my father's lap. Likely drooling all over his suit. He didn't seem to mind, though. He just stroked the dog's ears.

"Well, I'm sure your mother will be pleased you're feeding him well."

My mother called Charlie her grandson. Enough said.

"What's this about?" I asked, sitting down in the chair near his desk.

The night lights were on out over the slopes. I got a sudden urge to grab my board and hit the powder. Snowboarding at night was something I would always love. The crispness in the air, the quiet around the trees, and the millions of stars filling the night sky above the pure, white snow. There really was nothing like it.

"I heard you called a staff meeting today."

I groaned. *That's what this is about?*

"Well, if you already know, then you don't need to ask me about it."

"Apparently, I do because it's become clear you just aren't going to inform me or your mother on what's going on in your life."

Ah, shit. I winced. "Mom's upset?"

"If your mother was that upset, she'd already have been on your doorstep." He glanced up. "Or at the door of wherever it is you've been sleeping."

I groaned.

"Have you forgotten that BearPaw is sort of like a

giant family? Families gossip, son. Especially about the most popular member."

"People need to mind their own damn business," I muttered.

"Considering you held a meeting and made everyone aware of your business, I would say that statement is a moot point."

I sat up in the chair. "I'm sorry I didn't talk to you and Mom before I made an announcement. I didn't really plan it that way. It just needed to be said."

"This must be some girl." He started. "A suite under your name, ordering room service to be sent up every morning, purchasing a heap of outdoor gear in one of our nicest shops, bringing her to your lessons… staying in her room."

"I get the point, Dad. You know everything." And every single person in this place was a little tattle-tale.

"I'm not trying to lecture you. You're a grown man. What you do with your time and with whom really isn't my business as long as you aren't hurting yourself or anyone else."

"But?"

There was always a but with parents. Even when you were an adult.

"But this seems very extravagant for someone you just met last week."

"No one told you her name?" I inquired.

His forehead wrinkled. He looked tired. A feeling I didn't like pinged inside me, so I focused on the topic in front of us.

"No. But I don't really think it matters."

"It's Bellamy, Dad."

His face was blank for the first few seconds. Then

realization washed over his features, and he sat forward. "The girl you wanted to leave the pros for?"

I nodded. "The girl that got away," I murmured, repeating Alex's favorite phrase.

"You mean the girl that ran away."

My eyes flashed to his. I didn't like the implication of his words. My tone was flat, borderline unreasonable, when I replied. "It wasn't like that."

He spread his hands. "Then how was it?"

"She saw me kissing someone else that morning. I didn't know..." My voice trailed off as regret washed over me. I didn't fight for her back then.

Why the fuck didn't I fight?

Dad made a sound. "You were both very young. Not ready for love."

"Well. She's back now."

"I take it the feelings you had eight years ago are still the same?"

I met his eyes. "They're stronger."

"I see."

I shook my head. "She's in some kind of trouble, Dad. She won't say much, keeps saying she's trying to protect me. But she's jumpy. Skittish. She's running from some bad people."

"And you want to protect her."

I want to do so much more than protect her. "You're damn right I do."

"And telling the staff that she's your girlfriend was your way of doing that."

I made a sound. "She was worried they were thinking bad about her because everything is in my name."

My father smiled mildly. "So you set them straight."

I got up, restless. Prowling to the other side of the room, I said, "Why does this amuse you so much?"

"It's just nice to see you care about something other than snowboarding."

"I care about more than just boarding," I argued.

"So when do we get to meet her?" Dad asked. I wasn't sure if I should be annoyed or relieved he didn't argue back. "You know your mother is going to be relentless."

I made a sound. "She probably put you up to this."

He chuckled, and that pretty much proved that. "She's curious. She's heard all the gossip, too. But I was as well, especially since you were comping so much at the resort and calling staff meetings."

I grimaced. "She tried to pay me. More than once. I can't take her money."

"I understand."

I turned to him. "Do you really?"

He smiled wide. "I was young once. When I first met your mother, I was a besotted fool."

I barked a laugh.

"I am concerned, though. If she really is in trouble, then it could follow her here. I want you to be happy, Liam, but not at the expense of your wellbeing."

"Not you, too," I muttered and scrubbed a hand over my face.

"Come again?"

"Bellamy just told me the same thing."

"I like her already."

I rolled my eyes.

"Talk to her. If there is one thing I learned after all these years of marriage, you have to be honest. And you have to be a team. If you aren't, it will never work."

"Yeah." I agreed, thinking back to eight years ago. If we'd been a little more honest, maybe acted like a team, things might have turned out a lot differently.

"We'll get together this weekend. Bring her to Sunday dinner. I'll tell your mother. She can call you to finalize."

I nodded.

"So," he said in the tone he always used when he wanted to change the subject. I knew exactly where this was heading—to me taking over the resort. "Have you thought about what we discussed at our last meeting?"

There was a quick rap against his door, and then it opened. Alex popped his head in. "Sorry to bother you, Ren, sir, but I'm trying to find Liam."

I stepped forward so he could see me.

Alex's face softened with relief. "I tried to call you."

My chest tightened. "Is everything okay?"

He glanced at my father, then back. "Can we talk?"

We both looked at my father, and he waved us off. "Go on. Liam, I'll see you Saturday."

"See you then," I said, but right before I left, I stopped and turned. "Thanks, Dad. For everything."

"You're welcome, son."

Charlie was dancing around Alex when I stepped out in hallway. That's how I knew it was serious. Alex always goofed off with the dog, but tonight he didn't even seem to notice him.

"What's going on?" I asked, tucking my hands in the pockets of my jeans.

"I was at the tavern a few minutes ago, and these guys came in. I didn't think anything of it at first. I mean, there are new faces in and out all the time, you know?"

I nodded. A pit of dread was forming a hard knot in my stomach, and it was making me very impatient.

"But there was something off about them… Something didn't feel right."

"Are they guests here?"

Alex shook his head. "Don't think so. They paid cash

for their drinks… started asking some questions.

"What kind of questions?"

His brow furrowed even deeper. "They wanted to know about Bellamy."

My hands fell from my pockets, shoulders going rigid. "They asked about Bells?"

"Yeah. They were being casual about it, but there was something off. Then I remembered how you said she was in some kind of trouble…"

I surged forward and grabbed him by the front of his shirt. "What did you tell them?"

Alex wrenched away and made a sour face. "Like I'd tell them shit."

"C'mon," I said and took off down the hall. He fell into step beside me. "They still in the bar?"

"Nah, they left. That's when I came to find you."

"Where'd they go?"

"Not sure, but I told the guy working the front desk to watch them."

I hit the elevator button about fifteen times and then cursed. These things were fucking slow! With an impatient growl, I hit the button one last time and took off for the stairs.

"Where's Bellamy now?" Alex said, running right beside me, Charlie bringing up the rear.

"I left her in her room."

Alone.

Suddenly, it felt as if all the blood in my veins was replaced with ice water. I let out a string of curses and picked up my pace.

This place was huge. Just because men were here looking didn't mean they'd find her. She was fine. She was safe.

Please, God, let her be safe.

27

Bellamy

"Don't look so surprised," a man with dark, hollow eyes intoned as his palmed slapped the door and pushed.

I fought against it, but my strength succumbed to his.

The door flew wide when I stumbled back, keeping my eyes on the man.

He didn't smile. He just stared, stepped into the room, and folded his arms together, waiting.

He might have all the time in the world, but I sure as hell didn't. I snatched the first thing I saw, a ceramic coffee mug, and hurled it at him. It smacked him in the face and bounced off. I heard it shatter, but I didn't look to find out where. I rushed him, taking advantage of the distraction. Plowing into him, I shoved, trying to skirt past him and flee into the hall.

With a grunt, he shoved me back, barely having to move from his position at the entrance.

I flew backward, my body like a ragdoll. I hit the

corner of the bed and stumbled, falling onto the floor on my hands and knees.

Scrambling up, I prepared to fight some more. But the man now had a gun pointed right at me.

"The last time someone pointed one of those at me, I threw a pan of hot food in their face." I warned.

He didn't say anything, just held the gun as someone else came around the corner.

Flashbacks ripped through my mind. A red haze fell over me, and through it, all I saw was the night my father was killed. I smelled the urine and sweat in the room. I heard the slaps and grunts as my father was beaten. I heard the man piss in the toilet while I shook and swallowed down my own vomit.

I saw.

I saw the vacant, empty stare in my dead father's eyes. The blood… dear God, the blood.

"Remember me?" the second man asked as he shut the door behind him.

I blinked, focusing on the sudden perfect vision I had of the giant black spider tattooed on the back of his neck.

He had hair now, but that tattoo would be seared into my brain for all eternity.

"You were dead," I whispered, shocked.

He laughed. It was an ominous sound. "Because I had to be. Hard to put a dead man on trial."

The lengths at which these people would go to be free shocked me. Even now.

He must have seen it in my face because he laughed. "You think the only people that have witness protection are the police?"

I couldn't think. All I could do was stand there paralyzed—body *and* mind—from the shock of seeing him and having such vivid memories of that horrible day.

He chuckled. It was warm and cocky. "Oh, sweetheart. Where I'm from, we have this thing called hitman hiding."

The man who never smiled made a noise. Just a nondescript sound that meant nothing. Spider guy seemed to know what it meant, though.

"I don't care for the term either. Everyone knows guys like us are way more than just hitmen."

I opened my mouth to scream. I planned to scream so loud all the windows in this entire building would shake.

Spider guy launched himself across the room and tackled me. His large, bricklike body mowed me into the carpet. Before I could say or do anything, he hit me right across the face.

Pain exploded behind my eyes and radiated through my skull. My head lolled to the side for a minute before reality came back, and I tried to fight him off.

He made a sound and stood, grabbing me by the front of the T-shirt and yanking. One of the shoulder seams ripped, and something inside me broke.

This was Liam's shirt.

Tears welled in my eyes, and I tried to blink them away. They fell over my cheeks.

Liam.

The thought of him became clearer, and real fear settled deep inside me. He was coming back here. He could get caught in the crossfire.

I glanced around at the phone on the bedside table. Spider dude grabbed me by the back of the neck and squeezed so hard my knees buckled. I would have fallen, but he held me up, holding my limp body hostage.

I tried to hit at his arm, to smack it away.

He ignored the movements and leaned down into my face. "You got my buddy sent to prison for life. He's not getting any time off for good behavior. Know why?"

I made a sound and tried to break free. I couldn't breathe.

"Why's that, Spidey?" the man with hollow eyes asked.

"'Cause someone shanked him in his cell while he was sleeping." The fingers around my neck tightened, and a cry ripped from my throat.

He dropped me, and I fell onto my knees, gasping.

A gun appeared in Spidey's hand. There wasn't a silencer on it, though, and I wondered why.

He pressed the barrel against my temple, pushing it so hard I fell over, and he jammed it closer, pushing the side of my face into the carpet.

I kicked out, my heel connecting with his knee.

He cursed, and the gun left my head.

"You've caused us a lot of problems for a fucking little girl." He grunted and yanked one of my braids. I stood as he pulled.

"Let's go." The man by the door grunted.

"Go?" I asked, my voice hoarse and shrill at the same time.

"She thought we were gonna waste her right here," Spidey said, amused. All joking left his voice, and he shoved close again, so close his lips brushed against my cheek. "If you wanted to be eliminated the easy way, you should have let us kill you the first couple times we tried. That last time? That was the end of us being nice."

"If that was your idea of being nice, you really should take a class on manners."

Both men stopped and glanced at each other.

Spidey looked back at me. "You joking right now?

You got jokes before you die?" He shook his head. "Man, you are one crazy bitch."

He gestured with his gun, and the other man opened the door and gazed down the hall. "Clear."

"Let me tell you how this is gonna go," he whispered in my ear as he dragged me to the door. "You're going to walk out of here like we're all friends. And you ain't gonna cause a scene."

"And if I don't?" I spat. *Oh my God. Where is Liam? Please, please, let him not come back yet.*

"If you don't, we're gonna start shooting people. Everyone we see. And then once they're dead, we're gonna come back for your boyfriend."

My voice shook. "What boyfriend?"

"Don't play stupid with us, and we won't play stupid with you." He shoved me. I fell out into the hallway, ass in the air.

"Fuck," Spidey said. "Where's your pants?"

I stood, glancing down to the hall where a red EXIT sign was lit up.

"Go put some pants on. Shoes, too. And a coat."

"What difference does it make? She don't need pants to die," the other man remarked.

"Because people will notice some half-naked broad walking around with two men. Especially in the snow."

In the snow? We were going outside?

"Take her," Spidey ordered.

The other man came over, picked me up around the waist, and carried me back into my room. He threw me down on the bed, and I bounced up. "Get dressed."

I threw out one hand, grabbing the jeans I'd been wearing for days. As I snatched them to me, the man reached out and grabbed my wrist.

His eyes were still hollow, still black when they met

mine. His thumb caressed my wrist where he held. "If we had more time... oh, the things I'd do with you."

A scream built in my throat, and I jerked away from him. The action made me fall across the bed. The man leaned over me, caging me in with his arms. He smiled.

Oh God. It was the sickest thing I'd ever seen.

Lifting the gun, he used the muzzle and ran it up the inside of my thigh. I jolted up, trying to scurry back. He forced me down on the bed, holding me down with his arm. His chest was touching me. And so was the gun...

It kept going higher and higher until I felt it over my panties. He rubbed the cold metal against my core.

"You ever been fucked to death?" he asked, his voice near emotionless. "Imagine being shot from the inside."

He smiled again, and I screamed.

His hand slapped over my mouth, and I started to fight.

"What the fuck?" Spidey spat from the doorway.

The man holding me down stood. I scrambled back and got off the bed so it was between us.

Quickly, I pulled on the jeans. I wanted as many clothes on as humanly possible.

"We don't have time for that. Let's go!" he ordered.

The man came around for me, and I shrank back. My butt came up against the side table. I bumped into it, and a pen fell against my hand. Carefully, I pulled it beneath my fingers, slipping it behind my back.

"Now," the man demanded.

"I need my shoes." I pointed to the boots Liam bought me.

The man turned to get them, and I shoved the pen in my back pocket. It wasn't much, but it was something.

My boots were thrown at me. One hit the wall, and

one hit me. With trembling hands, I pulled them on. Next, he threw my coat at me. I pulled that on, too.

I left the room willingly. Spidey walked in front of me, the other one behind.

Instead of going the way I hoped, they forced me down the stairs but then off onto another floor where they forced me down a flight of service stairs, ones that clearly were not used by guests.

They hustled me through some part of the resort I'd never been in, a place that seemed to be maintenance. The corridors were dark and loud, and the hum of equipment drowned out the sound of them barking at me to move faster.

Eventually, we came to a door. Spidey shoved on it and it swung open. Snowflakes and cold air rushed inside and swirled around my feet.

The sky was dark, and everything outside felt still and quiet.

I stepped out into it all, the snow crunching under my loosely tied boots. The man from behind shoved me. I fell face first into the snow. Everything under the newly fallen powder was hard packed and unforgiving.

I cried out and pushed to my feet.

"Let's go, Little Miss Star Witness," Spidey mocked, pointing the gun at me from his side. "It looks like an awfully nice night to die."

28

Liam

I HAD A KEY TO HER ROOM, BUT I DIDN'T NEED IT.

It was open. The do not disturb sign hanging on the back had flipped around and gotten stuck between the door and the frame.

Alex and I glanced at each other. I put my finger to my lips, and he nodded, taking Charlie by the collar.

I pushed open the door and glanced into the room.

The lights were on. The TV was on. My empty plate and her untouched dinner sat near the window. I stepped inside. "Bells?"

Something crunched under my boots. I looked down and saw chunks of white porcelain all over the carpet.

"Bellamy!" I bellowed and stalked farther in.

It wasn't hard to see she wasn't in here. Her absence rang out like the nefarious vibes still wafting around. Panic unlike anything I'd ever felt grabbed my chest and squeezed. Pain lanced around my ribs and choked me.

Practically blind, I shoved past Alex and rushed into the bathroom.

It was empty, too.

"They have her." My voice was stricken. "They forced their way in and took her."

"Are you sure?" Alex said, worry written all over his face.

I bent down and picked up the handle of the broken mug. I chucked it across the room and it hit the wall, shattering. "They fucking took her!" I raged.

"Whoa," Alex said and laid a hand on my shoulder. "Chill."

"Don't you tell me to fucking chill!" I jerked away from him. "I gotta find her." I started to rush out.

Alex grabbed me, yanking me around. I glanced down where he held me. My chest was heaving. "I love you, man, but I will fucking rip off your arm if you try and stop me."

"I'm not trying to stop you."

"Then let go," I grumbled.

He pulled a phone out of his pocket. "Let me call downstairs see if anyone knows where they went."

I took a breath. "You have five seconds."

"I'll do it in four." He blew out a breath, and I paced to the other side of the room. The sheets were mussed and part of them were dragged toward the floor as if she'd fallen.

I made a choked sound and ripped at my hair.

"It's Alex. Hey, those men that were downstairs a few minutes ago? Where'd they go?"

My entire body tensed as I listened.

"You better find out right the fuck now, or you're fired!" Alex whipped the words out like lightning.

I made a rough sound and went to the window, flattening both palms on the glass. My body shuddered with energy, fear.

She swore she'd be here. She should be here. The only reason she wouldn't be was if someone forced her out.

When I was staring into that gun... all I saw was you. Her words filled my head. The anguish in them, the fear.

"I should have been here!" I roared and hit the glass with the side of my fist. The entire window shook under the hit.

I watched the glass wobble. That's how I felt inside. Wobbly. About to break. Cold.

Up on the mountain, off to the side of the lift and on the edge of the light, something caught my eye. I smacked my hands into the glass again. It nearly shuddered to a halt as I leaned in and stared.

There were three figures moving. Two large and one noticeably smaller. The light-colored hair on the small one stood out like a beacon for men lost at sea.

It was her. I knew it was. I could feel my soul trying to rip out of my body to fly to where she was. It hurt, so desperate it was trying to claw its way out of my chest.

"Watch Charlie," I ordered and rushed from the room.

"Liam!" Alex yelled, following me out into the hallway. "Liam, where are you going?"

I glanced back as I continued to run. "If I'm not back by morning, send a search party."

"Let me come with you!" he yelled, but I just kept on running.

29

Bellamy

IT WAS COLD. NOT JUST ANY COLD, THOUGH. THE KIND that reached through the howling wind with its scrawny, thin fingers and wrapped around your skin, searing past the flesh, reaching all the way to bone.

Winter was a worthy opponent. It didn't need to be anything other than what it was to win a war. It could bury you in snow, suffocate you with frigid air, or drop your body temperature to a point that the blood just froze in your veins.

And it could do it all while looking like a wonderland.

"Is all this really necessary?" hollow eyes asked as we trudged through the snow.

I didn't say anything. For two reasons:

1. I was terrified.

2. I was conserving my energy because I wasn't going to die like this.

"You heard the boss." Spidey tossed the words over his shoulder like a snowball.

Bitter wind blew, and I squinted against it. Jeans, a T-shirt, and a coat were not enough protection against a snowy mountain at night. My ears already ached inside, my fingers were stinging from lack of heat, and even pushed inside my pockets, they were stiff and unbending.

Snow coated my hair, and my nose was numb. I'd nearly bitten my tongue twice because my teeth were chattering so violently.

I stumbled and would have fallen if I hadn't caught myself with my hands. They screamed in pain when they sank into the icy snow. Funny how it looked so beautiful through a window, but the second you stepped out into its world, all bets were off.

"Get up." Hollow eyes grabbed me, forcing me to my feet. My knees ached from the cold.

Even if I managed to survive a gunshot wound, I'd never survive a trip back down the mountain.

"Where are we going?" I asked, shuddering.

He shoved me, and I started trudging again.

"To a place where your body won't be found until spring. And when it is, it'll be by the bears," Spidey replied.

"Why not just kill me now?" I asked, glancing back at the resort. It was getting farther away with every step.

Just keep going. Lead them away from Liam. The farther the better.

"I already told you. You earned a painful, frigid death. Not only did you put the boss and a lot of his people behind bars, but you made us all look like fools when you escaped. We're gonna make an example outta you.

Anyone who thinks they can follow in your footsteps will think twice."

"That why you came out of hiding?" I goaded. "So you could take care of me yourself?"

"I don't like loose ends," he spat.

My toes burned, and my legs felt wind burned through these stupid jeans.

"This way." Spidey grabbed me suddenly, forcing me in a different direction. So far, we'd been going up the mountain. Off to the side of the lifts. I'd tried to wave at some people riding on it about a mile back.

Spidey and friend laughed at me.

The snow falling from the sky had picked up. Visibility was lower than before. We weren't under lights, and all of us were dressed in black. Why couldn't I have picked a neon-yellow coat?

We walked some more, past a marker gesturing for us to turn back for the black diamond hill. It was darker the farther we got, so dark that Spidey pulled out a small flashlight and led the way.

He shined a light on another marker, one that distinguished the parameters of the resort. Everything beyond this point was unpatrolled and considered unsafe. They were making me hike through the snow up the side of a mountain to the place I would die.

I started to think about Liam. About everything we would never get to do. About how glad I was I got to see him again. How glad I was I got to at least tell him I loved him.

"Whoa," Spidey said, stopping abruptly. He shined the flashlight over what looked like a drop-off. The light stretched down to the untouched, smooth snow.

"We're here," he said, turning. The whites of his eyes

glowed in the dark, and his pale face stood out against the night and the black beanie he'd pulled on.

I bet it was warm under that hat.

Hollow eyes shoved me toward the edge, and I grappled for balance before managing to right myself.

Two guns lifted and trained on my chest.

Another flash from the night my father died slapped over all my thoughts. The way he jerked when the bullets hit him. The way his body dropped to the floor.

"Any last words?" Spidey asked.

"Yeah," I said, reaching around to my back pocket. My fingers were so cold it was difficult to force them to bend, but they did, and I grabbed the pen. "This is for my father."

I lunged, catching them off guard. Spidey fired a shot, but it went wide. The sound boomed through the night and rumbled the ground underfoot.

I kept going, not caring if I got shot. If I was going to die now, I was going to do some damage first.

My body collided with his, and we both fell into a tangle of limbs. The weight of my body caused his to sink deeper into the snow, so I used the advantage, shoved up, and swung my arm down, jamming the pen in his neck.

His eyes went wide with surprise, and the gun in his hand fell into the snow. Both hands came up to where the thin instrument stuck out of his flesh. Dark-red liquid seeped into his gloves.

Hollow eyes grabbed me from behind and lifted me off. I started kicking and swinging my arms with everything I had left. The cold butt of a gun pushed against my temple, and I froze.

Spidey stood, pulled the pen out of his neck, and

threw it on the ground. I watched it hit the pristine snow, splattering it with dark spots.

Well. That didn't really go as planned.

"You're going to pay for that," he spat.

"Because dying isn't already punishment enough?" I retorted. Then I kicked the man holding me in the shin. He grunted, but didn't let go.

Spidey walked over and punched me in the face.

Yep. That whole men shouldn't hit women thing?

These two didn't believe in that. Clearly.

My head rocked on my shoulders, and my body went momentarily limp. The smear of something warm on my face brought me back. It was actually a pleasant feeling because I was so cold, until enough focus came back and reminded me if I was feeling warmth, it was likely blood.

Whether it was mine or Spidey's, I didn't know.

Lifting my head, I felt the heavy weight of death. Like it was already here, already trying to entomb me.

A flash of something up above in the trees caught my eye.

I blinked, trying to see through the falling snow and my blurred vision. Whatever it was moved again.

Something familiar stirred inside me. Something that felt a lot like love.

Liam.

"I'll see you in hell, bitch," Spidey intoned and motioned for hollow eyes to put me down. He tossed me onto my feet near the edge of the drop-off, and I swayed.

The sound of a breaking branch drew the men up short, and they both spun in time to see a blur shoot from out of the trees and cut over the snow in a quick motion.

It was Liam. *He came for me.*

There was no moment to feel any sort of elation, though. Him being here wasn't a relief.

It just made this situation all the worse.

A fact that was undoubtedly proved when Spidey and his hollow-eyed friend lifted their guns and began to shoot.

30

Liam

THESE MEN WERE EITHER STUPID OR JUST INCREDIBLY arrogant.

Actually, nah. They were both.

Their arrogance made them stupid. They thought they could waltz into my resort, ask a bunch of questions about my girlfriend, and none of my friends would raise a red flag.

Assholes.

On top of that, they thought they could take Bellamy up a mountain without anyone noticing or even stop to think about the footprints they were literally leaving behind them in the snow.

If you hadn't been looking out the window, you might not have noticed.

The thought in my own head offended me.

Yeah, well, I did, I snapped back.

You knew a man was good and worked up when he

argued with himself. I was beyond worked up. I was damn near frothing at the mouth.

I saw which direction they'd been walking when I fled from her room, but by the time I got downstairs and into the instructors' quarters, I was sweating through my shirt. What if in the time it took me to grab some gear and follow, they'd disappeared?

What if I lost her all over again?

What if I never see her again.

The urgent, almost mind-numbing fear kept me moving, giving me a burst of adrenaline I hadn't felt since I'd been competing in the winter Olympics a few years ago.

I knew these mountains like the back of my hand. I'd grown up here, Alex and I had been all over the place as teens. I could use that to my advantage. These guys didn't know this place. They didn't know the mountain.

My leg muscles burned from the effort of running up the mountain in the snow while carrying my gear, but I didn't stop. Not even when I felt the familiar twinge of pain in my bad knee.

You're pushing yourself. You aren't supposed to do that.

I'd saw my fucking leg off before I let that injury slow me down. That voice of reason in my head? It could go fuck itself.

I picked up the trail they left behind and followed it until we got past the black diamond markings. The beam of a flashlight was faint up ahead, so I knew I'd found them. I just prayed to God I wasn't too late.

I listened over the whipping of the wind for her voice, hoping to hear it, straining to pick out that familiar sound over my own ragged breathing.

I knew they were going out of bounds the second the light disappeared into the trees. I also knew there was a drop-off close by, and it took everything inside me not to scream her name and warn her.

I couldn't give myself away. The element of surprise was on my side. I had to use it. It was all I had.

My direction veered from the one they went in. Instead of cutting across like them, I went up, everything in me quivering with effort. Once I hit the trees, I started to descend in their direction. Listening as I carefully went through the trees, I hoped they also hadn't changed direction and were heading straight toward me.

A few moments later, I heard Bellamy shout, followed quickly by a gunshot. I started running, no longer caring about the noise I made or if they heard me coming. My snowboard was hitting against the ground and the backs of my legs as I ran. I nearly stumbled but righted myself before I fell.

The snowboard hit the packed snow in front of me, skidding down the mountain a little ways before it hit a tree and stopped.

What the fuck was I doing? Running down the mountain when I could be on that board. Hell, I was better on it than I was on my own two feet.

I rushed down, braced my hand on the tree, and snapped my feet onto the board. My knee ached, but I ignored it.

Once I was good and balanced, I cut through the snow, weaving through the trees until I nearly shot out into a clearing right before the drop-off.

Reaching up, I grabbed a branch and stopped just in time to see some bulky guy in black punch Bellamy in the face.

Rage so strong rippled through me my entire body shook with it. I told myself to calm down, to collect myself so I could think clearly. The man holding Bellamy tossed her. She nearly pitched right off the edge.

The branch snapped under my grip, and thought was no longer an option.

With an angry shout, I burst out of the trees, cutting over the powder with more control than I'd used in a long time.

The sound of firing guns barely registered, but the way the ground shook under my board did.

Fuck!

"Liam!" Bellamy screamed, her voice echoing through the night.

More gunfire went off, and I zigzagged down the distance between us as bullets peppered the snow around me.

I watched through wild eyes as my girl leapt at the man who hit her, jumping on his back, and made them fall to the ground. As the pair grappled, the ground underfoot shook more.

This wasn't good. Not at all.

They needed to stop firing those guns.

As if they just wanted to be dickheads, a gun went off once more.

Bellamy screamed, and I looked up wildly, nearly pissing my pants in relief when I saw she hadn't been shot. The asshole shot right over her head, scaring the shit out of her and starting it all.

The deep, angry rumble of the mountain sliced through all the other chaos.

"Bellamy!" I roared.

Everything beneath us started to shift and give way.

There was only one thing I could do.

Only one way to not die in an avalanche….

Outrun it.

I flew past the man Bellamy had jumped on, cut my board into the snow, and sprayed a wave of powder at him and Bells. He let go of her to shield his face, and I kept going, knocking right into her, lifting as I continued to move.

"Hold on," I yelled, feeling her wrap her arms and legs around me.

The next moment, the ground completely fell away and we were flying.

31

Bellamy

THE GROUND BENEATH MY FEET BROKE APART AND crumbled. One moment, I was standing on both feet, and the next, I was staring down where the ground used to be as chunks of ice and snow fell into a giant, loud cloud that was angrier than anything I'd ever seen before.

Avalanche.

Holy shit, we were in the middle of an avalanche.

"Hold on!" Liam yelled, his voice barely even audible over the sound of the mountain roaring around us.

The ledge stretching out over the drop-off shattered just as Liam leapt off, taking us airborne over the chaos. I didn't look down. I couldn't. Plastering as tight as I could to him, I felt the churning in the atmosphere around us, heard the shouts of the men who tried to kill us both.

The ground came fast and hard. The jolt of Liam hitting the ground below us with the board made my teeth gnash together. A sound of pain ripped out of his throat, but his body locked up, exhibiting a level of skill and control I honestly couldn't fathom.

He continued to board down the mountain. I glanced up over his shoulder and gasped.

Nature's fury at its finest. That's exactly what I was seeing.

I'd heard the reports. I'd seen footage on TV. Nothing could ever do this justice. It was absolutely terrifying.

It was like a tsunami of snow. The sound was deafening as I watched great amounts of white roll and rumble toward us. Everything it touched, it took over. Everything in its path was destroyed.

It actually looked almost light the way the white puffed out and bloomed over everything, but I knew that was a lie.

That snow was heavy.

It was deadly.

"Don't let go," Liam yelled, locking his arm around me as his lower body swiveled with the board.

I clutched him tighter, unable to rip my eyes off the horrific monster literally chasing us down the mountain. It was gaining on us. I was slowing him down.

"Drop me!" I screamed against his ear. "Put me down!"

If he did, he could get away. He could survive.

In response, his arm clutched me even tighter, to the point of pain.

God, this man. Why couldn't he understand that I didn't matter? As long as he lived, *nothing* else mattered.

The rumbling got louder. The spray from the rush slapped me in the cheeks.

We're not going to make it.

We were too small, too powerless against such a force.

"C'mon!" Liam grunted and swiveled his body in a different angle. I felt our position change, almost as if we'd somehow become airborne again.

"Swim, Bellamy," he bellowed. "Remember to swim!"

And then the white swallowed us whole, crashing down around us, forcing us apart even as I screamed and tried desperately to hold on.

My body was flung and bent. The loud roar of the avalanche became deafening... until everything went hauntingly silent.

3 2

Liam

THE AFTERMATH OF AN AVALANCHE WAS JARRING. WHAT once was violent and explosive became impotent and peaceful.

Even if you managed to survive, those first couple breaths made you question if you were dead. The silence. The endless white. The momentary detachment to everything around you.

But then it came back just as violently as it all left.

The silence is interrupted by the sound of your pounding heart, the pain in your limbs, and the ragged way you draw in a breath.

"Bellamy!" I roared, launching up. The speed in which I sat up made me woozy, and I threw out a hand to steady myself on something.

There was nothing.

Nothing but a sea of white, a blanket spun by winter, covering everything as far as the eye could see.

"No." I gasped, forcing myself to my feet. My knee gave out and I fell, but I pushed back up just as fast.

"Bellamy!" I screamed. My voice echoed through the air.

I hoped it had been enough. *Please, let it have been enough.*

The second I knew that avalanche was going to overtake us, I hit a natural bump in the mountain, getting some air as the white reached out its claws.

I hoped I had enough air to not get pummeled completely. I hoped it gave us a shot of not being buried under tons of snow that packed down like concrete.

After thirty minutes, the chances of being found alive in an avalanche decreased drastically.

After three hours, you were as good as dead.

"Bellamy!" I roared again.

I had to find her. The clock was ticking. I wasn't coming off this mountain without her. If she died up here, then by God, I would, too.

Ignoring the searing pain in my knee, I jogged forward. My board was long gone. I'd probably never see it again.

"Bells!"

I staggered around, scanning the white, looking for something… anything.

A sound, muffled and almost lost, brought my head around. I froze and looked in the direction I'd heard it come from.

Cupping my hands around my mouth, I called out, "Bellamy?"

A muffled yell replied.

I took off, the sound below me. My knee gave out again, but I kept moving, rolling down toward the sound.

The second I sprang to my feet, a slim, colorless hand

poked free of the white. It wiggled and moved like a flag against the backdrop of night.

A strangled sound forced up the back of my throat, and I croaked as I lunged, falling onto my hands and knees and clawing at the snow around that hand.

She kept moving, her hand forcing down, coming back up, down again, until I could see her wrist and her other fingers poke free.

I grabbed her hands and pulled, releasing a yell into the sky.

Bellamy's body burst up from the packed white, and I fell back, bringing her with me. She collapsed across my chest. Her gasping for air was the best sound I'd ever heard.

"Thank you!" I rasped up to the sky. The stars blinked down at me. "Thank you."

Bellamy began coughing, and my focus shifted. Taking her face in my hands, I glanced up. "You okay? How bad are you hurt?"

"Liam." She wheezed. "Liam." Her eyes became misty and a tear fell over her cheek. "I really tried to hold on."

A small laugh bubbled up in my chest. The pressure of it coupled with the profound gratefulness that she was alive hurt, but it was a pain I would carry the rest of my life if I had to. "I got you," I said, collapsing back into the snow with a heave. "I got you now."

"You saved my life."

I lifted my head, meeting her eyes. "No, sweetheart. I got us pummeled by an angry mountain."

She shook her head. "You told me to swim. It kept me from getting stuck under there, right? You told me to swim."

In a burst of energy, I sat up to clutch her against me.

"Yes," I said, pressing a kiss to her forehead then to her nose. "Yes," I murmured again and kissed her lips.

It was one of the things always drilled into my head. If ever in an avalanche, swim. The snow, once packed, was nearly impossible to move. You had to swim to get out.

Bellamy ripped her lips from mine with a gasp and sank into my chest. Her body was scarily limp.

"Hey." I pulled her completely out of the snow. "Tell me where you're hurt."

"I-I'm not sure," she replied.

"Okay, let's stand up. Take stock of how you're doing."

"Liam?" She clutched at my arms before I could move.

"Yeah?"

Her eyes were so wide when she glanced up. "They tried to kill me. They were going to kill you." Her lower lip wobbled, and I was lost.

"Shh," I crooned, pulling her back into me. "They tried, but they failed. We're okay now. We're both okay."

She gasped and shoved away from my chest. "Oh my God! They could still be looking for us. They're still here!"

I held her when she tried to scramble up. "Calm down," I insisted. "Everything's okay."

"No!" she cried. "Everything is not okay!"

She was in shock. Her eyes were wild. Her lips were taking on a hue of blue I didn't like.

She had no gloves. No hat. And was dressed in a pair of soaking-wet jeans.

I pulled her in, rocking her back and forth, holding as tight as I dared. I was incredibly afraid I'd hold too hard and worsen something that was already injured.

Her teeth chattered and her body shivered.

"Up," I said, feeling the same urgency as when I rushed down the mountain, trying to get free of the avalanche.

Without shelter and heat, she was going to die.

Ripping the hat off my head, I stuffed it down on hers, pulling it so far down it nearly covered her eyes. Next, I pulled off my jacket and wrapped it around her, zipping it all the way up. "Put your hands inside against the lining," I ordered. When she didn't automatically obey, I took her hands and shoved them into the coat myself.

"W-w-what about you?" Her teeth chattered.

"Don't you worry about me." I assured her. "I've got snow in my blood."

Using my hands, I rubbed briskly up and down her arms, trying to get any kind of heat into her I could. She whimpered, and her body jerked back.

My eyes narrowed, hands hovering over her body. "What hurts?"

"My shoulder." She looked toward her right shoulder. I glanced at it but couldn't see anything because my coat was around her.

My eyes roamed over her face. Her cheek was split. The blood was frozen on her face. Her eye was darkening, and one side of her lip was swollen.

"He hit you," I rumbled as my own avalanche of anger whipped up inside me.

"Could be worse," she replied. A stricken feeling sliced me open. "The men!" She perked up, glancing around.

"They're probably dead," I answered flat. If by some divine act of God they were alive, I'd kill them myself.

"Try and walk," I murmured, wrapping an arm

around her waist. Her movements were stiff and wooden. Every step she took, I anticipated a cry of pain.

But as one foot slowly went in front of the other, I began to feel a little more hopeful.

"How are you?" she asked, glancing up at me.

How could I think about myself when half her face was swelling, her shoulder was wrecked, and second after second, she was more exposed to frostbite?

"Liam!" Her sharp voice cut into my thoughts. "Are you hurt?"

"Uh, don't think so," I said, shaking my head as we stepped. My knee buckled.

"Don't lie!"

"My knee," I told her. Slowly, I took stock of my body, actually turning my thoughts inward, fighting myself to keep them there. It was hard to think about me, especially when I had her to think of. Especially with the splitting headache sawing through my skull.

"You're bleeding!" She huffed.

"What?"

Her fingers poked out of the coat I'd put around her, reached up, and fingered behind my ear. I winced. They came away red.

"You hit your head, Liam."

Well, that would explain the headache.

I grabbed her exposed fingers, ignoring the blood smearing them, and pulled my jacket down to cover them. "Keep your hand covered."

"But your head!"

"The cold will slow the bleeding." I really wasn't concerned. I'd had worse.

"We need to get back to the resort." She worried. "You need to a doctor. We both do."

"It's too far," I replied, shaking my head. "We won't make it. Not without my board."

She grabbed the front of my shirt, her fingers curling into it even through the sleeves of my coat. "We don't have a choice." Her forehead wrinkled. "Where is your coat?" As if finally understanding what was happening, she glanced down at her own body, and a noise of alarm ripped out of her.

Bellamy started tearing at the coat, trying to get it off. I knew she would. I grabbed her arms and pinned them to her sides as she struggled.

In her haste, she jolted, and a bolt of pain struck through her eyes. She bit back a whimper and went still. I let go of her right wrist instantly, afraid I'd pulled her shoulder.

"I'm not wearing your coat!"

"Yes, you are."

"You need it!" she demanded.

"You need it more."

"No!"

I grabbed her face and forced our eyes to collide. "Look at me."

She went still and listened. My eyes bored into hers, searching. Her pupils were dilated. I cursed.

"What?" She whimpered.

"I think you have a concussion."

"Me?"

I was pretty sure we both did. She definitely was in shock, but her level of delayed understanding and movement... She'd hit her head at some point. Maybe whenever she injured her shoulder.

I picked her up, careful of her shoulder and making sure the right one was facing out and not against me as I cradled her against my chest. "We're going."

"Your knee!" She gasped.

"I don't give a damn about my knee!" I roared.

She fell silent, slinking against my chest. The curse I spat floated behind us as I walked. "I'm sorry, sweetheart. I just... Just let me get us somewhere safe."

"But where?" she asked, laying her head against my chest.

I glanced ahead, hoping like hell it was still there. "I know a place."

33

Bellamy

I was fairly certain he was favoring his left leg, and it was making me queasy. I wanted so badly to tell him to put me down, but I didn't. Liam was surly, and I knew if I pushed the issue, he'd yell at me again.

Don't get me wrong. I wasn't someone who would roll over and let anyone yell at me.

But this was different.

Liam was clearly very agitated and borderline irrational. He knew we were both hurt, but he was so focused on me nothing else mattered to him. Fighting would only make this situation worse. I settled for holding myself up as much as I could to hopefully make me easier to carry.

"You weren't this stubborn eight years ago," I muttered against his chest, feeling a little surly myself.

A sound rumbled out of him and the breath he released as he spoke puffed out in a white cloud around me. "Yeah, well, eight years ago, I hadn't lost you yet. I hadn't lived without you."

"Liam," I crooned softly, putting my hand on his chest.

He paused and glanced down. Our eyes collided. His held something beyond pain. "I gave up on you, Bells." That cold, stricken look gave way to hard determination. "I'll never do that again. Ever."

Pushing my hand out of the coat, I reached up, placing my icy fingers against his cheek. "I love you."

He started walking again, more determined than before. My heavens, he was stubborn. I was damned, though, because that stubbornness coupled with his reasoning behind it melted me even in the center of an avalanche.

I don't know how long he walked. It felt like forever. However, I was pretty certain my perception of time was sort of skewed. It didn't help that the sky stayed dark, no hint at all in its shadows.

Eventually, Liam slowed. "Think you can walk a little?"

I suppressed an eye roll. "I'm pretty sure I can handle it."

Carefully, Liam stood me on my feet, hands hovering around me as if he were afraid I would break.

"I'm okay." I assured him, ignoring the pain in my shoulder.

He pointed past me. "We're almost there."

Following his direction, I gazed across the snow to a dark structure perched ahead. "Is that a house?"

"A cabin," he replied, placing a hand at the small of my back to get me moving. "Years ago, one of the property managers lived out here. He was kinda eccentric and liked being out here on his own."

"What happened to him?"

"He retired, moved to Florida to be near his grand-kids. Guess he'd had enough of the snow."

"And no one else moved in?"

Liam chuckled. "No one else wanted to live on the side of a mountain alone. Alex and I used to run around out here. Sometimes Paul would take us fishing a few miles down the mountain. Come to think of it, maybe he didn't like being as alone as he said. Why else would he put up with two teenage boys?"

"Maybe he just liked you."

"Maybe my father paid him extra to keep us busy." He chuckled.

I giggled.

"Anyway, I don't know what kind of condition the place will be in, but it will get us out of the elements for a bit. Get you warmed up."

"Think there's a first aid kit?"

His eyes turned sharply to me. "Are you bleeding?"

"No. You are." I reminded him. "Liam?" I asked as the cabin drew nearer.

"Hmm?"

"How did you know where I was?"

"Alex came and found me. I guess those assholes were asking questions about you in the tavern, and he was worried. We went to your room." He paused. "The door was open and there was broken glass... The bed was kinda messed up."

I made a sound.

Liam stopped walking and turned abruptly. "Bellamy, did they... did they hurt you?"

I knew what he was asking. "No. They didn't. He just hit me a couple times."

An intense look swam over his features. I knew he

was angry and I knew he hated this situation, but he managed to control it, to push aside the worst of it. "I looked out the window and I saw you. Your hair actually... You just passed close to one of the lights, and it was enough for me to see you."

"And you followed." I surmised, kind of awed. It almost felt like fate. For him to have been looking out the window at the exact moment I happened to walk in a spot where he could see.

"Of course, I followed. I almost didn't grab any of my gear, but it's a good fucking thing I did."

"I'm sorry you lost your snowboard." I knew he loved it. And now it was gone.

He made a dismissive motion with his hand. "It's just a board. I have more at home." Then after a pause, he said, much quieter, "Probably won't even need one anyway."

"What?" I wondered. Something about that quiet statement made my stomach flip. It seemed very ominous.

"Nothing," he answered, then changed the subject. "I wonder if it's locked."

The cabin was literally just feet in front of me. I hadn't even realized we'd gotten this close. I'd been too focused on Liam and what he was saying. This close, I was able to see it better in the dark. It wasn't much, just a small log cabin that appeared a little weathered from being empty for a few years.

It had a single door in the front and two windows with no shutters.

Liam tried the handle, and it didn't open. Without any hesitation, he punched through one of the small panes above the handle. The sound of the glass shattering made me wince.

"Liam!" I gasped. "Your hand!"

His arm was already through the hole he'd punched out, and seconds later, the door unlatched. Pulling his arm free, he held up his hand to show me it was fine. "I'm wearing gloves, sweetheart."

I sniffed. I still didn't like him punching things.

He held out his hand. I swear I saw a hint of amusement around his lips. "C'mon."

I moved, and he whispered for me to stay close.

The pair of us moved into the dark cabin, my eyes seeking every dark corner they could find, just waiting to see if something moved.

"Anyone here?" Liam asked.

I scoffed. "Like they'd answer."

Liam chuckled, backtracking a little to close and lock the door. I don't know why he bothered to lock it. There was a hole in it. Once that was done, he went over toward the small, basic kitchen and opened a few cabinets. The sound of them opening and closing seemed loud and disruptive. I kept worrying it would somehow give away where we were.

I wondered again about Spidey and his creepy friend. If they had survived the avalanche. Liam seemed to think they were dead… but I knew.

I knew that if he and I could survive, then those men could, too.

The striking of a match brought me out of the shudder-worthy thoughts, and the glow of a flame filled the space as Liam lit an oil lamp. Soft, warm light filled the room, chasing away the worst of the shadows and revealing the small, sparse cabin.

"No electricity. But this will do," Liam said, carrying it across the room to place in front of a fireplace.

The room dimmed again when he stuck the lamp

inside the opening and followed it with his head. Seconds later, both he and the lamp came back out. "Well, here's hoping the chimney is clear enough so this cabin doesn't fill with smoke when I make this fire."

"You're making a fire?"

"You need to warm up, sweetheart. Come over here."

Why did he have to call me that? Why did he have to call me that so tenderly while he was trying to take care of me? I couldn't handle it. Not right now. Not much more. After everything that happened tonight, I was a bundle of overexposed nerves.

I followed his voice because I would literally follow it anywhere. Liam handed me the lamp and then went about using the few logs in the rack beside the fireplace and some paper that had definitely seen better days to start a fire.

As he worked, I glanced around the small cabin, noting a sofa, two chairs, and an old wooden coffee table. Near the door, there was a wooden coat rack, and across the space was a doorway I assumed led to a bedroom. On one of the walls hung a stuffed bird, its wings stretched out as if it were going to fly.

It was creepy. I tried not to look at it.

Liam appeared in front of me, setting the lamp on the coffee table not far away. The crackling of the logs in the fire drew my attention, as did the delicious heat already reaching toward me.

The flames were actually a good size, and I knew they would only grow stronger. My one hand wiggled free of the long coat sleeve, and I held it toward the warmth. I thought about tugging off the coat completely so the heat could get to the vulnerable arm and fingers against my side, but in the end, I didn't bother.

I heard Liam moving around in the house, but I didn't turn to look. I stared, almost transfixed by the bright-orange glow of each flame. The scent of burning wood and paper began to wrap around me, and I breathed in deep.

The pain in my shoulder cut the breath short, and I blew it out, stretching closer to the fire.

"I grabbed what I could find," Liam murmured, coming close.

I turned, watching him set down a stack of towels and a heap of blankets that looked like they had been ripped right off the bed. Before coming to my side, he grabbed the blanket on the back of the couch and dropped it close by.

"Your teeth are chattering." His voice was soft yet concerned when he reached for the zipper on the coat around me.

"My fingers hurt," I told him, trying not to sound like a whiner. Maybe I was in shock I went from barely processing to processing all at once and blurting out stuff I would otherwise hold in.

"I know." He lifted them and kissed them before returning to the coat. "That's good. You need the feeling to come back."

"What are you doing?" I asked as he peeled the coat off me. "I thought I was supposed to warm up."

"This stuff is soaking wet, Bells. It's gonna make it harder." After he put aside his coat, he unzipped mine and started gently tugging it away.

I hissed a breath, and he stopped. His mouth was a hard line as his eyes roamed over me. "Your shoulder?"

I nodded, biting my lower lip. Without saying anything else, I peeled my coat off me the rest of the way. I wasn't going to make him do it. He'd already done enough for me. Tears pricked the backs of my eyes, but I ignored them.

"All you have on under here is my shirt," he growled, staring.

"I was waiting for you."

He sighed. "I know. But this shirt is not enough protection against the cold outside." He bent, untying the loose, barely tied laces on my boots and tugging them off. He cursed, but I didn't acknowledge it.

I knew he was pissed to see I wasn't wearing socks. Hell, I'd been lucky they let me put on pants.

Working back up my body, Liam unbuttoned my jeans and slid them off in one motion.

"Liam," I said, my teeth knocking against each other. "Wh-what—"

"We need body heat, Bells." His voice was clipped.

When he reached for the hem of my shirt, his eyes found mine, asking. I nodded once, and he tugged.

"I can't lift my arm." I said apologetically when the shirt was half off.

"It's okay," he told me gently, then worked it down over my body. When I was down to nothing but my panties, his eyes raked over me, but not in a heated way. It was as if he didn't see my bare skin at all. All he was concerned with was injury.

When his stare fell on my shoulder, his eyes darkened. "It's separated."

"What?" I glanced down.

Something was off. It didn't look like it should. It was swollen and a little… misshapen. Reaching up, I fingered near my collarbone and winced.

Taking my hand, he folded it between his, pulling it away from the shoulder. "It's separated. Probably happened when the avalanche slammed into you." He groaned as if it physically hurt him, too. "I'm sorry."

"How do you know it's separated?" I asked.

"I've done it a few times while boarding. You need to get an X-ray and get it in a sling. It needs ice, but I'll be damned if I put anything cold on you right now."

"It's okay." I tried to soothe him. Clearly, seeing my shoulder was upsetting him. "It doesn't hurt much."

He gave me a look, and I returned it.

"Can't you just pop it back in place?" I asked.

"It's separated, not dislocated. There's a difference. And no, I'm not doing anything with it until we know how bad it is."

Liam stepped back and pulled his shirt over his head, then the T-shirt underneath it. Next, he pulled off his hat and reached for the snow pants and boots.

When he was down to nothing but a pair of very formfitting boxer briefs, he shook out some blankets and tossed a thick one on the floor in front of the fire. He sat, spread his legs, and glanced up at me expectantly.

I barely noticed. I was too busy looking at his incredibly strong, suddenly bare body... concealed only by underwear.

"Bellamy," he intoned.

I snapped to attention, glancing at his face.

He smiled knowingly. "Come here, sweetheart."

I sat between his legs. The heat from the fully roaring fire caressed my cold skin, and I sighed. A towel landed on my head, and Liam began drying my wet hair.

"Dry your braids," he instructed.

I reached up with the arm that didn't hurt to finish as he grabbed me around the hips and pulled me into his body. I gasped the instant our skin met. Liam's sharp intake of breath and the way he froze momentarily told me he was affected, too.

The towel fell from my head, and my hand dropped away. We gazed at one another, Liam holding my stare with his silvery eyes.

"Tell me if I hurt you," he murmured, rubbing heat into my body with one hand while he held me against him with the other. He worked gently but thoroughly, somehow managing to avoid my shoulder.

"We need to get that stabilized," he said, drawing back enough to look at it.

"It's fine," I murmured, snuggling back into his bare chest.

The skin-on-skin contact was sinful. It was enough to make me forget I almost died, was swept away by an avalanche, and now was hiding in some old cabin with no electricity until my limbs absorbed enough warmth to work again.

"Closer," I whispered, pushing into him a little more.

He made a sound and lifted me into his lap. My legs locked around his waist, our bare chests smashing together. I pressed my cheek into his shoulder and slipped my good arm around his waist. Liam snatched a thick blanket off the ground and wrapped it around us, rubbing up and down my back.

My eyes slipped closed. The sound of the crackling fire, the feel of his skin, the warmth he seemed to generate even though he'd been outside, too…

"Bellamy."

My eyes snapped back open, and the unfamiliar room came back into view.

"You can't go to sleep, sweetheart."

"Wasn't going to," I argued.

He chuckled. "Let me see your hands."

Begrudgingly, I lifted my cheek and sat up enough to push my hands between us. Inside the blanket, he rubbed at my hands and fingers, trying to hurry up the warming process.

"How about your toes?" he queried a few minutes later.

"I'm not getting out of your lap," I insisted. "They're fine." As if to prove it, I wiggled my toes behind his back.

His low laugh slid over me like honey, so sweet and sticking to me in all the right places. Liam grasped my face and pulled it down. "How's your head?" His stare bounced between my eyes. "Do you have a headache?"

"Not much," I replied. "My shoulder hurts more than anything."

How can he be so focused right now? How can he not be as utterly distracted by me as I am by him?

My eyes traveled downward to his chest and abs. His skin was soft and smooth-looking. I loved the way it stretched out across his chest, molding to all the muscle and strength beneath it. He'd turned into a man in the last eight years. His body was honed and experienced. The urge to run my hands all over him, relearn him all over again, eclipsed everything else in my mind.

"Your teeth aren't chattering anymore." He observed, rubbing the pad of his thumb over my lower lip.

"I guess you're warming me up," I purred. Unable to stop myself, I sucked his thumb between my lips.

He groaned. "Don't make this harder than it already is, Bells."

I raised an eyebrow and released his thumb. "What do you mean?"

"You know damn well what I mean," he murmured, palming my hips and rocking into me. His rock-hard erection was unmistakable.

I rocked against him again, and pleasure rocketed through my core.

Liam moaned. His face fell into my neck, his lips grazing over the skin. Pulling back, he blew out a breath. "All I want to do is be inside you. To prove to myself you're really okay. I know you're sitting here with me. I know you're mostly fine… but it's not enough, Bellamy." He glanced down. "I want to feel you come alive beneath my hands. It might not even be enough then."

I caught his chin, pushed it up. "I'm not saying no."

Silver lightning struck through his eyes. Temptation so strong passed over his face, but he shook it off. "I am."

Before I could respond, he kissed the tip of my nose, then gently set me away. After tucking the blanket around me, he laid out our wet clothes and put our boots near the fire.

My eyes stayed with him the entire time, devouring everything about him I could. Not only was unbridled desire coursing through me, but he was my lifeline. Without him, I probably wouldn't be here.

The thought made me shiver.

"Hey," he murmured, coming back. "You cold again?" Liam sank down on the blanket, setting aside a white kit, and opened his arms. He had a blanket draped around his back so when he folded me close, I was wrapped in him and an extra blanket.

My eyes strayed to the first aid kit, and I sat back. "Let me clean up your head."

"You first." He grabbed the kit and opened it, pulling out some supplies to line up along the floor.

"I'm not bleeding," I demanded.

"Yes. You are." He glanced pointedly at my cheek.

"Guess that wasn't Spidey's blood after all," I muttered.

"What?" Liam's voice was sharp.

"I stabbed him in the neck with a pen. He pulled it out and hit me. I felt blood on my cheek, but I was hoping it had been his."

Liam didn't look thrilled. At all. "Yeah, well, it's yours."

Turning my head so he could see the area, he worked quietly at cleaning up the split in my cheek. I winced when he touched it at first, but the look in his eyes scared me. So I held it back and forced my expression to be passive as he tended to the tender flesh.

I guess being out in the freezing cold had been good for something. Numbing all the pain. Now that I was warming up and trying to clean up the wounds, the hurt was becoming easier to feel.

I don't think I did as good of a job as I hoped concealing the fact my face hurt. Occasionally, the muscles in Liam's jaw would contract as though he knew, and my belly would tighten.

"Why'd you call him Spidey?" he asked, reaching for a bandage.

I stared into the fire. "He has a big spider tattooed on the back of his neck."

Liam moved on to my lip, dabbing. It stung, too, so I figured it must also be split. When he was done, he tossed aside the cotton pad and glanced down at my shoulder. "Try not to move that around, okay?"

I nodded and reached for the supplies.

His hand settled over mine, and I looked up.

"You need to tell me."

My voice shook. "Tell you what?"

I knew.

He knew that I knew.

He knew I was trying to evade. Up until now, he'd let me, but all that ended tonight.

"Tell me why those men came here. Why they want to kill you," Liam answered. "It's time, Bellamy. You need to tell me everything."

34

Liam

"I NEED TO LOOK AT YOUR HEAD." AS SHE SPOKE, SHE avoided my stare and reached for some first aid supplies.

My hand covered hers, stopping her movement. "Bellamy, I need to know."

Beneath my touch, her hand went slack. "I know you do," she whispered. "It's not fair for me to stay and keep you in the dark."

"Turn on the light, then, sweetheart."

The breath she blew out was shaky. Her eyes met mine. "Can I fix you up while I talk?"

Half a smile lifted the corner of my mouth. I'd probably let her saw my arm off if it made it easier for her. "Yeah."

A fraction of relief came over her face, and it was with that small change I realized just how hard this was for her. How scared she was.

"Turn this way." She motioned for me to spin. "So the light from the lamp is on this side of your head."

I did as she requested, noting the way my skin brushed against hers when I moved. God, this woman was a walking, talking test of patience. In every single way.

As bad as this situation was right now and as worried as I was for her, being inside her body was still a need that pulsed through my every cell. Probably *more* so now because of the situation we were in.

Using only one hand, Bellamy's cold fingers caressed the side of my face, gently guiding my head so she could see.

"Your hand is still cold." I reached for it, but she snatched it back.

"It's your turn, Liam." She insisted. I reached for her again, but she smacked away my hand. "Don't you push me, mister. I've had just about enough."

Pressing my lips together, I sealed in the humor just itching to get out.

Bellamy scooted closer to me, and I used it as a chance to cover her lap with an extra blanket. As I did, she gave me a warning look, so I swooped in super fast and planted a quick kiss on her lips before moving back. Then I grinned. "Go ahead,"

With an eye roll and a cute little smile, she titled my head back where she wanted it and grabbed a sterile wipe to gently dab at the cut behind my ear. I gritted my teeth against the stinging pain.

"It's swollen a bit," she murmured while gently cleaning. "It bled a lot." After retrieving another wipe, she began dabbing again. "I don't think it needs stitches…"

"Does it hurt much?" she whispered when I said nothing.

My voice was hoarse when I answered, "No."

Truth was any pain I might have felt was muted

beneath her touch. Bellamy had an effect on me that no one else ever had. When she was around, it was like it was only her. Even when she was sixteen years old, she had a hold over me so strong I would have willingly given up my pro athlete dreams.

She cleared her throat, continuing to work. "I didn't have much of a relationship with my father."

I glanced at her. I was surprised. "It seemed like you did."

She nodded, smiling sadly. "The truth was that time I spent with him here at BearPaw was the most time I spent with him ever. We went years and years between visits, and usually, when I did see him, it was for less than a day at a time."

"I didn't know," I murmured, feeling sad for her. I couldn't imagine not having my dad in my life, not knowing he was there.

"My mom was pretty adamant he stay away. She didn't want him to come around at all. Ever." Bellamy set aside the wipe and picked up a cotton pad. "My father was involved in things he shouldn't have been. Dangerous things…" Her voice fell away, then returned. "He wasn't a very good man."

"He loved you," I told her, turning to catch her eyes. "He might not have been a good man, but he loved you. I saw it."

A sad, wistful look crossed her eyes, and it pierced my heart. "Thank you for saying that."

I grabbed her chin, lifting it. "I mean it. It was obvious back then."

"Yeah." She smiled sadly and pushed my head back around. "I know he loved me. Why else would he risk my mother's wrath for even just a day visit?"

"You're worth it," I whispered.

She went back to cleaning my head and applying ointment. It seemed to take longer because she only used one hand. I was sorry she was hurt, but I wasn't sorry for the additional time she had to spend touching me.

"After I graduated high school, I went to culinary school. I love to cook and be in the kitchen. I'd always hoped to have my own restaurant or be a chef at one of the hotspots in L.A."

"I'm still waiting on a meal from you." I reminded her.

She laughed.

"I got a job in a place, started out as a dishwasher and managed to work myself up to cooking staff. Kitchens are very strict that way. You have to work your way up. Prove yourself."

"I'm sure you were the best in that place."

"I was getting there." Her voice was soft and gentle, just like her touch. I knew she was cleaning out a wound, but it felt more like she was caressing me. Caressing my body and my senses. Chills of pleasure rushed across my scalp, down the back of my neck. Every so often, a tinge of pain would cut through when she hit a tender spot, and that pain mixed with the pleasure was giving me a hard-on.

"Almost done," she said. "I'm not sure if I'll get a bandage to stick, but I can try."

"Keep talking, Bells," I murmured. I just wanted the sound of her voice.

"About two years ago, my father called me. I hadn't seen him in years. He said he was in town, gave me an address, and asked me to meet him. I went…"

My stomach tightened. "Something happened."

"It was in the worst part of town, but I didn't think about what that meant. I knew my mother didn't want me to meet him… but I just wanted to see him. He was my father."

Was. Jesus.

Her fingers were trembling. I felt the fine tremors as she tried for the third time to stick some giant bandage to the back of my head. Slowly, I reached up and pulled her hand away.

"It's not on there yet," she fussed.

I pulled it away from my head and looked down at the faint smear of blood. "I don't need that." I tossed it down and tried to pull her into me. She resisted, picked up a piece of gauze, and carefully pressed it against the gash.

"At least hold this on there until it completely stops bleeding."

I took the gauze and motioned to her. "Sit with me."

Bellamy climbed into my lap, and my heart rolled over. She sat facing the fire, her back against my chest. I folded my legs and arm around her (the one not holding the stupid gauze against my head).

Ducking my head, I kissed her on the shoulder.

"When I got to the place, he was really nervous and jumpy. I knew something was wrong. He shoved a bunch of money into my bag. I tried to get him to go to lunch…"

"What happened?" I pressed, wanting her to just get to the bad part. I didn't want her lost in the past, reliving something that clearly changed her.

"Some men showed up. My father had this hiding spot… between the walls. He shoved me inside right before they busted in the door…" Her whole body was trembling now.

I began rocking us gently, pressing kisses to her shoulder.

"They beat him up, and one of their bullets went through the wall where I was… like a peephole in a door… There are never good things when you look through a peephole in a door."

I gave her a little shake. "Bells."

"I watched them kill him."

I sucked in a breath.

"They shot him twice. Then they laughed about it, talked about going to get lunch."

She witnessed a murder. Not just any murder, though, the murder of her own father. Through a bullet hole. I couldn't even fathom the amount of mental torment she must live with daily.

"Did they see you?" I worried. The thought of her seeing that was heinous, but her getting caught was much worse.

"No." Her voice was hoarse, her body stock still against mine. "I sat inside that wall for hours, waiting to see if they'd come back. Just staring at his body through the hole."

It was almost as if she was back there, tense muscles, still form, low, rough voice.

A deep growl ripped from my chest as I tossed aside the stupid gauze. Both arms embraced her. I wrapped myself around her as much as I could and held tight, still trying to be mindful of her shoulder.

Her small hand found its way around my forearm and gripped.

"Have you ever heard of Perry Crone?"

"The most infamous crime boss this century?" Everyone in this country knew who Perry Crone was. If they didn't, they were living under a rock.

I felt her nod. "How much do you know about him?"

"A good bit, actually," I said, rubbing my chin over her

shoulder as I stared into the fire. "That big trial that put him away about a year ago was on every channel when I was in the hospital."

She turned, her eyes concerned. "You were in the hospital?"

See. That right there. That was why she was the only one who would ever own me. It didn't matter that some men just tried to kill her. It didn't matter her shoulder was fucked up, that she'd been punched in the face by assholes, or even that she was telling me about witnessing her father's murder.

I'd mentioned a hospital stay, and all those things stopped existing. Her blue eyes bounced between mine, searching... worrying.

Using my thumb, I smoothed the wrinkles between her brows and smiled. "Torn ACL, remember?"

Realization and even more worry clouded her eyes. She gasped and turned toward my knee. "You hurt it again." Her hand hovered over it. Then cautiously, she caressed it. "It's swollen."

"It's not important right now." I reminded her, my chest squeezing a bit. I wondered how different my recovery would have been if she were part of my life back then. I wondered if the depression that nearly drowned me would have been so intense.

Bellamy's eyes lifted to mine once more. "It is important."

I nodded, accepting the fact that, yeah, it was. But it also wasn't something I was prepared to deal with right now. I was very afraid of what the pain in my knee could mean. Of what it might do to me... again.

"You know, I'm sitting here filling you in on my past, and it's making me see that we haven't really talked about yours either."

A quick smile formed on my face. "That's because no one is trying to kill me." *Because the time we spent apart doesn't even matter. All that matters is here. Now. You.*

"Not everyone can have such a charmed life," she countered, cheeky.

I chuckled.

When her eyes met mine again, they were somber, less teasing. "I know it hasn't been charmed, Liam. I can… feel it in you sometimes. I know you've been through some stuff. I want you to know I care about it. All of it. I want to know."

The lump in my throat was tough to swallow. It took several tries, and even then, it felt as though all I'd managed to do was push it down into my chest where it settled like a weight. "I know, sweetheart. We'll get to my stuff. Yours is more urgent right now." I glanced around the sparse cabin for effect. "Clearly."

She appeared wary once more. That look I'd come to recognize in her eyes resurfaced as she spun back toward the fire. I wrapped my arms around her again, resting my lips right beside her ear. "I'm not going anywhere."

The feel of her body exhaling should have made me feel better.

It didn't.

"So you watched the coverage of the trial?"

I nodded, thinking back. "Yeah, it was the case of the year. Hell, of the decade. The Feds had been after Crone for a long time, and finally, they managed to get a witness with enough info to put him—" What I was saying sank in.

The way Bellamy was rigid in my arms, silently staring at the fire…

I went motionless. *"Holy shit,"* I whispered. Then a

low keening sound erupted from my throat. "Oh, no, baby. *No.* Tell me it's not what I'm thinking."

She shivered. "I wish I could."

I moaned and pulled her even tighter against me. When she yelped softly because of her shoulder, I only shifted my hold.

"You were the star witness? The one the prosecution had under lock and key until you could testify."

"That's right." The words seemed to claw out of her throat, leaving it raw and scratchy. "I'm the witness. I'm the one who put Perry Crone away for life."

And now I understood. Why she showed up here with barely anything to her name, why she didn't want to tell me anything. Why she was so hesitant to stay.

Perry Crone was a mobster. Certainly, no one to tangle with.

But here was my girl, twisted up with that bastard like a pretzel.

35

Bellamy

The words were out.

There was no going back.

Liam pushed up off the floor, leaving me unanchored and in danger of floating away. Before pacing away, he draped a blanket around my shoulders and tucked it closely beneath my chin.

I decided the best thing to do was to push on and not drag this out.

Liam had a choice to make. I had to let him make it.

"Turns out the reason my mother didn't want me around my father was because he was in bed with some pretty nasty New York mobsters." The sound I made was too harsh to be a laugh, but not quite sad enough to be a cry. "Who even knew mobsters existed outside of comic books and movies?"

Liam continued to pace behind me. I felt his movements, heard them, but I didn't look. I didn't really want to see the expression on his face when he fully understood that he was involved with someone who could literally bring the mob down on him.

"Before I was even born, she packed up and moved to California, all the way across the country. She told him to stay away, but he didn't listen. And I was just a girl. I didn't know what a relationship with him could cost. I just wanted my father. I wanted him to love me."

"Bells." Liam sounded broken.

When his hand slid across my back, I flinched.

I couldn't accept his comfort right now. If I did, I wouldn't be able to finish.

"I guess he'd done something to betray Crone and his organization. In court, they said my father had been trying to get out, to cut ties with it all."

"You don't get out of the mob," Liam murmured. "Even I know that."

"You're right. You don't. But he was trying anyway."

"He wanted to be a man worthy of a daughter like you."

A broken sound ripped out of me. My heart felt pummeled. "Please don't say that," I murmured. "I don't want to live with thinking he got killed because he was trying to get out for me."

Liam swept in close, picked me up, and carried me to the couch. He sat down with me in his lap and adjusted the blankets around us. "I didn't mean to put that on you, sweetheart." His voice was soft and cajoling. "There is nothing about this situation that is your fault." He pulled my face up to meet his. "Nothing."

"I know that, but sometimes it's hard to feel it. You know?"

His lips grazed my temple. "I know."

I laid my cheek against his chest. "Maybe he was tired of looking over his shoulder. Maybe he did want to be a better man. I don't know. I won't ever know the reason my father wanted out, just that he did.

"That day he was killed, the men who did it... They said Crone's name. Twice. They even called someone while I watched to make sure Crone knew they'd done what he ordered. It was the proof the DA needed to put him away. One of the men who was there that day, he got arrested and gave up some information, thinking he would be protected... but Crone's people got to him anyway. He died before the trial." That made me think of something Spidey said earlier. "He got shanked in his sleep," I murmured.

Maybe that's why Spidey wanted me dead so badly. Not because I got his friend sent to prison and killed, but because he knew Crone would do the same to him. Maybe he thought by taking me out, it would make him less of a target.

Liam made a sound and tugged me closer.

"I barely saw daylight in the six months leading up to the trial. They put me and Mom into protective custody. Mom wasn't a witness, but she was the only thing Crone could use against me. They made an attempt on me once, almost managed to kill me. After that, the Feds moved us around constantly. I looked over my shoulder every time I moved. When I slept, it was restless, and if I managed to sleep deeply, I always dreamed of that day..."

"I wish I'd been there," Liam murmured, stroking my damp, messed-up braid. "I'm so sorry you had to go through that."

"I'll never forget the look on Crone's face the day I saw him in court. The cold emptiness in his stare. After I testified, after I pretty much put the nail in his coffin, he smiled. He looked right at me and smiled. I'd never felt more threatened in my entire life."

"What happened?"

"They put me into witness protection. Mom, too. But we were separated. It was safer for us to be apart. I haven't seen her since the trial ended. The last time we met, she gave me a number. I have no idea where it came from. She told me I could call her on it if I ever had to. Our code was to ask about roses; that way we knew it was actually us."

"You were afraid to call her, though."

I nodded. "I was worried they were watching her, waiting to find out where I'd run off to." I lifted my cheek and glanced at him. "I'm still terrified I gave her away. But I had to know. I had to see if she was okay."

"I know." He soothed, tucking my face back into his chest.

"They promised I would be safe in witness protection. I got a new life, a new name. A new address. I left behind everything about who I was before. I gave up my job, my mother... everything."

"You went to Chicago, right?"

I nodded. "Seems kinda stupid if you ask me. The woman who put a mobster away was sent to live in Chicago where Crone has connections. But they assured me it was safe. And for a while, it was."

"How'd you end up here with me?"

"One night, a delivery man came to my door. I hadn't ordered anything, and I just had this feeling, you know? Like I was being watched... like something was wrong."

I felt Liam nod, so I continued, a little lost. Reliving the night just a week ago. God, it felt like a lifetime.

"I told him to leave the package and go." I swallowed thickly. My mouth was dry and so was my throat. "He said he would... but he didn't. He picked the lock and came inside."

Liam's body was taut beneath mine, nearly vibrating with stress. Wanting to comfort him, I slid my arm up and hugged around his neck.

"He had a gun with a silencer on it. We, ah, got into a struggle. I'd been cooking on the stove, and when he shoved me into the kitchen, I grabbed the pan and threw the hot food in his face. I ran then. I had that duffle packed in the closet by the door. Maybe I always knew I was going to have to run. I grabbed it and hid downstairs. When I saw him run the other way, I got a cab and got the hell out of there."

"You came here," Liam said. I could practically hear him digesting everything I'd told him.

I nodded. "After I went into a local gym and stole some shoes and a hat and after a couple stops on a train, yeah. I got on a bus and came here. It was the only place I could think of."

"You didn't tell the FBI you're here?"

I shook my head. "No. They had their chance to protect me. They failed. Crone's guys still found me, and I know they aren't going to stop. They're going to keep coming until I'm dead."

"I won't let them kill you."

I made a sound. "Don't you understand what I'm saying, Liam? These men… they're professional killers. I betrayed them. And what's worse is I got away. More than once. Anyone associated with me will get caught in the crossfire. I'm like a walking time bomb."

I climbed off his lap, despite his attempts to not let me go.

"This is why I can't stay here!" I said, flinging my arm wide. "This is why I can't be your girlfriend. Technically, Bellamy Cutler doesn't even exist anymore."

The severity of this situation seemed to crash down

on me full speed. I felt like I was being pummeled by that avalanche all over again. My body slumped under the weight of it all, and my shoulder ached. Tears I didn't even know I'd been crying dampened my face and dripped into my lips, leaving a salty tang across my tongue.

I'd been stupid. Blind. Liam made me blind. He gave me a sense of security and the love I'd always desperately wanted.

I loved him. Fiercely. Almost stupidly.

And by being here, I signed his death warrant.

Shame filled me. The kind of soul-crushing humiliation I'd honestly only ever known when I'd seen my mother that first time after my father's murder. The time she looked at me with a sad, almost damning look in her eyes.

She'd tried to tell me. I didn't listen.

I never fucking listened.

Security wasn't mine to have. His love wasn't either.

A sob ripped out of my chest, and I rushed toward my clothes, slapping my hands on the fabric, feeling it was still wet but knowing it was going to have to do.

Maybe if I left right now, if I took off and never came back, those men would follow… and they would forget about Liam.

Maybe if I just let them kill me, then everything would stop. Liam would be safe. My mother would be safe… I wouldn't have to run.

Another sob ripped through my chest, and more tears splashed across my cheeks.

"What are you doing?" Liam demanded, appearing by my side.

"I have to go," I said, picking up the jeans. "Just let me go."

The wet denim was ripped out of my hands and thrown across the room. I reached for another article of clothing, my shirt.

The shirt Liam had given me to wear.

Clutching it to my chest, deep, wrenching sobs ripped out of me.

Warm, strong arms encircled me from behind. Liam pulled me against him, hunching around me like a protective shield. "You're not leaving," he murmured.

"If I stay, they'll kill you. They'll kill us both." I sobbed.

"I'd rather die *with* you than live *without* you."

I sucked in a breath. The sobs shaking me stopped, and I stood frozen against him, his body holding up mine. "W-what?"

"I mean it, Bellamy," he intoned, his voice dangerously low and sincere. "If you leave, I'll follow. I'll chase you around this damn globe if I have to. I *will not* live without you."

I shuddered under the sheer power in that statement. I couldn't even fool myself into believing he didn't know exactly what he was saying. He knew.

He meant it.

My lungs trembled when I finally sucked in a breath. I turned to face him. The second he pulled back to let me, I folded toward the floor.

With a grunt, Liam caught me, pulling me right into his chest.

My entire body was shaking, teeth chattering again. It was too much. He was too much.

"Why?" It was all I could manage. All I could think of.

"Because I love you. Because one day with you is better than a lifetime without."

More tears fell.

The crushing emotion in my chest coupled with the weakness in my limbs overcame all thought. Even fear.

Fear, the strongest emotion I'd ever known, the strongest arguable emotion of the entire human race, had succumbed.

To Liam.

The pads of his thumbs were warm and slightly rough when he dragged them over my wind-burned, tear-soaked cheeks. My breathing hitched, and he smiled tenderly, making me feel I'd just been wrung out and hung in the sun to dry.

"You're staying here, Bells. You're staying home with me."

"Home," I whispered, tears filling my eyes anew.

He nodded, and I found myself nodding back. My hands closed around his wrists, holding on to him while he held on to me.

We stood there for a long time, the light of the fire creating an orange halo around Liam, giving his already strong body a superhuman glow as we held each other, just staring.

A log in the fireplace fell, and the sound of it was loud and interruptive. I jolted, taken off guard. Liam steadied me before easing back to add more wood and stoke the flames.

When he was done, he piled a few more blankets on the floor in front of the warm glow and then reached for my hand. Our lips met just seconds after our hands. His mouth was gentle and cajoling. A veil fell over everything. On one side, it was just him and me, and on the other was the rest of the world. The only sound in the room was that of our lips meeting again and again. The only light was from the flames of the fire and the one inside the lamp.

Outside, the wind howled. A stream of the icy air entered through the broken window on the door and brushed across my lower back, almost like a skeleton reaching out to me from a grave.

I shivered and pushed closer. Liam closed around me and turned, putting himself in the path of the air and blocking me from its clutches. Warmth reached out from the fire, wrapping around my legs and caressing my skin.

Lifting his head, Liam looked down with heavy, silver eyes.

I thought about speaking. Of saying something to try and convey exactly how he made me feel. In the end, I said nothing because there were no words that could explain, and no words could match the ones he'd just spoken.

Wrapping an arm around my waist, he lifted and pushed. My body went willingly onto the pile of blankets, landing softly beneath his.

Firelight stretched across his side and climbed over his defined shoulder. I traced the shadows with my fingertips and watched with bated breath as his nipples tightened. Lowering again, his mouth brushed mine, and we kissed endlessly, using our tongues to explore each other. I felt his erection brush against me every time he moved restlessly, and each time, I felt my own restlessness grow.

My fingers explored the contours of his back and sides. The way his body responded and rippled beneath my touch was intoxicating. His mouth ripped away from mine, and I gasped when he latched onto the side of my neck and sucked. I arched into him, turning my head to the side to give him all the access he desired.

Too soon, his lips gentled, and I made a sound of frustration and pushed up toward him farther. Liam kissed across my collarbone and flicked his tongue across my nipple.

I sucked in a breath, then expelled it when the pressure of his lips closing around the swollen pebble shot a tingle of pleasure through me that ended between my legs.

I grabbed at his hair, filling my hands, and ran my foot up the inside of his thigh.

Liam lifted his head. The glint in his eyes was hot and dangerous. "Watch that arm, sweetheart," he rumbled.

I blinked, not really hearing what he said.

God, just the sound of his voice was sexy.

I must not have done what he wanted because he smiled, lopsided, and kissed his way back up my body.

Pushing up onto his hands, Liam pulled my one hand away from him and pressed a kiss to the palm. "You can't be moving around too much," he said, placing the arm at my side.

My shoulder. Right. I'd forgotten about it.

In this moment, I didn't fucking care.

I reached for him again, ignoring his order.

He drew back, arching an eyebrow. "Don't make me stop, Bells," he intoned deliciously. "Please, don't fucking make me stop."

My arm fell back to my side, and he lowered again.

"This really isn't the time for this," he said, pressing kisses against my mouth as he spoke. "But *goddamn*, I want you so much."

Curling my hand around his waist, I pulled his body down until we molded together. His eyes flickered to mine, and I opened my legs so his body fell between them. His rock-hard cock nudged exactly where I wanted it to.

Both of us shuddered, and his hips thrust forward.

He'd have been inside me with the movement if our underwear wasn't in the way. I moaned and moved restlessly beneath him.

Rising to his knees, he hooked his thumbs in the waistband of his boxer briefs and tugged them down. I sucked in a breath, gazing upon the strength in his body and the way his long, lean torso gave way to a sinful V-shaped muscle that turned the inside of my mouth into the Sahara.

Curling a hand around the back of my knee, he lifted my leg, propping it up on his shoulder. Slowly, he dragged the panties over my legs using his fingertips as foreplay all the way down the inside of my thighs and past my knees.

Once the panties were gone, he kissed the inside of my ankle and nipped at my calf.

I watched him, feeling like the fire wasn't beside me anymore, but inside me. My fingers curled into the blankets beneath me, pulling up fistfuls as I waited so impatiently for his body to touch mine again.

The way his eyes lingered on my naked body was making me crazy. I was soaking wet and ready for him, and he didn't even have to touch me.

"Liam," I murmured.

"Tell me what you want, sweetheart," he whispered.

I pulled my foot from his shoulder and opened my legs in stark invitation, beckoning. "Come home, Liam."

His eyes flared, and then we were skin to skin. I felt his wide head at my entrance, but he didn't push inside. Shuddering, he rose over me, a low curse dropping from his lips. Balancing on his elbows, he met my eyes. "I almost forgot." His voice was gruff.

Liam pushed up, moving away. With a cry, I surged

up, wincing a little at the sudden movement of my shoulder.

"Careful," he rasped, coming back and dropping a kiss to my mouth.

"Don't stop." I reached for him.

"I'm not stopping, sweetheart. Hang on." He went to his coat, reached into an inside pocket, and pulled out his wallet. Seconds later, there was a foil packet in his hand.

"You on the pill?" he asked, looking between me and the condom.

I shook my head sadly. "Never needed to be."

He chuckled. "Can't say I'm sorry to hear that."

"I wish I was now," I murmured.

Dropping between my legs again, he rolled the rubber down over his length.

"We can fix that soon." Reaching between us, he stroked a finger up my center. I arched and cried out. I watched him stick the finger slick with my desire between his lips and suck. "For now, though, this will be enough."

He rose over me again, blocking everything so all I saw was him. In one movement, our bodies joined. My mouth opened, but no sound came out. Liam froze above me, pushing up onto trembling arms. "Did I hurt you?" he asked.

The effort it took him to not move was evident on his face.

I shook my head. "You feel good."

He moaned. "You are so fucking tight."

I moved beneath him, stroking against him. His face dropped into my neck, lips latching onto my skin to gently suck.

Slowly, Liam began to move. It was torture. He felt so

good, stretching out my walls, filling me up completely. Need and desire built inside me until it felt I might blow apart if he didn't give me what I wanted.

Reaching around, I grabbed his butt and pushed him deep.

We groaned at the same time.

He thrust deeper, and I whispered his name.

And then he was moving. He looked like the definition of control as he pushed up over me and pumped his hips, hammering into my body.

My head drifted to the side, and my eyes rolled back in my head as wave after wave of intense pleasure surged over my body.

"Bellamy," Liam rasped, the sound sort of like a prayer.

Turning my head, our eyes locked and I met him thrust for thrust. Lifting my hips each time he came down. The intensity inside me built and built until I was gasping for breath and there was no holding back anymore.

His name ripped from my lips as mind-numbing pleasure burst over me. My body shuddered and shook as the orgasm seemed to go on and on.

Above me, Liam shouted, his body stiff as he emptied inside me. Every quiver of his cock sent more ripples of insane pleasure shooting through my entire body.

I didn't come down until he did. Until he gathered me close and rolled, carefully draping me over his chest, anchoring his arms around me.

"Promise me you won't leave," he said a little while later as his fingertips dragged down my spine.

"I'm not sure you understand how bad this could get." I didn't know what else to say to him. I'd told him everything. It was as though he wasn't even afraid.

His voice was all rumbly when he replied, "I understand, Bellamy. I choose you."

He chose me.

That was his choice.

My heart swelled with love… and with guilt.

Still, I made a choice.

I chose him.

"I promise."

36

Liam

THE SKY WAS JUST BEGINNING TO SHOW SIGNS OF DAWN when I forced myself out of the tangle of blankets and limbs I was caught up in.

At first, I thought it might be tough to stay awake all night. After what happened, our injuries, and the fact I was totally fucking satiated from sex, I'd been concerned we wouldn't be able to manage.

It ended up not being an issue. Worry would do that to a man. Worry and the desire to protect what was his. I did think the men who forced Bellamy up the mountain were dead, but I would be a stupid fool not to realize there was a slim chance the assholes lived.

I lay awake listening for any signs of them approaching the cabin, either looking for us or just seeking some kind of shelter. They never came, and the hope I had they were dead grew.

No. I didn't feel remorseful for hoping those men were dead. They deserved that and more.

There was also the fact Bellamy was the target of a mobster. I had to make her safe… but fuck me, I wasn't sure how.

"Is everything okay?" she asked as I gazed out the window for probably the hundredth time, searching the snowy horizon for signs we weren't alone.

"Yeah, sweetheart, it's fine." I turned in time to see her shiver lightly and pull the blanket tighter around her.

The fire was starting to die down. I'd used the last of the wood. I could go out and get more, but it was wet and would take a while to burn. With the sun coming up, the best thing for us to do was get moving. We could be back at the resort in an hour.

"Liam?"

I made a sound, acknowledging her.

"Do you have your phone?"

I shook my head. "It was in my coat pocket, not the inside one. I lost it during the avalanche."

"Well, now I don't feel so stupid for not even thinking of it before."

"You aren't stupid. A lot happened last night." I strode across the room and poked at what was left of the fire. "It's almost light out. I think we should head out, get back to the resort as soon as possible."

"I'm going to call my contact at the FBI."

I turned. "I thought you didn't trust them."

She made a face. "It's not like I think they're dirty or anything. I just don't have much faith in witness protection. They're going to be pissed I broke their rules and did something that connects me to my old life."

I felt my eyes narrow as a thought occurred to me. "They gonna try and take you away?"

"I'm sure they'll want to."

A low growl rumbled up from deep inside me.

Bellamy hurried to say, "But I'll refuse. I'm not just going to blindly accept everything they say is the best thing. I want some say in my own life. I want some of what I lost back. I want you."

Bending down, I lifted her onto her feet, pulling her into my arms. "Fuck, I love hearing that."

"I love saying it."

"C'mon. Get dressed." I gathered up her clothes, getting angry all over again at how little she had to wear as protection from the elements. The jeans were still damp and so was some of the other stuff.

Bellamy plucked her T-shirt out of the pile I was holding and frowned. "They ripped your shirt," she commented, fingering a rip I hadn't noticed last night.

My gut tightened, and again, I had to fight back that instant rage threatening to take over. "It's just a shirt," I told her.

She shook her head. "It was yours and you gave it to me." Her blue eyes lifted. "It was my favorite."

It pierced my heart the way she looked at me. How even after everything, my shirt still meant something to her.

"I'll give you a new one, sweetheart," I murmured. "Hell, I'll take you to my place and let you have anything in the whole damn closet."

"I haven't been to your house yet." She was intrigued.

I smiled. "There's still lots of firsts we need to have. All the more reason to get the hell out of here."

Smiling softly, she lifted the shirt to her nose and sniffed it. I was about to ask her what the hell she was doing when she made a sound. "It's ripped, and it doesn't smell like you anymore."

I laughed and tugged it out of her hand. Then I handed her the one I had on last night. "Better?"

Her eyes lit up as she reached for it and tugged it over her head, struggling a little to get it over her sore arm and shoulder. After I helped pull it over her, she smiled, fingering the hem that fell past her thighs. "This one smells like you still."

I kissed her forehead, then threw on everything I had, including the ripped shirt that no longer smelled like me. When I was done, I helped Bellamy put on her coat, then began pulling mine around her on top of it.

"I can't," she said, stepping back.

"I'm not arguing with you about this, Bells. You're wearing it."

"What if I just put a blanket or two around me?" She offered.

I thought about it, then shook my head. "The coat is waterproof. Sit." I pointed to the coffee table.

With a huff, she sat down and glared. Suppressing a smile, I grabbed her boots so I could tie them up for her. Before sliding the first one on her foot, I tugged my sock over her bare toes.

Bellamy gasped, as I knew she would, and pulled her foot up out of my hands. "What are you doing?"

"Tucking your jeans into the socks. It will help keep the heat in."

"These are your socks," she ground out.

I sighed and rubbed a hand over my forehead. "I have a headache, baby. How about you just indulge me?"

An empathetic sound ripped from her throat. Her small hand covered my cheek and lifted my head. "Let me see." She leaned close to the gash she'd cleaned just hours before. After another small sound, she pulled back. "It's not bleeding anymore, but it's still pretty swollen. We really need to get it looked at."

"Foot," I said, holding out my hand.

She surrendered it without a word.

It was a dirty trick, playing hurt to get her to cooperate. My head *did* hurt, but it wasn't anything I couldn't handle. Hell, my knee hurt worse. I didn't want to argue with her, though, and we needed to get the hell out of here. So yeah, I might have used my injury to get her to cooperate.

"What about you?" She worried, biting into her lower lip.

I finished tying up her boots and smiled. "My boots are waterproof and warm. I'll be fine."

She nodded, looking doubtful.

"You keep your hands inside the coats, okay? I'll wear the gloves."

She nodded, and I pulled my hat down over her ears.

Another look of protest darkened her eyes, so I put my arms around her bundled body and kissed her. Her sweet lips parted instantly, and my tongue swept inside to stroke over hers. A feeling of rightness washed over me, a feeling I allowed myself to enjoy before pulling away.

As I did, a faint sound drifted in from outside.

Our eyes collided, both of us silently asking if the other heard. I put a gloved finger up to my lips and turned, automatically tucking her behind me.

The sound grew a little louder. It was a sound I was familiar with. It was a sound I wouldn't normally think twice about, but today wasn't a normal day.

It was barely light.

We were out of bounds of the resort perimeters, so whoever was out there wasn't just taking a snowmobile for a joy ride.

There was a reason it was out there. There was a

reason the sound of the engine grew closer and closer with every passing second.

"What if it's them?" Bellamy worried, her hand closing around the back of my shirts.

It couldn't be. Where the fuck would they have gotten snowmobiles? Unless they had them stashed in the woods somewhere. Unless they'd survived the avalanche, gone back to the resort, and took one to come looking for us.

I turned toward Bellamy. "Stay inside. Don't come out until I come for you."

Her eyes went wide. "Where are you going?"

"To see who it is."

"Liam." She reached for my hand, grasping it. "Stay here with me."

"You know I can't do that, sweetheart," I told her reasonably. I wasn't about to sit in here like a sitting duck. I was going to find out who the fuck was out there.

And I was going to do it now.

Bellamy

As Liam's hand wrapped quietly around the handle to the front door, I couldn't help but wonder.

Would there come a time when I wasn't afraid? Would there come a time when everyone around me wasn't in danger?

Would life ever be normal again?

Would I ever truly be free?

Was I doing the right thing by staying here?

All the questions swarming my mind instantly vanished the second he pulled open the door and glanced back.

"Please be careful," I whimpered.

"I'll be right back."

I wanted to scream after him as he stepped out into the snow. Didn't he know that was the worst thing he could say? Every person on every horror movie in the history of horror who said, "I'll be right back," *never* came back!

Screw his headache! I wasn't just going to stand here. If he was going out into the snow like a bonehead, then by God, I'd be a bonehead, too.

I paused in the midst of marching toward the door. It occurred to me that either one of us being a bonehead was… well, boneheaded.

Well, at least we weren't alone in it.

Wintry wind kissed my cheeks when I crept out the door. It wasn't a good kind of kiss either. Not the kind like Liam gave. It was more of the kind your eighty-five-year-old grandma gave you right before squeezing your cheeks and telling you how adorable you were.

Instantly, my exposed skin stung a little, but I ignored it and tried to keep the snow from crunching too much underfoot.

The sky was lightening, but the sun wasn't totally up yet. The white layer of snow outside did offer some sort of brightness so I could see. Squinting against the snow flurries flying wildly around, I sought out Liam.

He wasn't far, standing behind a large bush near the corner of the cabin, gazing out toward the snowmobile that cut quickly over the snow.

A few moments later, Liam stiffened, seemed to lean toward the person approaching, and then stepped out from around the concealment.

I gasped and went rushing forward. What was he thinking? It could be the men coming back to finish the job.

"Liam!" I yelled, rushing through the snow.

He turned abruptly. "I told you to stay inside."

"If you're going to act like an idiot, then I am, too!" I burst out.

I would have laughed at the look on his face, but this

wasn't funny. He had to know what kind of risk he was taking.

"I'm not being an idiot, sweetheart," he countered. A small smile pulled at his mouth. "But later, we're going to have a talk about you following me into a potentially dangerous situation."

I made a face. He was one to talk, Mr. I-followed-you-and-two-men-with-guns-up-a-mountain. "Isn't that what you did last night?"

His face darkened. "That's different."

"Don't you pull that sexist crap on me." I warned, planting my feet into the snow, ready to argue.

The snowmobile engine cut off, and someone yelled out, "Liam!"

I winced, remembering this was not the time for an argument.

Liam lifted his hand and waved, then started forward. After a couple steps, he stopped and held out his hand to me. "Come on, then."

I hurried to catch up. "Is that Alex?"

"Sure is," he quipped, pride in his voice.

Alex jogged over the snow, looking way more graceful than I ever would. "Seriously, man, I have been worried sick," he said, barely out of breath.

"I told you to search if I wasn't back by morning," Liam said as they one-arm hugged each other.

"Sun's almost up. I couldn't wait any longer." Alex glanced at me, his eyes resting on the bruises I knew covered my face. Then he looked back at his best friend. "What the fuck happened?"

"Long story," Liam muttered.

"Short version will work for now," Alex retorted.

"Some bad men are trying to kill me. Liam intercepted them, and their gunfire set off an avalanche last night. We almost died."

Both men turned their eyes on me.

I shrugged. "What? You wanted the short version."

Alex glanced at Liam. "When you said you thought she was in some kind of trouble, I thought you meant lost her job or was hiding from an ex."

"I wish," I muttered.

Alex barked a laugh. "Well, how about next time you give a guy a heads-up on what he's dealing with."

I blinked. That was it? That's all he had to say?

Liam saw my shock and chuckled. "We aren't the kind of men who run from trouble."

Alex made a sound of agreement.

"How about mobsters with big guns?"

Alex pursed his lips, but it didn't take long for him to shrug. "Them either. What do you think we are? Pansies?"

I made a choked sound, but the guys turned toward each other to have their own conversation. Frankly, I thought it was rude.

"A report came in about an hour ago about an avalanche on this side of the mountain last night. Since you haven't been answering your phone, I knew I had to come out here. I remembered this place, hoped you might come here if you needed somewhere."

"Good looking out," Liam told him, holding out a fist for a bump.

Why did guys always do that? They might as well just beat their chests.

"We were just about to hike it back to the resort." Liam continued.

"I wasn't sure what I'd find when I got out here," Alex

said, his voice low, revealing some of the torment he'd obviously been going through.

"I'm sorry I just ran off like that, man. I didn't mean to worry you."

"I'm just glad you're okay." He looked at me. "Both of you."

Alex's genuine concern touched me. I forgot what it was like to have people around who cared.

Liam reached for my hand. "C'mon, we need to get the hell off this mountain."

"Think the sled can handle three of us?" Alex asked as we moved toward it. The sky was growing lighter, and a beautiful shade of orange streaked just above the treetops.

Liam grunted. "I'll drive."

"What about your knee?" I worried. "You should let Alex drive."

Alex swung around, staring immediately at Liam. "You hurt your knee?"

Liam nodded, a dark look crossing his features.

Something passed between the two of them. Something that made me squirm around in my boots. Obviously, there was more going on than I was privy to. I wanted to ask. I wanted every detail.

Now wasn't the time, though, and I didn't like knowing I had to wait.

"I'll drive." Alex's voice was gruff. "You just hold on to your girl."

Liam nodded again.

"How come you don't argue with him?" I wondered, slightly disgruntled.

"Don't be jelly." Alex teased. Though, I couldn't help but wonder if he could sense that maybe I was a little jealous. His obvious close relationship with Liam and the sort of loyalty and trust they shared was something I wanted as well. "Not everyone has the power of persuasion like me."

I rolled my eyes, and Liam made a rude sound. "Dude. No."

Alex swung his leg up over the sled. "Thank you, Alex," he cracked. "I appreciate you coming out here at the ass crack of dawn to search for me, Alex."

I smiled and leaned over to peck him on the cheek. "Thank you, Alex."

His piercing blue eyes flew to mine. He hadn't been expecting that, and for a second, I'd rendered him speechless. Something I think probably didn't happen very often.

"I'm grateful Liam has such a good friend in you."

He lifted the thick scarf around his neck and patted it against his eyes. "This damn wintry air is making my eyes water. Shoulda brought my shades."

I giggled.

Dropping the fabric, Alex smiled, reached over and tugging on one of my messy braids. "Anytime."

"You two can bond later," Liam muttered. "On the sled, Bells."

I climbed onto the snowmobile behind Alex. "What about you?" I asked Liam.

He straddled the machine behind me, carefully sliding me forward until I smacked into Alex's back. "It's a tight fit, but we can make it work."

Alex peered over his shoulder at us. "Hey, look at that. A Bells sandwich."

Liam smacked Alex in the back of the head. "You are not part of any sandwich that involves my girl."

Liam's arms slid around my waist, and my body

shifted back into his. "You need to hold on to Alex, sweetheart."

After what he just said, that was literally the last thing I expected to hear.

"Come on, then, girl. I have some driving to do," Alex quipped and patted his side.

I glanced at Liam, and he nodded, so I slid my good arm around his side and anchored it at Alex's waist.

"Hold on," Alex called out over the engine as he revved it.

The next thing I knew, we were flying over the snow down the mountain and cutting through the trees. Alex was a horrible driver. Like my life flashed before my eyes. I was kinda tired of that happening.

The feel of Liam's arms tightening around my waist gave me a greater sense of security, and I leaned into him again, the arm around Alex sliding loose. Liam scooted closer against me, using his body to pin mine more firmly between him and his best friend.

After clearing one of the last hills, the resort came into view below, and I nearly cried in relief. I knew I wasn't actually safe yet, but just seeing BearPaw after I honestly thought last night had been my last made me incredibly grateful and sentimental.

Alex slowed to a pace that actually felt more normal and glanced behind him at Liam. Mirrored goggles covered his eyes, but I felt them drift over me before settling on the man I was leaning into.

He didn't even say a word, but he didn't have to. Liam knew what he wanted to ask.

"My place!" he yelled, and my body jolted back when Alex shot forward without any warning.

My hand dug into Alex's coat, and the rest of me

knocked into Liam. His arms tightened, and the sound of his low chuckle over the motor filled my ears. He hadn't even so much as jostled when Alex sped off like a demon!

Alex cut away from the resort, and I forgot about his hellish driving because I realized we were heading to Liam's cabin. A place I had yet to see.

As anxious as I was to discover a new piece of the man I loved, I couldn't help but worry. I couldn't help but glance over my shoulder as we drove on, scanning all the pristine snow for anyone who might be following.

We might have made it out of the avalanche, but I knew better than anyone that I was still far from safe.

38

Liam

THE ACHES WERE SETTLING IN. THE THROBBING IN MY knee was getting harder to ignore.

Now that the imminent threat to Bellamy was gone and all the adrenaline that pumped through me most of the night was dissolving, my body was letting me know it needed some recovery.

As an athlete, I knew how important recovery was. I also knew if you weren't able to properly recover, the body—and mind—would never quite be the same.

"The Extreme at the resort?" Alex asked the second the sled was parked beside mine on the side of my cabin.

I nodded. "Yeah."

Alex glanced between me and Bells. "I'll go get it and meet you back here. Then we'll head to the hospital."

"Thanks, man," I replied. "The extra set of keys are in the kitchen. My set is still in Bells's room."

"House key with them?"

I nodded.

"I got this." Alex pulled out a key ring from his coat pocket and went up the deck to the back door. Here at BearPaw, the back of the house was more like the front because it was usually the back that looked out to the slopes and the views.

"He has a key?" Bellamy asked as I helped her off the sled.

"Of course," Alex and I replied at the same time.

I pecked a kiss on her cheek, and into her ear, I whispered, "You're gonna get one, too."

Bellamy smiled, her eyes going soft for a moment before they shifted to the landscape behind us. The tension in her body was still palpable. It was almost as if her nerves had increased since we got off the sled.

"It's okay now," I told her, wanting her to feel safe.

"But for how long?" She worried, her eyes coming back to mine.

I didn't have an answer for that. I wished I did. I didn't want to see her like this. I didn't want her to live like this. She deserved so much better.

Charlie barked and nearly leapt off the back deck, bounding through the snow toward us. Bellamy laughed and held out her arm to the dog. He launched himself at her. I moved fast, putting myself between them so he didn't pummel her into the powder.

"Easy, boy." I laughed as he licked my face.

Bellamy scratched behind his ear as he leaned on me and let out a satisfied groan.

Alex came out of the door, holding up the spare set of keys to my truck. "I'll be back in just a few. Be ready."

"I really appreciate this," I told him.

He barely paused. "You'd do the same for me."

"Yes. I would."

I led Bellamy into my place as the snowmobile started up and took off.

"He's a terrible driver," she told me, grimacing.

I laughed. "Actually, Alex handles himself well on one of those."

"Your cabin is beautiful, Liam," she said, glancing around as we walked inside. "I've been wondering what it looks like."

I half smiled. "Not what you were expecting?"

"Maybe a little cleaner than I thought." She teased, then stepped farther inside.

I made a sound. "I haven't been home enough to make a mess."

Charlie lumbered across the room and grabbed a giant squeaking ball out of a basket and carried it over to me. I grabbed it. The familiar feel of slobber coated my fingers before I tossed it out the back door, and he took off after it.

I glanced back at Bellamy, who was still gazing around with an almost wistful expression. I tried to understand what she might be seeing through her eyes, but it was hard because I'd seen it all a million times before.

It was a simple log cabin, typical of what you would find at BearPaw. Or on any mountain. It had wood on the outside and wood on the inside. The ceiling was pitched in an A-frame style with beams running across it. The windows were large, giving views of the slopes, and were trimmed with the same wood that was on the walls. Everything was pretty basic, really. I wasn't a guy who needed much.

The table was handcrafted by a local furniture maker and so were the wooden benches that slid beneath it. Old snowshoes and snowboards hung on the walls, and all the pillows and blankets on the living room furniture were red plaid.

The fireplace in the center of the room was made of stone, and a rough-hewn log served as the mantel. It was pretty masculine in here, actually, but the kitchen was updated with white marble counters (my mom picked them) and had a bunch of open shelving with white dishes, bowls, and mugs.

I crossed the room over to the fireplace, suddenly feeling a little nervous about the place I never really gave much thought to. It was just home to me. Flipping the switch, the flames in the fire roared to life at the same time Charlie rushed back into the house, tracking in a ton of snow with him.

"I guess this place is pretty much a bachelor pad," I said, crossing to shut the door and keep out the cold.

"I love it," she murmured, gazing out the window, wrapping her arms around herself. "It feels like a real home."

Understanding coursed through me. As well as pleasure. It thrilled the shit out of me she thought it was comfortable here. "Something you haven't had in a long time." My voice was knowing.

Tearing her eyes from the view, she looked at me. "I think I forgot what it felt like to really have a home."

My chest ached. Slipping between her and the window, I tugged her gently, and she came, laying her head against my chest. "You have a home now, Bells."

I wanted to stand there with her all day. I wanted to take her on a tour of the place, show her both bedrooms and the loft. It was all going to have to wait.

"C'mon," I said, taking her hand and pulling her down the hall to the master bedroom. While she looked around, I pulled out some clean, dry, warm clothes, tossing it all on the bed. Next, I went into the attached bath, reached into the glass-enclosed shower, and turned on the spray to warm up.

"Alex will be back with the truck any minute now, but I think a shower would be good before we head to the hospital. You up for it?"

Her nod was eager, and I stripped off all my clothes and then helped her do the same.

"I should call the police." She worried, but I shook my head.

"We will, but we're going to take care of you first."

Bellamy relented, and I liked to tell myself it was because I was standing there naked in front of her.

Inside the shower, I took stock of her body, noting her shoulder was still swollen and there was a lump near the collarbone. She needed X-rays and a sling, hopefully nothing more.

"Will you help me?" Her voice floated around me like the steam from the shower. Ripping my eyes from her body and the way the ribbons of water cascaded over her, I saw her trying to undo her braids with just one hand.

With a sound, I brushed away her hand and slipped my fingers into her hair, making short work of the braids.

She sighed when her head tilted back beneath the water. Lust grew heavy in my belly as the water saturated the long strands, pulling them straight and making them cling to her neck, shoulders, and chest.

The heat of my stare must have been palpable because she opened her eyes and lowered her chin, meeting my gaze.

We stared at each other silently as steam floated around and water rained down over our skin. "If we weren't in a hurry right now…" The words rumbled out of me. "I would have your back against the tile and your legs around my waist."

Reaching out, her palm covered my chest. "I miss you already."

I groaned. "That's not making it easier on me, sweetheart."

"Kiss me."

I obliged. Thin cascades of warm water ran between our lips as they moved against each other. Her body was slick against mine, and the exhaustion that clung to my limbs was gone for long moments as I sank into her mouth.

When I started to ease back, she came with, pulled my bottom lip into her mouth, and sucked, drinking down the water clinging to my skin. I swear she somehow managed to drink a piece of my soul.

I groaned when she released me. Her arm slid around my waist, and she pressed close, hugging me as if she were afraid she'd never see me again.

My heart was thumping quite heavily against my ribs, my stomach was doing all kinds of flips, and my fingers itched to explore her body, to push her beneath me.

Above all, though, there was this sense of soul-crushing emotion. A depth of love I truly had never known. Not even eight years ago. It was even stronger than my need to be inside her. It was stronger than anything I'd ever experienced in my entire life.

I had to protect it.

To protect her.

But how?

39

Bellamy

"It's Bellamy."

"Who?"

I sighed. "Bella Lane."

"Ms. Lane, I've been waiting for your call."

I glanced down at the floor and Liam's socks that were covering my feet. "You know what happened?"

"We know that your location and identity were compromised and that you were found by Crone's men. For a while, we really weren't sure if you made it out alive."

"I did. I felt it best that I keep a low profile."

He grunted. "Going back to your original identity was not recommended."

Something inside me sparked with anger. I was exhausted, hurt, and people kept trying to kill me. Yes, I probably pissed off the good ol' FBI by not calling, but didn't I have a right to protect myself?

"It's not my original identity," I snapped. "It's who I really am."

"You are Bella Lane."

"I'm well aware of my new identity. I haven't actually gone back to the old one. I'm just with some people who knew me as Bellamy." *The real me.*

"Are you talking about professional snowboarder and Olympic medalist Liam Mattison?"

It didn't even surprise me that he knew I was with Liam. I mean, if Crone's men could find me, I guess the FBI could, too.

What a freaking mess.

"Yes."

"And Alexander Carter?"

"Do you know the name of my hotel maid, too?" I snapped.

"This morning, a Jennifer Fray was attending your room."

Holy crap! I snorted. "That was a joke."

"This is no joking matter, Ms. Lane."

"I'm well aware, especially since I'm on my way to the hospital right now."

"So his men made contact?" He wasn't surprised by this either.

"Yes. They took me up into a snowy mountain to die."

"We have a team en route to you now, including me," Agent Frost said, not even showing any kind of reaction to the fact someone tried to kill me. Again.

How many times did this make? Three? Four?

I didn't even know anymore.

"My mother—" I started, but he cut me off.

"Has already been moved to a safe location."

"I want to see her," I said, feeling my lower lip wobble.

"That's not advised at this time."

I knew he'd say that.

"I don't give a damn!" I yelled into the phone.

Liam, who had been lounging against the island, listening, pushed off and came forward. I couldn't help but notice his limp. It seized all the anger and fight right out of me. After our shower, he strapped on some kind of serious-looking knee brace to stabilize it.

He needed the ER.

"I have to go," I said into the line.

"We will meet you at Caribou Memorial in about an hour and a half."

I hung up. "They know where I am. They're on their way."

Liam scooped me into his arms and held me tight. A few stray tears leaked out, and I rubbed them on his sweatshirt. Then I pulled back. "Let's go."

We held hands on the way out to the truck, and when I moved to climb into the back, Liam stopped me and sat in the back instead.

The drive to the hospital was silent, even though I knew Alex had about a hundred thousand questions. Maybe he sensed my stormy mood, or maybe he thought he'd get more answers when it was just him and Liam. Either way, I was glad for the quiet.

I had no idea what was going to happen when Frost and friends showed up. He wasn't going to be happy at all when I informed him I had no intention of returning to witness protection.

He would tell me what a huge mistake I was making.

Part of me knew he was right.

4 0

Liam

HOSPITALS SUCKED.

I'd spent enough time in them to last me the rest of my life.

Yet here I was. Again.

The second we rolled into the ER, we were given a room. I guess there were some benefits to being town royalty and an Olympic medalist.

An Olympic medalist who was washed up... one who probably wouldn't see the slopes again.

I tried not to focus on the blizzard forming inside my brain. Instead, I focused outward on my girl and making sure she got the same level of treatment I would.

Every nurse or doctor who walked into the room got introduced to my girlfriend, something that was starting to irritate me each time I said it.

She wasn't just my girlfriend.

She was my life.

How did I make that clear to people? How did I articulate exactly what I would do if they didn't take care of her as though she was the ruler of my world?

I took comfort in the fact that the word girlfriend seemed to work. We were put in the same room, but they pulled us apart for X-rays and shit. Something I really didn't like.

In addition to Bells calling her FBI contact (who I already hated because he seemed to upset her), I called the local cops. There was a party going out to look for the bodies of the men who tried to kill us, and there were also a few sticking around on our floor to make sure no one else tried anything stupid.

Aside from the general questions, we hadn't had time to answer much else because the first priority was our injuries.

I knew the questions would come, though. A lot of them. Hard ones. I wasn't ready yet, but I was going to have to be.

I wasn't ready for the results of the MRI I just had either.

I was saved from the depths of my own head when the door opened and Alex strode in. I glanced behind him, expecting Bellamy to appear. When she didn't instantly, I glanced to him.

"She's coming. Nurse wouldn't let me push her down the hallway."

"Because he's a terrible driver," Bellamy announced as she came around the corner.

"Am not," Alex protested.

"Are, too," the nurse countered.

Bellamy snickered. It did my heart good to see her. She was like the sun on a stormy day. Even with the sling anchoring her arm to her side.

"How'd it go?" I asked.

"Separated, like you said," Bellamy replied.

The nurse parked the chair beside Bellamy's bed, but she got up and came to mine instead. The nurse started to say something, but I caught her eye and winked.

She didn't say anything else.

My knee was propped up, an ice pack covering it. Bellamy carefully avoided it but scooted toward me between my legs.

"The doctor will be in shortly," the nurse said, then left.

"I'm exhausted." Alex yawned and went over to Bellamy's bed and stretched out across it.

"Make yourself comfortable," she said, watching him.

"Thanks, I will." He yawned again and closed his eyes. "I was up all night, worrying about you two."

"Thanks for staying with Bells," I told him.

His eyes reopened, the full weight of their icy color settling on me. "How's the knee?"

"Waiting," I clipped.

Bellamy glanced over her shoulder, peeking around the curtain of hair falling over her face. "How bad is it?"

"It'll be fine."

I felt Alex's stare, and I returned it. He made a sour face, and I gave him the finger.

"You two need to stop it."

We both looked at Bellamy.

"Stop what?" I asked.

"Having conversations I can't hear."

Alex cackled.

"We don't do that, sweetheart," I said, giving him another hard look.

Her eyes levelled on my face. "You're doing it right now."

"I like you, girl who got away. I like you a lot," Alex mused.

"I didn't get away. I came back," Bells retorted.

I put an arm around her waist and rested my chin on her uninjured shoulder. "Thank God you came back," I murmured.

A little shiver worked its way up her back. I felt it move through her. Then she turned her head and kissed me softly.

The door opened again, and I glanced up at my doctor. My body went rigid. Drawing up to my full height, I nodded. "Dr. Brackner."

"Liam," he said, glancing over at Alex lying on the bed.

"Hey, doc." Alex waved but made no move to sit up.

He inclined his head. "Alex."

Doc knew Alex because he'd been here for a lot of my previous recovery. The staff here was used to seeing us together, so no one batted an eye when Alex made himself at home.

Dr. Brackner was a lot more curious, though, when it came to the girl sitting between my legs. I'd already introduced them, but just like the rest of the staff, everyone was curious. It was the first time I'd ever introduced a woman around as a girlfriend.

"How is the shoulder, Miss Lane?" he asked. It was weird hearing her called that. But she'd checked in using what I thought of as her fake name. She told me it was her actual legal name, but to me, she would never be Bella Lane. She would always be Bellamy Cutler.

"It's separated," she replied. "But it will be fine."

He nodded. "Yes. Rest, keep it mobilized, and then maybe some light physical therapy should do the trick. You'll be good as new in a few weeks."

Her head bobbed. "That's what my doctor said."

"I can help you out with the physical therapy," I told her.

Her head whipped around, and a pink flush darkened her face. *"Liam,"* she hissed.

I bit back a laugh. She had a dirty little mind. I fucking loved it. "I know all about physical therapy for a separated shoulder. I've had one a few times," I explained.

Her eyes widened when she realized I was actually talking about physical therapy for her shoulder and not the *other* kind of physical therapy. Again, I stifled a laugh, but I was pretty sure my eyes were twinkling.

Across the room, Alex was choking, trying not to make some lewd comment.

"Thank you," she said, her voice a little strained, her cheeks still blooming bright pink. "I might take you up on that."

I winked.

She blushed even harder.

Dr. Brackner cleared his throat. "I have your results here, Liam."

I stiffened. Alex sat up on the bed.

"I assume it's okay to discuss this in the company of your friends?"

"Of course," I said without missing a beat.

"Friends are just chosen family, Doc," Alex told him.

"Yes, I suppose so."

"How bad is it?" I asked, my voice harsher than I intended. I didn't want to know, but now that the moment was here, I didn't want to beat around the bush.

"Not as bad as I'm sure you're thinking," the doctor replied. "It's not re-torn."

"Praise Jesus!" Alex exclaimed.

I could feel the confusion in the way Bellamy glanced at me, then back to the doctor.

"But it is stretched."

I nodded even as the news hit me in the gut like a fist.

"What does that mean?" Bellamy asked, reaching for my hand and closing hers around it. I took a deep breath and slowly exhaled it.

"Means our boy still has a shot at returning to the slopes!" Alex announced, relief heavy in his voice.

Bellamy turned to me with wide eyes. "You planned to return to snowboarding?"

I cut a harsh glare to Alex, and he looked like he'd swallowed a canary. "My bad."

I made a face, and he winced. "Sorry, man. I thought you talked to your girl."

"I do talk," I barked. "We've just been busy."

"Should I give you all a moment?" the doctor asked.

"No," I said, dismissing Alex and giving Bellamy's hip a gentle squeeze. I'd explain everything to her as soon as I could. "Please, go on."

"The recovery time on this is a lot less significant than when your ACL was torn. You won't need surgery again, but I think I will suggest a procedure called thermal shrinkage."

"What's that?" Bellamy asked.

I already knew. I learned all about ACL procedures and shit a year ago. "It's where they heat up the stretched collagen in my knee to tighten it back up."

"Is that dangerous?" she worried, glancing back at my doctor.

"Not at all. It's a same-day procedure, so he will be back home with you by the end of the day." My doctor glanced to me. "As you probably already know, after the procedure, you will likely be able to bear full weight on the knee."

I nodded.

"We don't do that here, so I will make some calls to arrange for you to have it done elsewhere as soon as possible."

I nodded again, my stomach dipping a little. I didn't want to do this shit again. Even if it wasn't nearly as bad as before, it still stirred up bad shit. Shit I thought I put away.

"I'll call my trainer and see if he can make a call to the doctor who did my last surgery. See if I can get in with him."

"If that's what you want, then of course. Have them call me, and I will discuss everything with them and send the records."

"Thanks."

He inclined his head. "You need to stay off the knee. No boarding. No lessons. Main focus right now is swelling and pain management."

"Yeah, I know," I muttered.

"If the swelling doesn't subside in a day or two, you're going to need to come back. Don't wait. I'll prescribe—"

"No pills," I snapped.

Bellamy jumped, and I rubbed her back in apology for the outburst.

The doctor paused. "Nothing too heavy or habit forming, but I can give you a prescription for a larger dose of Motrin so you aren't having to swallow so many pills."

My voice was gruff when I replied, "Thanks."

"I know this type of injury is upsetting for an athlete such as yourself. I also know you have been doing everything right in the last year. This could be a lot worse. It's going to heal."

"What about the pros?" I asked, feeling Bellamy's stare again. I avoided it.

"Time will tell."

Time is my enemy right now.

"What about his head?" Bellamy cut through the level of finality in the doctor's words and the way I was reeling from them.

"You do show signs of a mild concussion, and normally, we would keep you overnight for observation. But since this happened several hours ago, I think we will probably be able to release you later on this evening, baring no complications."

"And he doesn't need stitches?" She pressed.

"They already said I didn't, sweetheart," I told her gently.

"I still worry," she told me, and I smiled.

"No stitches. Just keep it clean. Any complications or pain, come back in."

Bells glanced over her shoulder. "That's what they said about my face."

I kissed her on the temple.

"The nurse will be in periodically to check on you and make sure you have everything you need. The police are already waiting to speak with you, but I've kept them out until the results of your tests came back."

I nodded, grateful.

"I'll be back in later this afternoon, as I'm sure the doctor attending to you will be, Miss Lane. Then, barring no complications or trouble, we'll have you both discharged later this evening to get you home for some rest.

"Can we go to sleep?" Bellamy asked, hopeful.

The doctor chuckled. "After you've been awake for twenty-four hours, which I believe you will hit before we discharge you."

She sighed. "I was hoping you'd say something different than my doctor."

Dr. Brackner chuckled. "I'm afraid not."

"Alex can keep us awake," she said and looked over toward my best friend.

He was back to lying on the bed. Snoring.

"Maybe not." She amended.

I laughed.

"Any other questions?"

"No," I said and held out my hand. "Thank you for not making me wait."

He nodded once. "Of course. I imagine you have both endured a very trying time the past several hours. If it's any consolation, you two are very lucky, considering the avalanche. It could have been much, much worse."

Bellamy leaned into me, and I hugged her.

When the doctor was gone, she turned to me, her eyes wide and sincere. "Why didn't you tell me?"

I wasn't about to insult her intelligence by pretending not to know what she meant or even evading the question.

I leaned down so my forehead rested on hers. "'Cause I was too busy trying to get you to tell me what was going on with you."

"I'm not any more important that you are, Liam."

"To me you are."

"Well, I feel the same about you."

"I never meant to make you feel like I was keeping it from you. Your stuff is just a little more time sensitive."

"I feel guilty."

I rested my hand against her cheek and sighed. "Don't."

"It's not that simple."

I half smiled. "It is that simple."

She shook her head once. "I crashed into your life and brought down so much drama. You're a target for the mob now, Liam. If Agent Frost knows who you are, then so does Crone."

I started to say something, but she kept on going, rolling right over my words.

"Clearly, you have a lot going on yourself, and I didn't even think of that. I just showed up and"—she gestured between us—"this happened." Then in a softer, almost whisper, she said, "I didn't mean for this to happen."

"How long have you been completely alone, Bellamy?"

She pulled her forehead from mine and sighed. "Even if I went back into witness protection, you'd still be in danger now."

"How long?" I pressed.

Her shoulders slumped. "Almost two years."

It hurt to hear. It hurt to know. Both of us had suffered in the past couple years, but unlike her, I had family. She had no one.

Slipping my arm around her waist, I flattened my palm on her lower back. "You aren't alone anymore. You won't ever be again. You aren't going back into witness protection, and we're going to work this out. Together."

We were so close I heard her swallow. Felt her intake of breath. "You shouldn't drag the people you love into horrible situations."

"You aren't dragging me. I'm walking into the situation willingly. Hell, I'm running."

The way the sapphire of her gaze reached deep into

me and squeezed my heart made the hand against her back spasm. "I should have marched over to the car that day, yanked Kelsey by her ponytail, and made my claim."

I laughed low. "A cat fight in my honor?" I wagged my eyebrows at her. "Behave."

Her lips curled up in the most delicious smile, and I closed the distance, kissing her, claiming that smile and tucking it deep inside me.

"I love you," I murmured against her lips.

"I love you, too, Liam. So much."

"That was seriously the most touching thing I've ever heard in all my life, and my mom and sister watch some hella sappy shit."

Bellamy jumped and probably would have fallen off the bed backward if I wasn't holding her. I just turned my head. I really wasn't surprised. Alex was an eavesdropping asshole.

"Seriously, dude?"

"I thought you were sleeping!" Bellamy exclaimed, her cheeks pink. She was fucking adorable.

Minus the cuts, bruises, and swelling on her face. That shit just pissed me off.

I didn't care this was courtesy of the most notorious modern crime boss. That guy could suck a dick after I punched him in his jaw. I wasn't going to back down from him. Not when he was threatening Bellamy.

A threat to her was a direct threat to me. To my entire life.

This bastard was in for the fight of his life.

"How am I supposed to get any sleep while you two are over there chatting away like we're on Dr. Phil?"

"You shouldn't have listened!" Bellamy declared.

Alex yawned and sat up. "I needed to know what I was getting involved with." He shook his head. "Perry

Crone, huh? I don't know how you managed to piss off that guy, Bells, but damn. I don't know if I should be worried or impressed."

"I told you not to call her Bells," I growled.

Bellamy looked incredulous. "That's all you have to say to him!"

I shrugged. "I was going to tell him anyway."

"You aren't involved." Bells warned Alex.

We both laughed.

Her eyes narrowed.

I stopped laughing and took her hand. "Now, sweetheart. Alex and I are a package deal. You know that."

She shook her head. "This is dangerous."

"I'm a dangerous guy." He hopped down off the bed.

"This goes way beyond bad driving," she intoned.

He made a rude sound, his body language shifted, and the shield of smooth swagger he wore lowered to reveal a much more private side that Alex didn't show unless he had to. Crossing the room almost like a panther, he kept his piercing eyes on Bellamy. Her fingers curled around mine a little tighter.

I almost told him to knock it the fuck off, but I held my tongue.

Bellamy was in our lives now, and though the threat to her was most important, it was time she learned about me and Alex and who we were now versus eight years ago.

Deep down, I worried it would change the way she felt about me.

The way she loved me.

Maybe that's why you weren't in such a hurry to tell her about your own life.

Alex dropped down, squatting so he was eye level

with my girl. I gave him a warning look, which I know he saw even though his eyes remained on her.

"Trust me when I tell you I haven't just been sitting on a mountain for the past eight years, just riding some skis and chasing bunnies."

Her eyes never left his. Her voice was slightly hesitant. "What were you doing?"

He stood, the look in his eyes going flat. "Learning how to deal with dangerous people, some worse than the ones you're running from."

Bellamy shivered a little, and I slapped Alex on the arm. "You made your point. How about some coffee?"

Alex blinked, and the shield came back up. He smiled. "Coffee sounds good. Cream and sugar, Bellamy?"

"Yes, please."

When he was gone, she looked at me with wide eyes. "What was that?"

"Alex spent some time in the army. You can trust him. He has what it takes to keep you safe."

Her eyes strayed back to the door where he'd gone.

I took her chin and pulled her face around. "Make no mistake, though, sweetheart. Alex has some skill and experience I don't, but I'm just as capable of handling this situation. There is no one else on this earth as motivated to keeping you safe as me."

"I don't want someone to save me."

I knew that, but it didn't stop me from wanting to protect her anyway. "How you feeling?" I murmured caressing her swollen cheek.

"They gave me some pain meds."

I caressed her lip close to where it was split. "Come home with me tonight."

"What?"

"No more room at the resort. No more not waking up together. It's time to come home, Bells."

She seemed surprised. "You want me to move in with you?"

"I want you to come home."

"Don't you think it's too soon?" she asked, concern darkening her eyes.

My stomach flipped, and that little voice in the back of my head warned me that this was a bad idea. That once she knew all of me, she'd leave.

I told it to shut the fuck up.

Even silenced, though, doubt was still there. So was fear.

"No," I said, pushing on. Reaching for what I wanted. Reaching for her. "I mean, it's kinda backwards I guess, considering we need to get to know each other better as adults. But we can do that at home. Together. I love you, and that's not gonna change."

Please say it won't change for you.

"You'll tell me about your knee? About the pros?"

"About everything." Damn the way my voice went hoarse.

"About Alex?"

"If you want. But maybe you should let him do that."

A beautiful smile lit up her face. "Home is where my heart is."

"Is that a yes?"

She nodded. "Yes."

I lunged at her, scooping her into my chest. She winced at the sudden jostling of her arm, and I pulled back, leaned down, and kissed the bare part of her shoulder.

"How's your knee?" she asked, glancing down at the ice pack.

"Time will tell," I muttered darkly, repeating the words the doc had said.

Questions swirled in her eyes, and I braced for them. I wasn't really ready to talk about this. Not here. Not now.

But I would.

If she asked, I would.

I was saved when the door opened and Alex appeared, carrying three paper cups with lids. "Yo, look who I found," he announced.

Bellamy and I both looked up.

My mom and dad rushed into the room.

"Oh my God, Liam! What on earth happened?" Mom fretted, rushing across the room to my bedside. Her eyes went to Bellamy and widened. "Oh, you poor thing." Her hand hovered toward her swollen cheek. "What's happened to you?"

"Mom, this is Bellamy. Bellamy, this is my mom, Holly."

"It's nice to meet you, Mrs. Mattison."

Mom made a sound. "Call me Holly. And yes, I've been anxious to meet you. Everyone at the resort is all a twitter with the news of Liam's new lady."

"All *a twitter*," Alex echoed.

I suppressed a smile.

Mom gasped. "Liam! Your knee! Oh, what's happened?"

"Mom, what are you doing here? How did you know I was here?" Jesus, did the staff call them? That was a damn violation of patient rights or something, wasn't it?

The last thing I wanted was to freak my parents out, and I'd been trying to avoid the whole meeting my girlfriend right after a near-death experience thing.

I glanced at Alex, wanting some kind of explanation.

He shrugged. "Found them wandering around in the hall." An odd expression rolled over his face, and his eyes cut toward my father who was standing off to the side, letting my mother hover.

I sat up and looked around her.

My brows wrinkled when I saw him standing there. "Dad?"

Our eyes locked and this... *look* passed between us. He was wearing a hospital gown.

"We weren't wandering." Mom hushed Alex. "We were looking for you. Imagine our surprise when we heard all the nurses giggling and going on about the local Olympic medalist being admitted."

"Imagine," I said, looking back at Dad. "Why are you dressed in a hospital gown, Dad? What the hell's going on?"

Mom stopped fretting over me and went quiet, turning to glance at Dad.

He came forward. "It's nothing to be concerned about, son. I just had a checkup with my doctor this morning, and I was having some tests done. You know how they are in this place. They think everyone needs to wear one of these damn gowns."

"They're very drafty." Bellamy agreed.

Dad chuckled and turned his attention toward my girlfriend. "That they are. So nice to meet you, Bellamy." He held out his hand. "Liam speaks very highly of you."

"Of you as well," Bellamy replied, looking a little shy. She glanced back at my mom. "Both of you."

Mom came forward again. "Tell us what happened."

I groaned. "It's a long story, Mom."

Alex handed Bellamy a coffee, and she tucked her hands around it and sighed. I noted the goose bumps coating her arms and frowned. Snatching my zippered hoodie she'd worn on the way here off the bedside table nearby, I leaned up and draped it around her shoulders.

She smiled as I tugged the neckline closer around her. "Shoulder okay?" I asked low.

Her head bobbed. "Thanks."

"Liam?" Mom asked, trying to get me to spill.

Fuck, I was tired. I just wanted to grab up Bellamy and shut ourselves inside the cabin for a few days.

I knew I couldn't.

"What kind of routine tests?"

"What?" Mom asked.

"What kind of routine tests are you having done, Dad?"

Alex shifted, and Bellamy took a sip of the coffee.

The door opened again. This time, a man in a suit walked in, followed by a woman dressed in a pencil skirt and dress shirt. Behind the pair was the police chief of Caribou.

"Frank!" Mom exclaimed upon seeing him. Her hand flew to her neck. "Is this a police matter?"

"I'm afraid so." Frank agreed.

The man in the suit cleared his throat. Bellamy shrank back against me. "I'm going to need a word with Miss Lane and Mr. Mattison." He glanced around. "Alone."

"Now wait a minute. You can't just waltz in here and take over my jurisdiction." Frank cut in.

The man flashed his shiny FBI badge. "Actually, we can."

Ah, so this was Agent Frost. Douchebag.

"The FBI!" Mom exclaimed.

I looked toward the ceiling. This room was becoming a shitstorm of people and underlying conversations that had yet to be had.

"I'm Renshaw Mattison, Liam's father. What's this all about?" Dad stepped forward, sounding every bit the powerful businessman he was. The hospital gown he was dressed in seemed even more out of place.

I frowned, and a sick feeling crawled around in my stomach.

A doctor poked his head in the room. It wasn't my or Bells's doctor. "Mr. Mattison. I thought I might find you here."

"Doctor," my dad replied stiffly.

"I have those results if you wouldn't mind coming back to your room?"

"What's going on?" I looked at Mom.

She averted her gaze.

Routine my ass.

Suddenly, the pressure to start training this spring to take over BearPaw made a lot more sense. Realization smacked me in the face so hard I wondered if maybe my concussion didn't just get worse.

I started to get out of the bed. The ice pack on my knee hit the floor, and the bed scooted a little askew as I tried to get around Bellamy.

"Liam." She gasped, reaching out to grab me.

"Son." Dad appeared. "Get back in bed. Keep the ice on your knee."

"My knee is fine," I snapped. "I'll come with you," I told him, finally managing to stand, most of my weight on my left leg. "I want hear what your doctor has to say."

"That's not necessary," my father replied quickly.

I made a rude sound. I didn't know why he bothered talking. I was going.

I managed to herd my parents to the door, near the doctor who was standing there waiting patiently.

"We'll need you to wait outside while we question Miss Lane," Agent Frost said behind me.

I froze and turned to see him looking at Alex. I glanced between my parents and Bellamy, who was sitting on the bed alone.

Fuuck.

I couldn't leave her in here with these vultures. I was one hundred percent positive these agents were going to try and scare the shit out of her to get her in the back of their government-issue SUV. She was already confused and scared enough.

I had to be here. I *wanted* to be.

"Just stay with Bellamy, son. You clearly have a statement to give to the police. Your mother and I are fine. It's just routine."

"You can stop saying that," I retorted, harsher than I intended. "We both know it's a damn lie."

My parents fell silent.

"Go, Liam. I'll be here when you're finished," Bellamy said, understanding and patience in her voice.

Turning to Alex, I said, "Can you walk down the hall with Mom and Dad. Make sure they get to their room okay?"

"My pleasure." He nodded, then handed me the coffee I had yet to even touch. I took it and met his eyes.

The look of understanding in those depths made me feel better. He'd keep an eye on my parents, make sure everything was okay.

"I'll come get you if I have to," he said quietly.

"I don't take too kindly to my son hiring a babysitter," Dad announced to the room.

"I'm insulted you think so low of me, Ren," Alex quipped.

Dad made a rude sound. "Come on, then."

The doctor, Alex, and my parents moved out into the hall.

"Mom," I said, and she turned back. She'd been moving slower than everyone else because she knew I would call out to her.

"How bad is it?"

"Everything is fine." She assured me.

I didn't believe her.

When she was gone, I turned back. Agent Frost was trying to banish Frank.

"He stays," I announced. My voice was hard and dark. I embraced a little of that darkness I always tried to keep put away. I needed it right now. "If you want any kind of cooperation at all, you will involve the local police chief who I trust implicitly." I levelled a hard stare on Agent Frost. "Which is more than I can say for you."

Agent Frost looked as if he'd swallowed an ice cube whole, but he nodded to the woman with him, and she moved to shut the door.

I went back to the bed. Bellamy stood to let me slide on, then replaced the ice pack on my knee and made sure the pillows elevating it were steady. When she was done, I pulled her beside me, anchoring an arm at her waist.

Before submitting to the round of endless questions I was sure were coming, I glanced back at the door my parents had just left through.

They had some explaining to do.

Bellamy

IT WAS LATE BY THE TIME WE ARRIVED AT THE CABIN. As the hours slipped by at the hospital, I became more convinced they were going to make us stay the entire night.

I underestimated Liam's power of persuasion and his popularity with the town. I knew he was an Olympic medalist, but it was something that barely ever crossed my mind until someone else mentioned it.

He wasn't Caribou royalty turned star athlete with medals and worldwide popularity. To me, he was just this handsome kid who once spent a few hours teaching a girl he didn't know how to ski. A guy who flirted to make me less afraid of a ski lift... and the one who took my virginity.

And my heart.

Now he was a man who'd morphed from that ornery bad-boy appeal into a sexy man with sharp instincts and unwavering intensity.

He still had my heart.

I was beginning to realize it didn't matter which version of Liam he was. It wouldn't matter. I would love him no matter what.

"If you were anyone else, we'd still be sitting in that hospital room," I mused, taking off my boots by the door.

He made a sound. "I'm just glad to be home."

"You should get off your knee." I went over to his side, looping my good arm around his waist, offering to take some of his weight.

He didn't give it to me, of course. I didn't really expect him to. I wanted him to know I would take it if he ever decided to give it.

"I'm tired of sitting down." He complained.

"Want me to make you something to eat?" I offered.

"You're finally going to cook for me?" He teased.

I laughed. "I'm not sure I'm up for making an entire meal," I said as we went into the kitchen. "But I could probably at least make you a sandwich."

"Probably all I got in the fridge anyway."

"I'll go to the store in a few days," I said, leaving him at the island to open the large stainless-steel appliance.

I'd barely gotten to glance at what he had inside before he reached over my shoulder and pushed the door shut. I spun, surprised, and he used his body to back me up against the cold metal.

"I thought you wanted a sandwich."

Liam ducked his head so his lips were beside my ear. One palm was planted flat on the fridge right beside my head. I was completely caged in by him… and it made my heart race.

"How can I think about food when you're standing in my kitchen, talking about going grocery shopping?"

"Uhh…" My heart was still fluttering, and every word he spoke brought the brush of breath over my ear.

"I see you standing here, and I can barely believe it. Do you know how many times I imagined this? Do you know how many years I thought of you, girl who got away?"

My lashes fluttered. My gaze tried to meet his.

Dipping his face, he pressed a kiss against my neck. "Knowing you're here. That you're staying…"

He kissed my neck again.

My head fell to the side, and my fingers curled into the front of his T-shirt.

"Knowing I'm going to cook for you," I joked, but it sounded more like a moan.

His throaty laugh tightened my nipples. The space between my legs started to ache. I didn't know how he did this to me. How he could make me ache and want after being awake for over twenty-four hours… after *everything*.

"You could hand me a pack of crackers, sweetheart, and it would be the best damn meal I ever ate."

"I love you." My hands slid down the front of his shirt into the waistband of his loose-fitting sweats. The thick band of the Calvin Klein boxer briefs I'd watched him put on earlier today enticed my fingers further, and I pushed beneath it.

His teeth nipped at my neck, and I smiled.

"Forget the food," he half growled and picked me up.

I gasped. For two reasons:

1. His hard dick rubbed me in all the right places when my legs went around his waist.

And

2. He didn't need that extra weight on his knee!

"Your knee!" I tried to get down.

"You should make it feel better."

I glanced down, worry mixing with the want inside me. "What can I do?'

He smiled. "Anything you want."

He carried me down the hall, despite my telling him not to. Charlie danced around like we were playing a game. Liam set me on the edge of the bed and reached into his nightstand for a giant chew bone. Charlie barked, snatched it out of his hand, and disappeared.

Reaching back into the drawer, Liam pulled out some condoms and tossed them on the bed.

I reached for his sweats and pushed them down his leg. They got caught on the thick brace around his knee, so I slid off the mattress and down his body to carefully work them off. When that was done, I did the same to his Calvins.

I felt the heat of his eyes as I worked, which made me even hotter. On my knees, I glanced up his body as my hand closed around his rigid cock. Liam sucked in a breath, and our eyes met. I pumped him a few times, and the muscles in his lower abs rippled. I leaned across and licked them, then moved down and sucked his head into my mouth.

With a groan, Liam's body went slack. He bent a little, resting one of his palms on the mattress. I moved up and down his rod, sliding my lips along the taut, smooth skin.

He made a sound and tried to pull me up, but I wasn't done. I pulled back but kept my hand around his shaft as I kissed and sucked on his sack.

He muttered a few curses, and I smiled.

Standing up, I licked my lips, still tasting him on me.

Liam's eyes flashed silver. He began stripping the clothes he'd given me to wear to the hospital off my body. The second he untied the drawstring at my waist, the pants fell right to the floor.

"You up for this?" he murmured, looking at my arm in the sling.

In response, I took his hand and guided the thick fingers between my thighs, brushing them against the slick wetness.

He shuddered the second he felt just how up for this I really was.

I climbed on the bed. His palm covered my bare ass, and his fingers slipped between my legs again. He stroked me, and I shuddered.

After I patted the mattress beside me, Liam did my bidding. The second he was on the bed, I pushed him down on his back. He lifted an eyebrow, and I gently pushed a pillow beneath his knee, giving it some support.

"How about you let me drive?" I asked, dragging a finger down the center of his chest.

His head fell back against the blankets, and a satisfied smile pulled at his lips. Settling a palm on my hip, Liam tugged. I straddled him, but not his hips, his waist.

Rocking against him, I shuddered. My desire coated his stomach, and his palms covered my breasts. "You are so goddamn beautiful," he groaned, kneading the flesh.

I let my head fall back, and he pushed up onto elbows so he could tug a breast into his mouth. I cried out and thrust against his abs again. Liam's fingers bit into my hip, and he urged me to move again. My inner muscles flexed and spasmed, wanting something more, wanting to feel him inside me.

I shimmied down his body, and he released me to grab one of the packets nearby. Our hands worked together, rolling the latex down his shaft, my fingertips lingering on his balls as he finished. When he was done, Liam held up his thick, hard length, and I poised above it.

Our eyes met and held as I slowly, torturously slid down over him. My body accepted his inch by glorious inch. I had to force myself to go slowly because, really, all I wanted to do was push down and take him completely.

When at last he filled me and our bodies where totally joined, he palmed my hips and rocked my body. Both of us moaned, and my head fell back. The long strands of my hair brushed the top of my ass, and my teeth sank into my lower lip.

I began moving on my own, riding him the way that felt right. Liam moaned, his hands fell away, and I took control. Before I knew it, I was panting and the room was blurry. My palm slapped down beside his head, and I leaned over him. We kissed the way we fucked. Fervently, deeply, and at times, manically.

The tension in my body became too much to bear, and I whimpered.

Liam ripped his mouth free, grabbed my hips, and looked into my face.

"I have what you want, sweetheart," he growled, then lifted his hips off the bed, surging up inside me.

I bore down, and pleasure exploded inside me. It was so overpowering that my eyes rolled back in my head and light burst behind my lids.

I whimpered again, and he rocked into me, milking my inner walls, stroking my swollen clit for every last ounce of pleasure.

I collapsed against his chest, lungs heaving. I was totally boneless as mini ripples still coursed through my limbs.

Liam moved beneath me, surging up again. Feeling

the way he pulsed inside me, I knew he was ready. I started to push up so I could ride him through it, but he made a sound, locked his arms around my waist, and held me to him.

I shoved down, and he surged up. His deep shout filled the room, and he thrust into me over and over again. I was pressed so tightly against him I could feel the pounding of his heart and hear the gasp of each breath he took.

Eventually, his body calmed and relaxed against the mattress. I lay prone over his chest, his body still cradled inside mine.

His fingers dragged slowly through the length of my hair as satisfaction curled around the room.

A short while later, I realized the air in here was cold. I reached for the blanket, only to realize we were lying on top of them.

"Up," he murmured and lifted me off him. I pouted a little because I wasn't ready for him to leave me yet. He chuckled and kissed my pouty lower lip.

My shoulder was sore. It was almost time for some pain meds, but I was too satiated to get up. I settled for resting my back against the plush headboard and pulling the covers up around me.

Liam kissed my shoulder when he crawled back into bed. He mirrored my position, and we both sat in bed together, holding hands.

"I feel like I could sleep for a week." I confessed.

"You and me both."

"You didn't get a chance to talk to your parents," I said, worrying about them. About Liam. I saw his reaction when he noticed his dad in a hospital gown. My stomach seized for him. Liam had the kind of relationship with his father I'd always wanted with mine.

If I was so broken by losing my dad, what would it do to Liam if something was seriously wrong with his?

"We were all so exhausted after the Feds left. If I made them explain, then they were gonna make us explain. I was tired of talking. Tired of trying to make sense of any of it."

"And maybe…" I began, my voice gentle. "You're scared to find out what's going on?"

"Maybe," he echoed, his voice barely there.

"Whatever you need, Liam, I'm here."

He lifted our joined hands and kissed the back of mine.

"We'll go see them tomorrow. After we've had some sleep."

I loved when he said we. Like it really was him and me now. Like I really wasn't alone anymore.

"Do you think they'll want me there? I know it's a personal family matter."

He made a sound. "You *are* family. And hell yes, they want you there. Most importantly, *I* want you there."

I wanted his parents to like me. To love me even. I would love to have a close relationship with them. I just prayed they would want that too once we told them everything I'd brought into their son's life.

"You know what Agent Frost said earlier today is true." I began.

He glanced at me swiftly, a sour expression forming on his face. "I don't like that guy."

I smiled. "You made that very clear. To everyone."

He grunted. "I'm not sorry. He needs to know I don't like him. I want him looking over his shoulder, knowing I'm watching. Because I am. I will watch every decision that guy tries to make when it comes to you."

"They only found one body up on the mountain." I reminded him. As if he could forget.

"Doesn't mean the other one isn't just too buried to find."

I nodded, praying he was right.

Still. There was this feeling inside me... deep down. The same kind of feeling that spider crawled up the back of my neck whenever Crone's men got close.

Spidey wasn't found on that mountain today. But a trail of blood was. Until it disappeared, just stopped suddenly, leaving the snow as pristine as it when it first fell.

They didn't find his body because he hadn't died.

He was still out there. I knew it.

He'd gone back underground again, skillfully hiding from the FBI and any other interested party who wanted to bring him in. Spidey would stay hidden, too. I knew he would. He would lie in wait like a cobra, ready to strike. Like an angry grizzly bear in hibernation.

He would heal from his injuries. Bide his time. Probably even somehow get word to Crone.

Agent Frost told us as much, and I knew he was right.

I'd gotten away from this guy more than once now.

To Spidey, I wasn't just a job. I wasn't just a target of the mob. This was personal. Liam and I might have bought some time up in that avalanche, but I wasn't stupid, and neither was the man beside me.

Crone's men would be coming back. And since I refused to run anymore, they knew exactly where I'd be. There wasn't much the FBI could do if I refused to cooperate with witness protection.

Liam sensed my troubled, dark thoughts and turned, wrapping his body around mine. "We'll be ready when they come back, sweetheart. There's nothing I won't do to protect this."

Charlie jumped up on the bed, making the mattress bounce beneath his giant body. He flopped down on the foot, stretched out, and continued chewing his bone.

My chest swelled. My heart felt so full here in this bed with my two guys. Turning, I swept a gaze over Liam's face. "All those times I wondered what might have been," I whispered, stroking his face. The stubble on his jaw tickled my palm and sent butterflies through my middle.

He kissed the tips of my fingers and smiled. "You don't have to wonder anymore."

"Now I know," I whispered.

A sound of agreement burst from his throat. "Now *we* know."

Resolve welled up inside me as I watched the dog and snuggled deeper into the arms of the only man I'd ever loved. We would survive whatever came at us. We had to.

Liam and I survived the surge, but a whole new blizzard was brewing.

THE END

AUTHOR'S NOTE

I'll tell you a secret. It's been a while since I truly dug into a book I was writing and truly got involved and felt sucked in by my own characters.

Don't get me wrong. I LOVE all my couples. I really do. They all have something great about them, some of them, MANY great things. However, some—for me—just have a certain kind of magic. Previous couples that I feel this way with are Romeo and Rimmel, Braeden and Ivy, and Trent and Drew (my favorite of all time). They just have a magic about them. You get what I'm throwing down?

In 2017, writing was sort of a struggle for me in many ways. I loved all the books I put out, but finishing up the *GearShark* series last year left me feeling a little lost. It's hard to explain really, but sometimes an author feels like they might not write anything as good as their previous books. Or may not feel that same *spark* they sometimes have with certain characters.

For quite a few months, I was ruminating on the idea that I wanted to write something set at a ski resort.

Probably because I spent all of November and half of December in front of holiday Hallmark movies (#addicted). I just loved the setting.

So when I started to feel burned out while writing *Toad* (Have you read that yet? Dooo it.) I knew I wanted to switch it up and write something different for a little bit.

I came up with the idea for *Avalanche* and really just thought it would be fun to write. I thought it would be a standalone novel. Just, in a sense, a "filler" book between series… And then I started writing.

I got sucked in so hard and so fast with this book. It shocked me. Even my husband was surprised at the amount of time I spent typing fast and furiously on the laptop. When I wasn't, I was spacing off into the world or writing down ideas on pages of notebook paper. This book took roughly three weeks to write (maybe a little less)… with more than half being written in the first week.

I often felt like Will Ferrell in *Elf* when he burst into his father's office and twirled around singing, "I'm in love. I'm in love, and I don't care who knows it!"

Except I cared.

I didn't want to tell anyone about Bellamy and Liam. I wanted to sit at my laptop and hoard them in secret. I was worried if I told anyone about them, my newfound mojo love would wear off. I was afraid their magic would slip through my fingers.

I still love them.

So much that I'm giving them another book.

I can't quit them, yo.

I'm even scared of admitting out loud how much I love Liam and Bellamy. I'm afraid the writer gods will come take away my mojo love.

Mojo love is a real thing.

Anyway, I have no idea if readers will feel this connection to them. It will be interesting to find out. No one knows about them yet, except a few select peeps, and even then, I guard them closely to me.

I really love this story. I feel, in a sense, it's unique for me. It's my first "second chances" story. My first "mob" story. It's a new setting for me. And I feel like it's a faster-paced book (maybe that just feels that way because I wrote it fast) with good action and some good angst. (Am I making this up or are you getting this, too?) Of course, it has some of my familiar "feels" in it and the sense of building a family—sort of reminiscent of the *#Hashtag* series.

I truly hope you guys love this one. I hope you feel a connection to Liam and Bellamy like I do. And to Charlie, too.

Thanks for reading and taking an adventure into a new book world with me. Reader support means so much, and I'm truly grateful.

Until next book!

XOXO,
Cambria

ABOUT CAMBRIA

Cambria Hebert is an award-winning, bestselling novelist of more than forty books. She went to college for a bachelor's degree, couldn't pick a major, and ended up with a degree in cosmetology. So rest assured her characters will always have good hair.

Besides writing, Cambria loves a caramel latte, staying up late, sleeping in, and watching movies. She considers math human torture and has an irrational fear of birds (including chickens). You can often find her painting her toenails (because she bites her fingernails) or walking her Chihuahuas (the real rulers of the house).

Cambria has written within the young adult and new adult genres, penning many paranormal and contemporary titles. She has also written romantic suspense, science fiction, and most recently, male/male romance. Her favorite genre to read and write is contemporary romance. A few of her most recognized titles are: *The Hashtag Series, GearShark Series*, *Text, Amnesia,* and *Butterfly*.

Recent awards include: Author of the Year, Best Contemporary Series (*The Hashtag Series*), Best Contemporary Book of the Year, Best Book Trailer of the Year, Best Contemporary Lead, Best Contemporary Book Cover of the Year. In addition, her most recognized title, *#Nerd,* was listed at Buzzfeed.com as a top fifty summer romance read.

Cambria Hebert owns and operates Cambria Hebert Books, LLC.

You can find out more about Cambria and her titles by visiting her website: http://www.cambriahebert.com.

Please sign up for my newsletter to stay in the know about all my cover reveals, releases and more: http://eepurl.com/bUL5_5

Made in the USA
Middletown, DE
22 April 2022

64597424R00220